D0896859

IN THE RING

IN THE RING

A DAN STAGG MYSTERY

BY JAMES LEAR

CLEiS
PRESS

Published in the United States by Cleis Press, an imprint of Start Midnight, LLC, 101 Hudson Street, Thirty-Seventh Floor, Suite 3705, Jersey City, NJ 07302.

Printed in the United States.
Cover design: Scott Idleman/Blink
Cover photograph: Shutterstock
Text design: Frank Wiedemann

First Edition.
10 9 8 7 6 5 4 3 2 1

Trade paper ISBN: 978-1-62778-236-4
E-book ISBN: 978-1-62778-237-1

IRAQ SUICIDE BOMB ATTACK: DEATHS IN BAGHDAD RISE TO 45

The number of people killed in Thursday's suicide bomb in the Iraqi capital, Baghdad, has risen to 45, interior ministry officials say. The blast also injured 120 people. A car packed with explosives was driven into a market square where civilians were doing their shopping, and exploded on colliding with a US military vehicle transporting personnel to a nearby base.

Only three American troops were killed. Their names have not yet been released, as next of kin are informed. The rest of those killed are thought to be Iraqi civilians. The so-called Islamic State (IS) has said it carried out the suicide attack.

SENIOR US OFFICER AMONG DEAD IN BAGHDAD BLAST

A US Army general was among the victims of the suicide bomb in the Iraqi capital, Baghdad, on Tuesday. Colonel Dan Stagg, 43, was one of three military personnel thought to have been targeted in the attack. Second Lieutenant Mark Williams (32) and driver Private Jordan Flowers (24) were also killed by the blast. The remaining 42 civilian casualties were all Iraqi citizens, including five children under the age of eight.

BAGHDAD TERROR VICTIMS RETURN HOME

The bodies of three US Army personnel killed in last week's suicide attack in Baghdad were today flown into Washington DC. Funerals take place next month at the Arlington National Cemetery.

01

A line of light. Greenish white, then gone.

The sound of dishes being washed, chink chink chink, or is it bells, distant bells?

Silence, a roaring silence like a never-ending explosion, and a sudden pounding in the chest, hard, like someone's hitting me with their fists, thumping into me, breaking my ribs. Panic, flight, a jerk in the spine and the legs, prepare to run. Fear.

Awake.

Everything is white and blurred. I think there's a TV on somewhere, a screen of some kind. Too much light. Movement, vague circles white out of white, puffy clouds coming closer and receding. Is this death?

A face at the end of a long tunnel, like looking down the wrong end of a pair of binoculars, ridiculously far away and tiny, so tiny it makes me laugh, the breath coming out through my nose.

The face getting closer, a brown sun in a blue sky, white clouds, coming towards me like a dolly shot in a movie, taking up more and more of the sky until all

I can see is brown skin and white teeth and eyes that look into mine and a mouth that smiles and speaks, *hey, you're awake, hey Dan, how are you doing, buddy? Welcome back.*

And then the clouds cover the sun and the picture goes down to a line like on the old TV at home, a line and then a dot and closedown.

It was the pain that woke me up in the end, a sharp sensation that cut through the last of my dreams. Awake, alive, and hurting. The pain is real, so I must be real.

My eyes felt like they'd been tumble-dried and rolled in sand. I tried to lift my hand to rub them, but it weighed about a hundred pounds. Craning my neck, I looked down at it, lying on the white covers of the bed. Looked like my hand—tanned, gnarly, hairy—but didn't feel like it. Didn't feel at all, in fact. Shit, I thought, it's been chopped off and left on top of the bed. It's no longer part of me. Am I going to get robot parts?

But the pain. Back to the pain. It was somewhere further down—below the hips, starting around my ass and travelling down to my right foot. Real strong good old-fashioned pain. At least I could feel my legs. I know lots of ex-soldiers who can't.

Jesus fucking Christ, it was beyond pain, it was getting into red-hot-blade territory, and I must have yelled because there was a sudden movement beside me, to the left of the bed, just beyond my field of vision, and then a voice.

"Ah! Dan! You're back."

Sounded familiar, like a dear friend, except I don't

have any friends, let alone dear ones, and God knows it couldn't be my family.

"Haahmmmfff." That was meant to be "who's that?" but my mouth wasn't working any better than my hand. Fuck, I thought, if my dick doesn't work either then I'm in real trouble. That made me laugh, which came out through my nose then got stuck and turned into a coughing fit. My lungs, it seemed, had been filled with hot ash.

"Okay, okay." An arm slipped round my shoulders, lifting me gently. "Take it easy."

Then the coughing made me belch, and I would have puked if there had been anything in my stomach to bring up other than a bit of foul-tasting bile that dribbled down my chin and neck. I tried to wipe it away, but of course—no hands.

"Take it easy, Dan." A soft cloth cleaned my mouth, and I was lowered back on to the pillows.

That's when it twigged. I'm a vegetable. Something has happened to me and I've lost the use of my limbs, I can't control my mouth, I probably have to piss through a tube and shit into a diaper. I always wondered about those guys who come back from war zones like this. Do they know what's going on—how bad it is? Well, apparently they do. Great.

"Do you have any pain?"

"Mmmmmm." I couldn't nod or form words, but I guess the intonation put it across.

"A lot of pain?"

"MmmMMMMMmmm."

"Okay. I'm calling the doctor."

He stepped away from the bed, into my field of vision, and for the first time I saw him, five foot eight inches of athletic American male poured into a nurse's uniform, a handsome face that I recognized from somewhere, a dream perhaps.

He spoke into a phone while I checked his back for wings. No: he appeared to be human, and mortal, which meant I must be alive, if not kicking.

He sat on the edge of the bed and put his warm, living hand on my cold, dead fingers. Maybe not so dead. Maybe a flicker of response. "He'll be here in a minute. Hang in there, Dan." He smiled, and I tried to smile back, which led to more drooling. He smiled and dabbed. "Pain relief is coming."

It occurred to me with a sudden jolt that I had no idea where I was. I've heard the question asked in a million movies—*where am I, Doc?*—but now I couldn't form the words. I glanced around, hoping for clues. My vision was still blurred, but I made out something that looked like the stars and stripes, high up on the wall. A US base, then, if not actually on home soil.

The pain blasted back, as if my shinbone was being sawn through, and I tensed up, squeezing my eyes shut, all sorts of hell going on in parts of my body I couldn't identify. A general cacophony of pain. And above it all, a gentle squeeze of my hand.

"Can you look at me, Dan?"

I opened my eyes and squinted out. A handsome face always makes me feel better.

"That's it. Try and listen. My name's Luiz. I'm a nurse, and I've been looking after you for the last few days, since you got here. You've been unconscious for quite a long time, but you're going to be fine. There's no brain damage."

I waited for the *but* . . .

"Your leg was pretty smashed up. They've pinned it back together, and now we're just going to let it heal."

But . . .

"The good news is, if it hurts, it's mending. If you couldn't feel anything, I'd be worried. The more it hurts, the better." That sounded like something I've said to a lot of young men before, which made me laugh again, with the same messy results. Luiz cleaned me up.

"Okay, okay. You'd better not laugh any more. Take a few deep breaths, it'll help with the pain until the doctor gets here. I'm just going to keep talking. Listen to my voice, and look into my eyes."

No great hardship. Beautiful brown eyes . . .

"You're in the Walter Reed National Military Medical Center in Bethesda, Maryland."

The Navy Med. I'd been here before, maybe four, five times in a career of being shot, blown up, and beaten for Uncle Sam.

"You arrived three days ago after spending two days in a military hospital in Baghdad."

Baghdad. That rang a bell. Baghdad. That's where I was. And now I'm here in Bethesda. Baghdad, Bethesda, Baghdad, Bethesda, Beghthesda, Big Bad, Bethlehem, Bthzzzzhzhzzh . . .

His voice muffled, fading, shutters falling again, into a chasm, a deep black chasm that might be death.

The next time I woke there were three doctors standing around my bed, and a man in military uniform. I recognized the rank before I recognized him: USMC major general, green coat, green trousers, web belt, khaki shirt, khaki tie, black shoes, two silver stars on the epaulettes. My right arm jerked upwards, trying to salute, but all I managed was a faint wave. I couldn't see his face.

"He's coming around," said a voice I didn't recognize. "Here he is."

"You're doing really well, Dan," said another voice. "You're going to make a full recovery."

All I could manage was "Hmmm."

They were whispering above me. I was too tired to hear what they were saying. I just wanted to sleep again.

"Dan . . . Dan? Are you awake? Dan? Can you hear me?"

"Yeah . . ." I was drifting off again. I tried to open my eyes. "Yeah, I'm here."

"There's someone here that wants to talk to you. An old friend."

"Wha' . . .?"

"It's me, Dan." I knew the voice. My father? Fuck, no. Someone I actually liked. "I'm here."

Perfect green service uniform. Gleaming stars. Of course. Major General Wallace Hamilton, the man who streamlined my re-entry to the corps after years in the civilian wilderness, and who made it his personal business to have my records cleared of any sexual wrongdoing. My champion. My mentor.

"Dan. It's good to see you. We thought we'd lost you there."

I tried to shrug. "Still alive."

"You had us worried. How do you feel, Dan?"

I could just about make out his face against the glare of overhead fluorescents. In his fifties, gray hair, a little weather-beaten, like a stern headmaster that you know has your best interests at heart even when he's punishing you. He'd been a good friend to me.

"Feel like shit."

The doctors coughed and glanced at their watches. Hamilton crouched down, his face level with mine. "You get yourself well, Dan. I can't afford to lose you." I looked into his pale gray eyes. "Not again."

"Yes, sir. Do my best."

He lowered his voice. "I'll come and talk to you later, when you're feeling better. But I just wanted to see you. Okay?"

"Okay." I felt his cool, dry hand on my forehead, and closed my eyes. I don't know how long he stayed there. When I opened my eyes again, he, and the doctors, were gone.

Luiz was standing at the end of the bed.

"Time for your bath," he said.

A bath? Jesus, when did I last have a bath? How long had I been lying there, drifting in and out of consciousness? How had I been shitting and pissing, let alone keeping clean? A bath—hot water, steam, bubbles, the full works—sounded like heaven. I tried to sit up. I wanted to get out of this damn bed, to walk, to run. More urgently, I needed to get to the bathroom.

"Hey, hold on," said Luiz, placing a gentle hand on my shoulder. "Let's not get carried away." He had an accent that I couldn't place—Spanish? Brazilian? Mexican? "I'll take care of everything as usual."

"I need to piss."

"How do you think you've been peeing since you got here?" He produced a gray cardboard dish. Oh, Christ. A bedpan. Did that really mean that for the last few days, Luiz has been . . . He pulled back the bedclothes. "Come on. It's too late to start being shy, Dan." He positioned the pan between my legs, tilted it up, and placed my cock over the edge. "There you go. Fire away."

"I can't."

"You can't? What do you mean?"

"Like this. It's . . . weird." Considering that my sex life has consisted almost entirely of things that most people would consider weird, this surprised even me. I've done things with my cock far worse than pissing in a bedpan. Why the sudden primness?

Luiz was laughing. "I'll draw the curtains if you like."

"It's not that."

"Do you want me to look away?"

Under normal circumstances I'd be more than happy to let him hold my cock—or do anything else he wanted. But now, vulnerable, exhausted, and in pain, I seemed to have gained a sense of shame.

"Try to relax." Patient fingers held my cock, resting it on the soft gray cardboard, but the piss wouldn't come. In fact, to my horror, I was starting to get hard. Not just semi-hard; this was the kind of sudden erection that could rip through plate steel.

"Sorry . . ."

"It's fine." He was smiling. "I've seen it all before."

"You mean me?"

"Dan, even while you were in a coma you seemed to be permanently horny. I don't know what they feed you out there in Baghdad."

"I hope I didn't embarrass you."

"I'm a nurse. I wipe stuff up."

"Oh, Christ." I wanted to hide my face, but there isn't much you can do when you're in a hospital bed, too weak to lift your arms but apparently well enough to have a rock-hard cock that's being gently held in the soft hands of a handsome man.

"I think we need to get rid of this before we can get you washed, Dan."

"Yeah."

"Do you think it'll go down on its own?"

I strained my head forward to look down at myself. I was relieved to see that my cock was unscarred, however smashed up my leg may be. It rose, thick and straight, the foreskin half retracted. "I doubt it. Sometimes I'm hard all night."

"Okay. Don't tell the doctors." He squirted a few drops of liquid soap on his hands, rubbed them together, and started running them up and down my shaft. Fuck, it felt good, even when I tensed my legs and sent all sorts of pain signals running up and down my central nervous system. I needed to cum very urgently, and I needed it to be in Luiz's hands. This gentle, smiling man who had looked after me for so many days, washed me, no doubt fed me and brought me my potty like a baby, while I was helpless, in his hands . . .

I started shooting within about thirty seconds, great ropes of the stuff flying through the air and landing all over the bed, my nightshirt, Luiz's arms. He started wiping up right away.

"I needed that," I said. "I mean, I haven't come for days."

"Are you kidding? You've been coming every day. Sometimes twice."

"What?"

"In your sleep. Sometimes when I've been washing you."

"I see. And you've . . . helped out?"

"Not deliberately. But, you know, I have to keep you clean down there . . ."

"Right. Well . . thanks, I guess."

He mopped up around my cock and balls. "Ready to pee now?"

"Nearly. You just keep holding it."

Somehow he managed to siphon about a pint of piss out of me.

"Better?"

"Much better."

"Now it's time for your bath. Which, I'm afraid, means stripping you naked." Luiz pulled the shirt over my head, carefully lifting my arms out of the sleeves. When I was naked, he sponged me with warm, soapy water. It felt wonderful.

"I can't do much to your leg, I'm afraid. Not till all the metalwork comes off."

I looked down; bolts protruded from four points around my knee, connected by metal strips out of a child's construction kit.

"How bad is it?"

"Your knee was fractured, and the top of your fibula is badly smashed. You were in surgery for over eight hours."

"Wow. I'll never get through airport security again."

"It'll mend. They'll take all this off in a week or so. You'll be walking within a month."

"You seem confident."

"I've seen guys worse off than you. We get them on their feet in the end."

"Will you help me?"

"I'll be with you every step of the way," he said, carefully wiping the sponge around my ass. "Now, let's get you dressed and dry. You need to rest."

"What about you?" I pointed down towards the front of his loose blue cotton pants, where the bulge of his erection was clearly visible.

"I'll take care of that later."

"Let me watch."

"Seriously?"

"Of course I'm fucking serious. Do it." I didn't want to resort to seniority—I was a colonel, and Luiz, as a military nurse, was unlikely to be more than a second lieutenant. He might even be a civilian. Whatever the facts, he seemed willing to take orders. He looked over his shoulder to check that there was no one at the door, then deftly lowered his waistband and hoisted out a big, hard dick and a pair of low-hanging balls. I'm not sure if this is a therapy recognized by the medical profession, but the sight of his junk did me more good than all the drugs in the pharmacy.

He licked his left hand and slicked up the head of his cock, then started working it, standing close enough to me that I could feel the body heat. Within half a minute, his balls were tightening; it wasn't going to take him much longer than it took me. Anyone looking through the glass window into the ward would simply see Luiz's arm working back and forth, and would assume that he was washing me or massaging me, rather than jerking off in my face.

"Closer. I want it."

He went on his tiptoes and unloaded over my face. I took as much as possible in my mouth. The rest of it ran down my cheeks, chin, and neck.

After the last spasm he wiped himself briskly on a towel, snapped his waistband back in place, and carried on cleaning me, wiping off the jizz with a washcloth.

"You'll do," he said, when I was clean and dry. "Ready for some lunch?"

"You going to feed me?"

We were both laughing about that when the door opened and a doctor came in. Luiz beat a hasty retreat, presumably to deliver various jizz-stained items to the laundry.

I'd been in the Navy Med for a week before anyone told me what had happened. Plenty of time to think, to piece together the shattered memories. There was someone I cared about back there in Baghdad. My usual type: a younger officer, straight until I persuaded him otherwise, then unstoppable every time he got near me. What happened to him? I racked my brains. I just assumed he was dead. Everyone I care for dies. You know about Will. I try not to think about him.

Major General Hamilton came to see me again. He was all smiles, never a good sign in a superior officer.

"Great news, Dan. I hear the metalwork is coming off in a couple of days." He gestured towards the nuts and bolts holding my leg together. "You can start rehab. They say you'll be up and running again in a matter of weeks."

"Yes, sir."

"You can call me Wallace, Dan. You're off duty."

"Okay, Wallace."

He sat. "How much have you been told about what happened?"

"Not a lot."

"You were in a car. You were rammed by another vehicle packed with explosives."

"Suicide bomber?"

"Nothing left of him. The blast threw you clear. Obviously you weren't wearing a seat belt."

"Are you going to court-martial me?"

"I think we can overlook it on this occasion."

"Thank you, sir."

He smiled, started to say something and then stopped. His face fell, and his eyes flickered around the ward. "The other personnel in the vehicle were not so lucky."

"I see."

"They were both killed."

"Right." What else could I say? "I'm sorry."

"Do you remember anything about that day?"

"I'm having trouble remembering much about my last posting. Baghdad, right? What was I doing there?"

"You were part of a team coordinating the deployment of US troops across the region. You were temporarily stationed in the capital as part of a high-profile public relations exercise."

"How did that go?"

"Badly." He started laughing again, the old gallows humor of the USMC never far from the surface. Then he remembered his mission. "Do you remember any of the men you were serving with?"

"I was thinking about that earlier. There was a guy . . . a young officer. What the hell was his name? He and I were close." I looked into Wallace's eyes; we'd had many discussions in the past about sexual relations between serving military personnel, about professional boundaries, about not letting sex interfere with work. He knew better than anyone that I would always have a bedfellow.

"His name was Mark Williams, Dan. Second Lieutenant Mark Williams."

"That's it! He was a really . . . oh. Shit." The penny dropped.

"I'm afraid so, Dan. He was in the car with you."

"Why?"

"You were on your way to a press conference."

Of course. I'd picked him for the job. I wanted him to be with me in Baghdad. Adjacent rooms in the hotel. No questions asked, as long as the locals didn't get wind of it.

"I see." I killed him, then. Not directly, but if it wasn't for me and my persuasive cock, Second Lieutenant Mark Williams would still be alive. His family and his girlfriend back home would be looking forward to seeing him.

"It's not your fault, Dan."

I couldn't think of anything to say to that. I liked Wallace Hamilton, and I had much to thank him for, but if he hadn't let me back into the corps, that beautiful young man with his light brown hair and tight pink ass would still be alive.

"I'm so sorry, Dan."

I didn't want him to see me cry. "Could you just leave me alone for a minute, sir?"

"Of course. I didn't mean to . . ."

"It's okay. Could you call the nurse . . . I think I'm going to . . ."

It was too late. I puked down my nightshirt.

The doctors wouldn't let me see Wallace again till the next day, by which time I'd been given a thorough checkup and a Valium. Luiz told me that it was only the major general's rank that allowed him on to the ward at all; the medical team were dead against any kind of conversation that might upset me. And it seemed that everything Wallace had to say was upsetting.

"There's something we need to discuss with you, Dan."

"We?"

"There's a team of people who are very . . . interested in you."

"And who might that be?"

"We've been working with the CIA."

"Right." The CIA? Fuck that. At least with USMC you know where you stand. Get in, kick some ass, get out, deal with the consequences in the sleepless hours of the night. But the CIA? The Company? Among old-school marines like me, they're feared and despised. "What do they want with me? Someone they need killed?"

"No, Dan."

"Then what? I'm not one of the suit and tie boys, Wallace. I'm a marine. That's all."

He blushed—Major General Wallace Hamilton, with all his medals and citations, his reputation for ferocity in the field and diplomacy off it, actually blushed. "You have a particular skill set that they think could be useful to them."

This could only mean one thing. "I see. They want someone fucked, and then killed."

Wallace laughed, thank God. "That's closer to the mark."

"Sounds like a job for Dan Stagg. Am I still a marine?"

"You always were, and you always will be."

"I get the impression there's a 'but' coming."

"Well . . ." Wallace looked around the ward, shifted in his chair. "There's a mission lined up for you, Dan. Just as soon as you can walk."

"Can you tell me what it is?"

"You'll be fully briefed, if you accept it. Let's just say that it's an undercover operation, and it involves travel."

"What's so exciting about that?" I've done enough undercover operations to know that there's no excitement involved, just hard slog. Some of them go well, some of them go badly. And then you pretend nothing happened. You weren't there. Fake news.

"There's a big difference with this one, Dan."

Jesus, I thought, spit it out. He can talk about people getting blown to pieces, but now he's struggling? "Go on."

"The thing is, Dan . . ." He paused, looked at his hands, picked a nail, looked above my head. "The thing is, you're dead."

02

I had a moment of clarity. Of course I'm dead.
That explains everything. The spooky white hospital
room, the angelic Luiz—how could I possibly have
believed that a military nurse would jerk me off and
come in my face?—and the eerie lack of information
about what had happened to me. Any second now I'll
sprout wings and start playing "From the halls of Mont-
ezuma" on a harp. So there is an afterlife. Maybe I'll see
Will. My heart pounded for a second.

"What the hell are you talking about?"

"Officially speaking," said Wallace, "you were killed
in that explosion in Baghdad, alongside Mark Williams
and the driver. There were no survivors. That's what
the news reports have said. No one knows you're here."

"My family?"

"Next of kin have been informed in the usual way."

I stifled a laugh. Dead to the world—isn't that what
I've always wanted? To be without ties, separated from
a family that rejected me, no responsibilities, no regrets
. . . Dead. Free.

"You're seriously telling me that my parents think I'm dead?"

"Yes, Dan."

"How can you do that? I mean, is that even allowed?"

"That's up to you."

"The corpse has a choice?"

"Exactly. If you want, you can stage a miraculous recovery. We'll smooth things over. We'll tell the people who need to know."

Who would care? Jody, maybe, but that was a long time ago. For all I knew he was dead too. Maybe he'd float by on a cloud any moment, sucking angel cock.

"And if I don't want?"

"Then you have a new life. A fresh start. That's what you always said you wanted, Dan. You came back to the corps to start all over again."

"I guess so."

"You got your wish."

I liked the idea of being dead. "How did they take it? My parents?"

"They're very proud of you."

"I bet they are. And I'm sure the death gratuity will help. They can do a lot with ten grand. Go on a cruise. Build a new lanai." Wallace said nothing, just looked at me. "What do you want me to say?"

"Just let me know whether you're dead or alive."

"How soon do I have to decide?"

"Your funeral is in two days."

"In Washington?"

"Yes. Arlington."

"Ten miles down the road."

"Thereabouts."

"Can I go? I'll put on a disguise."

"No." Wallace was smiling at last.

"I'll think about it. But you have to tell me why."

"Why what?"

"Why do you need me to be dead?"

"It's a question of security, Dan. There must be absolutely no way that your identity can be established. The CIA needs you to be operationally credible."

"What the fuck does that mean?"

"I don't know the details yet. The Company plays its cards close to its chest. What I do know is that you'll be issued with a new identity, new papers, everything, and there can be no trails leading back to Colonel Dan Stagg."

"I see."

"And there's another reason. Something I insisted be put in place."

"What?"

"Have you noticed the armed personnel outside the ward?"

"I haven't been outside the ward."

"You're sealed off by one of the tightest security cordons that has ever existed in a military hospital. You should see the guys at the entrance. Even I get searched."

"Why?"

"Because there's a very real chance that they'll try again."

"Who will try? And what?"

"ISIS. They tried to kill you in Baghdad. You were the target. The other casualties were collateral damage. ISIS don't like failing, so we've allowed them to believe that they succeeded. They're claiming that your death is a triumph."

"Why? What have I done?"

"You're a high-profile officer in the US intervention in Iraq. And they know your service record. As far as they're concerned, you're a sworn enemy of Islam."

"How do you know?"

"US intelligence is pretty good in this area, Dan. Besides which, they've released videos on the internet which make it perfectly clear. We issued photographs of your corpse."

"Nice. Anyone I know?"

"A clever mock-up from the graphics boys. ISIS lapped it up. Posted it everywhere. You're famous."

"A famous corpse."

"Exactly."

"And if they find out it's fake . . ."

"They won't be pleased."

"You haven't left me a great deal of choice, have you?"

"If you agree to this, Dan, you'll be given excellent security support before the mission."

"The mission. Yeah. I forgot about the mission. And afterwards?"

"That remains to be seen."

"What you're saying is that I might be dead for real."

"It's a possibility. You know that better than anyone."

"And if I survive?"

"The future is yours to do with as you please."

"Or as Uncle Sam pleases."

"Your usefulness has been noticed at the highest levels, Dan."

"They been talking to my ex-boyfriends?"

"Actually, yes."

"Oh." That took the wind out of my sails.

"First and foremost, you're valued as an excellent officer. But you have other skills that make you uniquely valuable."

"Fucking got me thrown out of the corps, and now it's my biggest asset?"

"Times have changed, Dan."

"You can say that again. The dead can walk. Queers are good. What are you going to tell me next? Pigs can fly?"

"There have been unconfirmed sightings, yes." Wallace reached out and took my hand. "I don't need an answer right away, Dan. It's a big decision."

"You know what I'm going to say, though."

"I do. But it wouldn't look good in my report if I didn't give you time for reflection. They'd say I persuaded you. As if I could ever persuade you to do anything."

I returned the pressure on his hand. Wallace Hamilton, for all the silver stars and medals, was the nearest thing I had to a father. "Come see me tomorrow. I'll have an answer for you then."

Of course I chose death. Old soldiers aren't afraid of dying, and I'm readier than most. I've never enjoyed life. It's great when I'm fucking or fighting or killing—everything else is blocked out. The rest is shit, and if it doesn't start out that way I can turn it around pretty damn quick. I never got on with my family; there's no love lost there, they'll be much happier with the compensation money. They were proud of me as long as I was serving overseas. When I was discharged, when I lost everything—the man

I loved, my job, my identity, my future—they were mortified. They barely tolerated my bridge-building visits. My
father shook my hand when I told him I'd been accepted
back into the corps; he wouldn't discuss the whys and
wherefores. He'd prefer a dead hero to a living son, and
as for my mother—well, she always did what Daddy told
her. She won't grieve for long. She has grandchildren to
withhold her affections from now, so she's set for the next
ten, fifteen years, whatever she has left.

If your parents don't love you, you're screwed. I've
never been good at friendships or relationships, at least
those parts that don't involve the genital organs. Who
are my friends? I don't mean the people I happen to be
working with or fucking—I mean the people who have
stuck with me over the years. Who do I turn to when
things are bad? Who do I celebrate with when things
are good?

Nobody. I have no friends.

There have been times when I thought maybe, maybe
him, maybe this time . . . Will, of course, and Jody,
the two men I might have had a future with. One died,
the other I betrayed and abandoned and did my best
to forget. I can blame my parents as much as I like,
but I know where the problem lies. It's me. I'm like the
Grinch. My heart is two sizes too small.

At least if I'm officially dead it saves me the trouble of
committing suicide. And if my mysterious new mission
puts me in the way of danger, so much the better. My
real death will supersede my fake death, and nobody,
save the CIA, will be any the wiser.

And if I refuse to play ball? My fans in ISIS will
get me.

All in all, a pretty compelling argument for death. I let Wallace know well before the deadline.

Days drifted by in a haze of powerful painkillers. Luiz took good care of me: I can only assume that he was acting under orders, keeping Dan Stagg calm and happy until he was useful again. Hand jobs graduated to sucking, and it was only my smashed leg that prevented me from fucking. We were never interrupted.

Soon I was able to sit in a chair, and to walk with the aid of crutches. The metal had been removed from my right leg, and the use returned. Luiz encouraged me to move around the ward, mobilizing my leg, starting the long process of rehabilitation. The muscles were wasted, the joints hurt like hell, but I began to believe that I might recover.

There were no reports from the funeral. Nobody told me how my parents were doing. Wallace visited me once more, but it was an official visit, a withdrawal. There were consultations with physical therapists, surgeons, and counsellors, all of whom agreed that I was doing fine and would soon be fit for active service. They wanted me out of the Navy Med and back in the field, where I could be killed all over again.

Of the CIA job, I heard nothing further. Perhaps it had been cancelled. I'm experienced enough in the ways of covert missions to accept that sometimes these things disappear without a trace.

And then, one afternoon when Luiz had fed, shaved, and sucked me, he said, "You have a visitor in about an hour, Dan."

"Oh, yes."

"Do you want to get dressed?"

"What, in actual clothes?"

"Sure. We have some things in your size."

"My uniform?"

"Civilian clothes."

So I'm not a marine any more, then. Not outwardly, at least.

He made me look presentable: slacks, a proper shirt with a collar, brown brogues. I could have been a stock-broker on a weekend break. He sat me in an armchair, made a few final adjustments, ran a cool hand over my forehead, and left.

The door opened, and a handsome man in a sharp suit carrying an attaché case walked briskly into the ward. "Dan Stagg?"

"That's me."

Someone must have been researching my sexual history, because my visitor was just the kind of guy I go for. What, I hear you ask, he was male and had a pulse? Well yes, my tastes in men are catholic, but this one pressed a lot of buttons: a little younger than me, say mid-thirties, medium height, slim, clean shaven, brown hair thinning on top, glasses. The nerdy kid at school who grew up to be hotter than hell, while the football and track stars ran to fat.

He put his case on the end of the bed, and extended a hand. Dark hair on the wrist, a blue-and-white striped shirt cuff. No rings. "Ethan Oliver."

We shook. "Agent Oliver?"

"If you wish. But we're not using ranks or titles."

"Okay. Mr. Oliver."

"You can call me Ethan. I'll call you Dan, for now at least."

"Before I get my new identity."

"Exactly so. Mind if I sit?"

"Be my guest."

He pulled up a chair and sat opposite me. "How's your leg?"

"Mending."

"Good, good. They say you're making great progress."

"I'm doing my best."

"Are you satisfied with the quality of your care?"

"What is this? Market research?"

He smiled. "We want the best for you."

"I see." Had they recruited Luiz? Was he some kind of CIA nurse-whore? "That's very considerate of you."

"You've probably been wondering what you're doing here."

"Getting my leg fixed?"

"I mean all the security. The secrecy. I don't know how much Major General Hamilton told you."

"You know exactly what Major General Hamilton told me."

He glanced at his neat fingernails, then smiled. "I wouldn't be doing my job properly if I didn't."

"So let's not bother with any pretense. Are you going to brief me? Or is this an audition?"

"It's certainly not an audition, Dan. We've had our eyes on you for some time. We know all about you."

"Is that so?"

"You're not exactly low profile. Even when you were in between postings . . ."

"When I was thrown out of the marines for being gay, you mean?"

"That's it. You couldn't seem to keep yourself out of the news."

"I didn't want any of that. I just wanted a quiet life."

"Tell that to the marines, as they say."

"Very funny."

"Fortunately, we managed to contain the stories. We kept your photo out of the media as much as possible."

"What do you mean?"

"We've been monitoring you for a long time, Dan."

"How long?"

"Since your discharge in 2009."

"Why?"

"Because men like you are useful."

"Gay men?"

He waggled his hand. "Let's say attractive people, no matter what their gender or sexuality."

"Okay. I know how to fuck, and I know how to kill. What does that make me? James Bond?"

"If you like, yes."

I looked him in the eye, wondering who would blink first. Hmm. Not him.

"Go on."

"When we identify a potential operative, we need to establish a degree of anonymity around him or her."

"So I don't get recognized when I go undercover?"

"Exactly. We've suppressed most of the published images of you. You were never very active on social media."

"My ex-boyfriend tried to get me on there."

"Jody Miller. Yes. Those accounts are now shut down."

"And how is Jody? You've probably seen him more recently than I have."

"He's fine."

"Good to know."

'You weren't thinking of contacting him, were you." It was not a question.

"Supposing I was?"

"That would be unfortunate."

"For who?"

"For the mission."

"Ah, the mission. I thought for a moment you were threatening me."

"Mmmm." He scratched his chin, which made a pleasant crackling sound. "The reports were right. You're aggressive."

"Is that what they said?"

"That's what they said. And that's why we want you."

I couldn't think of a smart reply to that one.

"Have you ever been to Britain, Dan?"

"Only to change planes."

"Do you know anyone there?"

"You tell me."

"No. You don't."

"Correct. Please don't bother asking me questions to which you already know the answer. It'll save a lot of time."

"Are you in a hurry?"

Sarcastic little fuck. One day, Agent Oliver, I am going to punish you for this. "My leg fucking hurts and I want some painkillers and I want to sleep."

That seemed to get through. "Sorry. I'll try to keep

to the point. You're going to be sent to England, to work closely with MI6."

"So I really am James Bond, then."

"Up to a point. You remain in the service of the United States Marine Corps. But they have seconded you to the CIA."

"And you're lending me to MI6. Understood. What's the objective?"

"You will penetrate an organization that we believe is funding extreme right-wing groups in the US."

"And kill them all."

"No. This is an intelligence mission."

"Then why are you using someone whose skill set is limited to fucking and killing?"

"Your control in London will fill you in on the details."

"Am I going to be told anything before I go?"

"You'll be told enough."

"And if I have questions?"

"Then you must ask them, of course."

Yeah, I thought, and you'll do your best not to answer them.

"Why is this important? I mean, there are crazy extremist groups all over the place. What makes these guys special?"

"The FBI recently uncovered a plot to set off a radiation device that could have killed thousands of civilians, including government officials."

"I heard about that. Some racist nutjob."

"That's what got into the news media."

"Carefully controlled by you, of course."

"Not just by us—but yes, there is some agency input into news releases."

"What was the truth, then?"

"We think that this particular group was part of a wider network. We've made some arrests, and as far as the media is concerned that's the end of the story. But there's compelling evidence that they have links to other small groups who have been attacking just about every target you can imagine. Mosques, women's refuges, abortion clinics, LGBT centers."

"Nice."

"And if you follow the money, several of them are being funded by the same source in the UK."

"Why not just bust them?"

"Because we don't have proof."

"Does that matter?"

"Up to a point. But we think they're planning something big. We need a man on the inside. That's how the FBI stopped them last time. They had someone from the Ku Klux Klan cooperating with them."

"I see. And this time, you need a queer."

"Yes."

I guess the look on my face was pretty eloquent.

"Well," said Oliver, "you told me not to beat around the bush. You know perfectly well that we don't think gay men are the equivalent of KKK members. I don't need to explain that to you."

"And why do you need a gay man?"

"Because we think it will help you to penetrate the UK operation."

Another staring match. This time I blew it completely, and laughed. "Are you for real?"

He allowed himself a slight smile. He had nice white teeth. Sharp. "Oh, yes."

"So I go to England, I penetrate, I report back to MI6—and then what?"

"You will be given further instructions as the operation proceeds."

"In other words, you don't know."

"It depends on what you find out. As I said, we think there is something big in the works. It may involve you."

"You mean you want me to become part of a terror plot?"

"It may be necessary."

"And I might get killed when you come storming in at the end. Is that right?"

"You know about operational risks, Dan."

"And if I survive? Do I ever get to be Dan Stagg again?"

"That depends on you. With the right kind of support and therapeutic intervention, if necessary, you will always be Dan Stagg."

"Some guys lose themselves."

"That's what I'm talking about."

"But you don't think I will."

"We have confidence."

"Based on what, exactly?"

"As an example, your relationship with Luiz."

"I see. He's been filling you in, has he?"

"Yes."

"And what does he say?"

"He has given you a glowing review."

"I see." I was getting hard. Perhaps Mr. Preppy Agent would like to find out first hand, rather than relying on paid informants. "So the fact that I was having sneaky sex in a hospital bed is a good thing?"

"In these circumstances, yes. It shows resilience."

"I recover quickly."

"So I gather."

His eyes flickered down to my crotch, and back up. CIA methods have certainly changed.

"What happens next?" I was hoping he would say, "I have to strip you naked and suck your dick," but that was a bit far-fetched even for the strange circumstances I'd been living in since my death.

"You work on your recovery. When you're ready, you'll be briefed on your new identity. It's important that you're confident with the cover story. You'll be issued with a new passport and a few other items and then you'll get on a plane to London."

"Sounds straightforward."

"It's anything but straightforward, Dan, and that's why we've chosen you for the job. Think you can handle it?"

"Sure. I go in, kick ass . ."

Oliver held up a hand. "No. That's exactly what you don't do. You take your time. You get to know people, and you make them believe that you're one of them. You'll have to do things that might go against your morals . . ."

"Morals? What morals?"

"You'd be surprised. Even tough guys like you have a sense of right and wrong."

"We'll see."

"You may have to go off radar, if we think things are getting dangerous. If we abort the mission, we may not be able to tell you. You could be abandoned."

"Oh, I'm used to that. I have an on-off relationship with Uncle Sam."

"That's one of the reasons we picked you for the job. You can deal with rejection."

"I've had plenty of practice."

"Yes." Was that a glint of compassion behind the shiny lenses of his glasses? If so, it didn't last. "It's a necessary qualification."

"Were there many other candidates for the job?"

"Of course. We keep a lot of people in mind for these things."

"And they never even know it."

"Correct."

He stood up. "And now, you must be tired. I'll leave you in peace. I'm glad to have met you, Dan, before you turn into someone else."

"Before I get killed for real?"

"I don't think you will, somehow. And when you come home, I'll be glad to welcome you back."

We shook hands. "Sounds good. Will we have a party?"

"Oh, I expect so." He smiled. "Something along those lines."

"That's worth staying alive for."

I watched his tight ass in his charcoal-gray pants as he walked out of the ward. How long before I spread those cheeks and push my cock in? How long before I see his self-control evaporate as I fuck him? They always tell you to visualize your goals. This was mine.

And that is how I died. Not with a bang, but with a conversation and a handshake. It felt good being dead. Calmer than I've felt for a long time. At peace with myself. I couldn't quite shake the suspicion that I was really, actually, physically dead, and that this strange dialogue with the USMC and the CIA was just a dream. The afterlife. I was hoping that heaven would be a nonstop orgy of hard cocks and tight asses, but it was more in keeping with my luck that it was a cross between an anxiety dream and an operational briefing. Luiz was at hand to stop me from going mad. I wondered how the CIA had recruited him? WANTED: qualified nurse and physical therapist, must be excellent cocksucker and good listener. Luiz certainly matched the job description.

"How do you feel, Dan?" he asked the next day, while I was eating lunch and he was changing the bedsheets.

"Oh, just dandy."

"Great." He tucked in the sheet. "You are allowed to talk to me, you know."

"About what?"

"All of it. I've been briefed."

"How much do you know?"

"As much as you."

"You're not much of a nurse then, are you? I died on your watch."

"You seem pretty much alive to me, Dan. At least, you were when you came in my mouth yesterday."

"Yeah—speaking of which, I wish you'd hurry up with that bed. I've got something I need to do."

"And what might that be?"

"I need to fuck you."

"I'm not sure that's a good idea."

"Don't you want me to?"

"You're not fit enough."

"Do I have to be signed off before I'm allowed to stick it in your ass?"

He smiled. "I should at least discuss it with the doctors."

"Come on, Luiz. I want to show the guys at the CIA that I'm ready for this job. As I understand it, I'll have to do quite a bit of fucking."

"That appears to be the case."

"So I need to demonstrate my abilities."

"Nobody doubts them."

"I do. I've lost confidence in myself."

"Have you indeed."

"And there's only one way to find out if I am still up to the job."

"If you say so."

I grabbed his ass. "Maybe you should get that cute little agent to come and see for himself."

"You liked him, then?"

"I wouldn't go that far. But I want to fuck him."

"I'm not sure I see the distinction . . ."

"Well, you," I said, caressing his firm, round buttocks, "I like. You're a nice guy, you're kind, and I feel great when we have sex. I'd like to spend a lot of time with you, preferably with my dick inside you."

"You're quite the romantic, aren't you?"

"Oliver, on the other hand, is a prick, and not in a good way. An annoying little pen-pusher who's risen to power without ever having to get his hands dirty. He just happens to have a cute face and a tight little ass. I want to show him who's boss. Get him sweating and drooling for my dick."

"They really chose the right guy for the job, didn't they?"

"I never said I was nice."

"The sooner they think you're fit, the sooner you'll be shipped out."

"I guess so."

"I'll miss you."

"Is that part of your job description?"

"No. Of course not." He knew what was coming. "But I can't help it."

"You don't want to get involved with me, Luiz. I fuck people up."

"Do you? I'd like to find out."

"You mean, when I get back? If I get back?"

"Maybe."

I pulled him towards me, and stroked his cock. "You'd wait for me?"

"Would it be worth my while?"

"It might be."

"And what about the others?"

"What others?"

"The men you left behind."

"Oh, they'll cope with their grief, I expect." I was thinking of Jody. "They'll find someone to fill the gap. Guys like me are a dime a dozen."

"That's bullshit." He leaned down, and kissed me on the lips. "You just don't know how to let yourself be loved."

"Is that what the briefing documents told you?"

"You're a cynic." He kissed me on the side of the face, the jawline. "You've been in the military for too long. You're suffering from PTSD."

"Go on."

He kissed my neck, cradled the back of my head. "You need looking after."

"By you."

"I'm pretty good at it."

"What about when I'm not in the hospital anymore? When I'm just a miserable old bastard who needs to get his balls emptied twice a day?"

"Shut up and fuck me, Dan."

"Without permission from your commanding officer?"

"Jesus. Do I have to put the condom on you myself?"

"Actually, yes. That's exactly what you have to do. You have to do everything."

"I see." He smoothed down the freshly made bed. "Let's get started, then."

"How are we going to do it?"

"You'll find out."

Luiz knelt in front of me, and unbuttoned my pants. I was already half hard, and by the time he'd pulled them down around my knees my dick was sticking up, ready for active service. He grabbed the bottom of my shirt and pulled it up over my head and arms. I was naked.

"Can you stand?"

"I think so." I pushed myself out of the chair. I'd done enough physical therapy by now to stand unaided. "There you go."

Luiz was still on his knees.

"Steady now. Don't make me cum. That's going somewhere else."

He stood up, stripped off his nurse's uniform in less than five seconds—it could have been designed for rapid removal—and procured a condom from one of the pockets. Obviously he was prepared for this. He rolled it on me with the same precision he brought to making a bed. Lube was pumped from a little dispenser. The quality of nursing care in the Navy Med really was excellent.

"Ready?"

"Ready."

He bent over the side of the bed, legs apart, his round, hairy ass pointing up, split down the middle. I was familiar with it, having managed to get three fingers and a tongue in it. Now it was about to do the job for which it was created.

I braced myself with one hand against the bed frame. Usually I can rely on my thigh muscles to provide the support and thrust I need, but after a bad smash and weeks in bed the strength was not there. I lined my cock up with Luiz's hole, pushed forward and glided in, encountering very little resistance. Once I was in, I could lean forward and put some of my weight on to Luiz's broad, smooth back. He pressed his ass against me, doing half the work; all I had to do was meet his backward thrusts with my own weak forward motions. We picked up each other's rhythm, and soon I was fucking him efficiently, if not particularly well.

Luiz reached around to squeeze my balls. "You're doing great, Dan." He used the same phrase during physical therapy sessions. I guess this was just physical therapy-plus.

Endorphins and adrenaline were deadening the pain in my leg, and I wanted to spin him around, fuck him in every position, take control. This was not to be. When I attempted to stand up and flip him on to his back, a bolt of agony shot from my hip to my knee. My cock slipped out of his ass and immediately started to soften. I swore loudly and bit my lip to stop myself from crying.

"It's okay. Sit down. We shouldn't have tried."

"No!" I'm not a quitter. "Bend over that fucking bed. I'm going to finish this."

He did as he was told, which was enough to get the blood flowing back to my cock, and after I'd watched him fingering his hole for half a minute I was fully stiff. I held on to his hips, pushed in, and fucked him as if my life depended on it, which I guess it did. Certainly my future employment did. I knew Luiz would report back. "Yes, sir, he showed great resilience in the face of overwhelming odds . . ." For all I knew, they were watching me on CCTV. I'd be surprised if the room wasn't full of cameras. Okay, Agent Oliver, I'll give you a show. I'll fuck Luiz's ass so you know just what's coming once I get back home . . . You're going to regret it when I'm tearing into you, when you're whimpering and begging me to stop and I just keep on fucking you . . .

And with those unedifying thoughts swamping my brain, I emptied my balls deep inside Luiz's guts.

03

I've only passed through England on my way to other places. Apart from one stopover for a briefing in some soulless satellite town, my experience of English culture is confined to airports. So London, after four and a half months in the hospital and rehab, was a shock. I wasn't used to crowds, or noise, or traffic, let alone traffic coming from the wrong direction. I was unprepared for the racial diversity; I guess I expected it to be white men in bowler hats. But this was like New York and DC and Boston and Baltimore mixed up with Disneyland, all those famous buildings that I always half assumed only existed in the movies. And the men— everywhere, from immigration onward, the men.

Being a temporary CIA agent on loan to the British Secret Intelligence Service, MI6, meant that I flew business class and was put up in a nice hotel right by the river. A large room with a view of the Thames, the Houses of Parliament, crowds coming and going along the South Bank, a huge double bed, a massive bathroom . . . Usually my first thought would be to find a couple of friends to share my good fortune with me, but this time I'd been told to keep a low profile and "avoid contact with unknown persons." That meant not fucking the locals.

The appointment was at 1000 hours the morning after my arrival. Eastbound transatlantic flights are a bitch, the jet lag is far worse than going stateside, but I've spent most of my adult life coping with disrupted sleep patterns, and an early morning workout in the hotel gym, a quick blast of steam, and a cold shower set me up nicely. I managed to avoid getting involved with the young guy who was cleaning the spa area, whose attention to the floor right outside the steam room seemed a little excessive, but I gave him a smile and a wink and a good view of my cock. I got dressed and walked over Hungerford Bridge, seagulls swooping overhead, blue skies, a cold wind, boats passing beneath my feet. My appointment was in a private members' club a little north of the river, all classical columns on the outside and marble and gold on the inside. I announced myself to the hall porter, and was immediately ushered up the grand staircase.

"You'll be in the smoking room, sir." He held a deeply polished door open. I stepped on to carpet so deep it seemed to suck at my feet. "Mr. Reeve will be with you shortly."

I'm used to these tactics. You show someone into an office and leave them on their own for a while. It's a great way of breaking down the confidence of the person you've summoned, and of asserting your own authority. I've done it hundreds of times with junior ranks, whether it's for a briefing, a disciplinary, or a fuck. Get them in and keep them waiting: they'll be much more obedient even after just five minutes. Try it sometime.

I'm wise to the game, but it still worked. I was in unfamiliar territory, not just a different country but a different world of privilege and tradition, where I was uncertain of the code of conduct. However much I reminded myself that I was Colonel Dan Stagg, hero and veteran, my palms were getting damp as I glanced around the panelled walls, the leather-bound books, the crazy old furniture that made it look like a movie set.

I jumped when the door opened, and wiped my hands on my pants.

"Colonel Stagg?"

I couldn't see him too well, just the vague shape of a tall man in a dark suit. The voice sounded—not old, exactly, but certainly not young.

"That's me."

"That was you, technically speaking. You are now . . . someone else." He stepped forward, and the light from the windows hit him. My age or older: could be a well-preserved sixty, even. Flat stomach, broad shoulders, neatly cut gray hair, blue eyes behind gold-rimmed glasses. A dark gray suit with a slight stripe, a bright white shirt and a tie that, I assumed, announced his membership of some elite. Far too refined to be a military man: all of us, even to the highest ranks, have a coarseness that never rubs off. This one reeked of government.

"Andrew Reeve. Nice to meet you." We shook. His hand was warmer and drier than mine. "I expect you're wondering why you're here."

"I'm too old to wonder about anything."

He raised his eyebrows maybe a quarter of an inch. "That implies a readiness for the unexpected."

"I'm sure I don't need to talk you through my CV, Mr. Reeve."

"I am familiar with it."

"I hope I'm here to be briefed."

"Among other things. Please take a seat." He motioned towards a couple of wing-backed armchairs set on either side of a fancy little table that was probably worth more than I earn in a year. "Coffee or tea?"

"Coffee, please."

He pressed a button on the wall. "I'll ring for it."

"I thought they only did that on TV."

"Here, at least, we retain a few of the old comforts." The door glided open, and a waiter appeared with a tray. He must have been waiting for the signal. "We'll help ourselves, thank you Radek." The waiter bowed slightly, arranged china cups and silver pots and withdrew, but not before I'd caught his eye. He was young, early twenties maybe, with cropped blond hair and blue eyes.

Reeve noticed. He didn't miss much. "Radek is one of ours." My turn to raise my eyebrows. "MI6, I mean. We're keeping this in the family. I trust you're maintaining a low profile as well, as discussed."

"I'm doing my best."

"Hotel to your liking?" He poured coffee.

"Very nice. Not that I've had much time there."

"And you haven't . . ." He looked me in the eye.

"Entertained? No. I see my reputation precedes me."

"Your reputation, Colonel Stagg, is why you are here."

"I never saw fucking around as a career move, but apparently I was wrong." See? Always the coarseness. Reeve seemed to approve.

"I'm going to tell you about the job. Please don't take notes."

"I never do."

"I understand you haven't been in the UK much."

"Correct."

"You've never been to Manchester."

"I changed planes there once, twenty years ago."

"I can live with that. Most of the people you will be dealing with were barely born twenty years ago. And what do you know about boxing?"

"You tell me. You've read the file."

"You're a black belt in various forms of martial arts, and you boxed a little in your teens and twenties."

"More than a little, but yes, that's about right."

"Think you could brush it up?"

"You don't forget stuff like that."

"Good. And you instructed at various levels."

"Tae kwon do, karate, judo. But mainly army combatives."

"And you're good at it."

"I am."

"You can kill with your bare hands?"

"Want me to demonstrate?"

"I have your superiors' word for it, as well as news reports of various civilian activities which we are trying to suppress."

"During my little holiday from the marines, you mean?"

"Precisely. You were busy, weren't you?"

"As a fighter?"

"Among other things." He sipped his coffee, perhaps mulling over the details of the report. How much was in there? Who had they talked to? There are plenty of guys who can testify to my talents in the sack, and there's a trail of dead and wounded to bear witness to the combat skills. "Now, to details. You will be assuming a new identity, and it's vital that you are absolutely confident in your new persona."

"Who am I?"

"Your name is Greg Cooper."

"Did you pick that out of a hat?"

"We have software for that. You were an officer in the United States Marine Corps, highly trained in combat skills, and you served in several theaters of war."

"So far so good."

"And you were thrown out of the marines for . . ."

"Fucking."

"This is where we depart from reality. You were discharged for racially abusing a fellow officer."

"Oh, I was, huh?"

"You called him, I quote, 'an Obama-lovin' sand nigger.' Unfortunately, one of your colleagues was filming you. You tried to dismiss it as barrack-room banter, but the authorities disagreed. It became quite a cause célèbre in the media. And although Greg Cooper was disgraced and discharged, he became something of a hero to certain so-called free speech advocates."

"On the extreme right."

"Exactly. You should see the amount of online coverage you generated. Quite the Twitterstorm."

"And you started planting this when, exactly?"

"As soon as you died."

"Very efficient."

"We have to be. Now, with this unfortunate reputation, you were in no hurry to pursue a career in the US, and you decided to take an extended holiday in England. Start a new life."

"I take it I have family here."

"You have an English grandfather. You will learn all about him."

"Good ol' gramps."

"You're looking for work. Your only real qualifications are in martial arts and combat training. You'll be travelling around, scouting out opportunities."

"And I'll find one in Manchester."

"You will gain employment with one Alan Vaughan, a boxing promoter and manager who owns a chain of gyms in the northwest. We believe he is funding an extreme right-wing organization in the US."

"And you want proof. That much I have been told."

"Hence the need for an agent on the inside. Your mission is to penetrate Vaughan's organization, find out exactly where the money is coming from and where it is going."

"Isn't that obvious? There's a lot of money to be made in boxing."

"That's already been pursued. He keeps the boxing side of things squeaky clean. All the money is accounted for, and it goes back into the business. Staff wages, premises and so on. His accounts are spotless. He makes substantial donations to charity from his own income, all completely aboveboard."

"But you think there's more."

"We believe so. Vaughan is very careful. If there are other branches of his operation, he keeps his distance from them. We need you to gain his trust, and that of his close associates."

"And that's where my cock comes into it."

"Vaughan is gay—discreetly so, but it's an open secret within the boxing world. He has a sort of Praetorian Guard that deters any investigations. His dealings with the media are highly controlled. He's a brilliant showman, he does a lot of charity work with disadvantaged young people, raises a fortune from his various celebrity friends. But the public knows nothing about the real Alan Vaughan."

"So I fuck my way into his confidence."

"We suspect that Vaughan is involved with a serious terror threat in the US. If this turns out to be true, we may need you to execute part of Vaughan's plan. If it comes to it, you will be in the firing line when US forces intercept the attack."

"And if Uncle Sam doesn't kill me, then someone in Vaughan's camp will do the honors."

"It's possible."

"Thanks. And what's in it for me, apart from a lot of hot young boxers?"

"We thought that might have been an incentive."

"Twenty years ago I would have been tempted. Nowadays I need more than just ass."

"You will be well paid, of course."

"And?"

"And what?"

"What's my future, when I deliver Vaughan? Or are you counting on me dying?"

"You may continue to be useful to us. Alternatively, you can retire in comfort. You'll want for nothing."

"So if I survive this job, I could be pensioned off?"

"Very handsomely."

"And you know perfectly well that I'd go crazy and kill myself within a year."

"We had assumed that."

My coffee was cold by now, but I needed something to wash away the nasty taste in my mouth. I was being played. I don't like the feeling. But it was pointless to deny that the job had its attractions. Secrecy, a new identity, however disgraceful, and a generous supply of young athletes. "What makes you so sure that Vaughan is involved in criminal activities?"

"We obtained information from a young man who broke ranks with the organization. According to him, Vaughan is involved in everything from prostitution to blackmail. There was compelling evidence."

"Can't he testify?"

"Unfortunately not."

"You mean he's dead."

"No body has been found, nor has he been reported missing by his family."

"What do the police say?"

"Their investigations were frustrated."

"Does Vaughan have friends in high places?"

"It's possible that he has a hold over some senior-ranking police officers."

"Blackmail?"

"We assume so."

"Fucking, killing, blackmail."

"And martial arts."

"Silly me. And martial arts."

"There's another thing I forgot to mention. Vaughan has a wife and children. They live in a very posh part of the country, in a nice big house. His youngest, a little girl of five, is disabled. He wheels her out for photo opportunities. That's made him a sort of saint in many people's eyes. As far as the popular press is concerned, he's untouchable. And he's highly litigious. There are stories about his past, and he has a criminal record from thirty years ago—drug-related. He keeps that very quiet, and threatens to sue if it's mentioned."

"Sounds like a real charmer."

"He is, that's the trouble. Wait and see. Now, if you've finished your coffee, we have a private room upstairs where we will be running a few tests." Reeve pressed the button again, and Radek materialized in the doorway. "Radek will show you up and get you ready. I will join you in, say"—he looked at his watch, a fancy gold number on his tanned, hairy wrist—"twenty minutes."

I followed Radek up the stairs, enjoying the view of his ass, little suspecting its central importance in the tests of which Reeve had spoken.

The upper floors were given over to private rooms— much like a hotel, except we appeared to be in the nineteenth century. Radek opened the door with a large brass key. No swipe cards here.

"Please." He stepped aside to let me in. Wood panelling, dark crimson carpets, a fancy antique bedstead, a velvet sofa in the window, old-fashioned casements. I looked out at a view of London rooftops, trees, parks, the river.

"Very nice. And what are we doing up here?"

"You will have a shower or bath."

"I had one already this morning." I looked at my watch. "Two hours ago. I didn't get dirty since then."

"These are my instructions." He picked up a white towelling robe from the bed. "Please undress and put this on."

"Seriously?"

"Yes please."

He stood in front of me, holding out the robe. As you know, I'm always happy to undress for good looking blond boys in their twenties, but I was also mindful of orders. Surely MI6 weren't so stupid as to put Dan Stagg, or even Greg Cooper, in a hotel room with a young man telling him to undress, without expecting consequences. You don't put a wolf in a cage with a newborn lamb. Reeve had spoken of "tests." Perhaps they were seeing if I could withstand temptation.

"What does Reeve say about this?"

"He is expecting you to be washed and naked when he joins us in twenty minutes."

"And you?"

"Me, sir?"

"Is he expecting you to be naked as well?"

He blushed. "If you want me to be."

"With my dick in you?" I was hard, and he could see. He shrugged, but said nothing. "What are your orders?"

"I am instructed to take orders from you."

"Well, that's the best news I've had for a while. In that case, you can . . . run the bath."

"Yes sir." Was that disappointment or relief on his

face? Either way, it wouldn't last for long. Radek scuttled off to the bathroom, and soon I could hear water gushing into the tub.

"Now come back here."

"Yes sir."

I snapped my fingers and pointed to the carpet in front of me. "Kneel."

He did as he was told, and looked up at me with wide blue eyes. They'd chosen him well. Someone must have studied the kind of guys I like fucking, and come up with a kind of composite picture. Radek fit the bill perfectly. Young, tough but cute, the kind that often ends up in the USMC. Blond, pale, good bone structure. Polish, I guessed.

"Go on."

"What, sir?"

"You want me naked. Undress me. Starting with the shoes." I lifted my right foot and thrust it towards him. "And don't get the laces knotted."

He cradled the heel of my shoe in one hand, and tugged at the laces with the other. The shoe glided off, followed by the sock. When both feet were bare, I said "Now my tie."

He stood up, and it was easy to see that he was as stiff as I was. I let my arms hang down by my sides while Radek removed my tie, whipped it out of my collar and started unbuttoning my shirt. He was so close I could smell his deodorant. He didn't need further instructions. He took my shirt off, and gave me an approving smile when he saw my hairy, lean torso. The months in rehab had paid off; I'd gone from being weak and skinny after hospital to full Stagg strength. I grabbed his wrist and brought his hand to my chest, pushing the fingers deep into the fur. Then I dragged it down over my stomach to the waistband of my pants.

"Carry on. The belt."

He knelt again, and now he was in a hurry. Buckles, buttons, and zippers yielded under his skillful fingers, and soon I was standing in my underpants. Nice tight white Y fronts, my civilian underwear of choice. Radek licked his lips. My dick was fully hard, pointing towards the two o'clock position, almost reaching my hipbone.

"Get it out."

He reached in via the leg opening, and pulled my cock out.

"Ready for your orders?"

"Yes sir."

"Then suck it."

He took hold of it and gave it a tentative stroke. Given the abstinence of the last few days—which, by my standards, was like a lifetime of celibacy—I was ready to explode. My cock kicked and jumped in his fingers. Luiz had done a great job of getting me back to full fitness.

Radek opened his mouth, put out a velvety pink tongue and took me in, just the head at first, but swiftly, smoothly sliding his lips down the shaft, over every vein and wrinkle of skin, until I felt myself entering his throat. No prizes for guessing how they'd selected him for the job. I gripped his chin with my thumb and fore-finger—he had a little bit of stubble there, not exactly a beard, just one of those indecisive patches that young men like these days, which look ridiculous but feel kind of good—and held him down on me. Tears oozed out of the corners of his eyes, and he obviously couldn't breathe, but he stayed put.

"Good man." I let him come up for air. "Now strip. And make it quick." I looked at my watch; about five minutes left before Reeve was due to join us. He was expecting a show, and I didn't want to disappoint him. Radek wasted no time, efficiently pulling off jacket, tie, and shirt. His body was smooth and slim—a sportsman rather than a gym rat, I suspected. Something that requires speed and agility rather than brute strength. I almost asked him: soccer? Basketball? But then he dropped his pants. His legs were hairy, almost shaggy on the calves and shins. He was wearing tiny black underpants, with a shiny, slimy wet patch at the front, silver against the dark cotton.

"Off."

He pulled them down, and his cock sprang up against the little mat of hair on his belly, light brown like his bush, and mercifully untrimmed. I've fucked a lot of guys, most notably Jody, who put a lot of effort into removing all the stuff from their bodies that I really like—hair, wrinkles, and so on. I prefer things to be left the way nature made 'em. Radek was scoring highly.

"Come here." I pulled him towards me. He was, maybe, four inches shorter than me: another plus. I put my arms around him and kissed him on the mouth. He opened up, let my tongue in, and then started kissing me back. Our cocks were pressed against each other, wet and sticky. Most of the precum was his, but I was getting there.

"Bath first, or do you want me to fuck you?"

"It's up to you, sir."

I did a quick calculation. Reeve would be here in a few minutes. The foot of the bed was opposite the door. I wanted to give him a good impression when he entered the room.

"Turn off the bath, and bring me condoms. I assume you have them."

'They're by the bed, sir. Right there."

I sheathed and lubed my cock.

"Bend over."

He stood in front of me, and parted his cheeks. His asshole was the same color as his tongue, rose pink. Without any preliminaries, I positioned myself behind him and pushed in. He cried out in pain, but didn't ask me to stop. I reached around and checked that he was still hard; I'm a gentleman like that. He was, with juice oozing down his shaft. I rested my ass on the edge of the mattress, and positioned Radek so that he was fully visible from the door. With one hand I explored his firm, tensed torso, his tight nipples, his strong, stubbly jawline; with the other, I jerked his cock. I fucked him at mid-tempo, not so hard that he exploded immediately, but hard enough to keep him on edge. His moaning must certainly have been audible from the corridor, unless the room was cunningly soundproofed.

As for me, I could have come any moment, but I've had plenty of practice at holding it back. I didn't want Reeve to arrive when I'd finished; I'm not twenty anymore, I can't recover in minutes. I wanted him to see what he'd bought.

Radek was throwing himself into his work. He twisted his head around to kiss me while I squeezed his tit, jerked his cock, and fucked his ass. Everything was going to plan—as long as I could keep one eye on the door handle, and not lose focus. The way his tight young ass was clamping around my cock, it wasn't going to be easy. He was close. His balls were tight. Hurry up, Reeve. You're going to miss the show. Radek's moaning was reaching a crescendo. I slackened off, stopped stroking him, slowed the fucking to a standstill. He didn't seem to mind. I think he'd have been happy to let me fuck him all day, depriving him of his orgasm until his brain was in shreds.

We went a couple more rounds like this, poor Radek approaching the brink and being held back. He was well trained; he didn't try to grab his own dick and finish the job himself. He let me take control. I was less disciplined. I was getting to the point when I just wanted to empty myself inside him, Reeve or no Reeve. But then I heard the click and creak of an ancient floorboard just outside the room. It had to be him. I started fucking, pinching, and stroking again; Radek was whimpering now, almost begging. And yes, at last the door handle turned. I picked up the pace, shoving my tongue deep into his mouth, and as the door finally opened Radek started coming, shooting great arcs of white across the empty space to land with an audible splat on the floor. I saw Reeve; our eyes met. Radek was too lost in the fuck. I let him finish his orgasm, milked the last few drops from his cock, kissed him and held him while he sweated and shuddered, my dick still inside him.

Reeve was silhouetted in the doorway, glints of light catching his silver hair. I could just about make out a smile on his face. He stepped forward. "I see you've

wasted no time." Radek jumped, but I held on to him.
"It's okay, Radek," said Reeve. "Stay just as you are."
He closed the door behind him. "How was he, Dan?"

"Very good, as I'm sure you already know."

He didn't deny it. "Have you had a bath?"

"Not yet."

"Go ahead." He stood and watched, arms folded
across his chest, as I withdrew from Radek's ass and
disposed of the condom. I hadn't come, so I was still
at full stiffness, and Reeve's presence wasn't doing
anything to lessen that. Radek stumbled off to the bathroom to clean himself up, leaving Reeve and me facing
each other, him in his crisp shirt and smart suit, me
naked, hairy, and hard.

"Did I pass?"

"So far so good." He started walking around me,
looking me over. "We needed some demonstration of
your powers. It's not that we don't trust our American
sources, but MI6 likes to check facts." He was around
the back now, checking whatever facts he found there.

"Feel free to touch," I said.

"All in good time."

He finished his tour. "How's the leg?"

"Not bad." I rubbed my right thigh. "Still hurts a
bit, but they patched me up pretty well."

"The medical reports said you have a high tolerance
of pain."

"I've been blown up, shot, beaten up, stabbed, all the
usual stuff. The novelty kind of wears off after a while."

"Do you like pain?"

"Not particularly."

"Do you enjoy inflicting pain?" He looked me in the

eyes, ignoring my cock, which was bouncing up and down, a thread of precum lengthening from the tip.

"Not for its own sake. But yeah, if I'm fucking a guy and it hurts him at first, that turns me on. I won't lie."

"You're not a sadist, though."

"Do you want me to be a sadist? Is that part of the JD?"

"Vaughan inhabits a rough world."

"Boxing? Come on. You're talking to a marine."

"I don't just mean the boxing. We suspect links to organized crime."

"I can fight if I need to fight. I can kill if I need to kill. If you want me to play the part of a psycho, I can do that for you."

"What about if you had to hurt or kill someone you believed to be innocent?"

"You mean collateral damage?"

"I mean a bit more deliberate than that."

"Murder."

"Yes."

"Is it likely?"

"Anything is possible."

"You're not going to ask me to kill Radek, are you?"

"Oh, no. Radek is perfectly safe."

Right on cue, Radek appeared in the doorway, a towel wrapped around his waist. "The bath is getting cold, sir."

"We're coming." He gestured me ahead. "After you, Dan." And as I walked into the bathroom, Reeve let his hand rest on my right buttock. He squeezed it gently. "Nice," he whispered, "very nice."

Those of you who are familiar with my career will

know that I only get fucked very occasionally, when I get the urge to submit to a higher authority. Most of the time I'm the boss, and I'm very happy to use my dick on any man who needs it. For many years I resisted the desire to take it; it was too compromising, too gay for a man who pretended for much of his adult life that he wasn't actually gay, he was just a guy who enjoyed the physical sensation of sex with other guys. I was adept at all the bullshit excuses. Time has taught me a few lessons, thank God, and now I'm quite comfortable with who I am, even if I still prefer to be on top. But in Reeve I recognized authority, seniority, a man accustomed to being obeyed. It didn't hurt that he was handsome and powerfully built. It didn't hurt that he was clothed and I was naked, or that his finger was running up and down my furry butt crack.

"Get in, then."

I climbed into the bath—warm, scented, foamy, and big enough for two. What would happen next?

Reeve started tugging at his tie.

"Are you joining me?"

"Any objections?"

"None whatsoever."

"Good." The tie came off, then the jacket. He unbuttoned his shirt. His chest was as hairy as mine, the dense black fur shading into silver. Radek stood like a valet, receiving every item of clothing as it was removed. He folded them carefully and laid them over a chair. Reeve stepped out of his pants. He was wearing blue and white striped cotton boxers. They looked brand new. His cock was straining at the button fly.

"Radek."

Radek knelt and pulled Reeve's shorts down. His

dick was long and thick and his balls would not have been out of place on a bull. Well, if you're going to get fucked, you might as well get seriously fucked.

"Think you can take it, Dan?"

I don't like having my abilities questioned. I knelt up in the bath, thick foam sliding down my body, grabbed Reeve's cock and started sucking it. I will never be a champion cocksucker; I lack practice, and usually find myself fucking a guy's throat before I get anywhere near tasting his dick. But I can muster a pretty decent blow job, especially for a man like Reeve. I assumed this was another test, and so I opened my jaws a little wider and concentrated on suppressing the gag reflex.

"That's enough." He pulled out of my mouth. "Shift up. I'm coming in."

Our legs entwined as the soapy water washed through the hair on his torso. Two stiff dicks broke the surface like periscopes. Radek, who had been standing passively watching, was rubbing himself through his towel. He was getting stiff again. What exactly did Reeve have in mind? Why the bath? Why Radek?

"That's better. I've been looking forward to this." He shifted around in the water, lowering his shoulders into the foam, rubbing it over his head. "You're probably wondering why we're here." He sat up and wiped the soap out of his eyes.

I grabbed his stiff dick and squeezed. "I assume it's something to do with this."

"Yes, partly. As Radek will tell you, I like to fuck."

"I guessed as much."

"But I also need to make sure that you can take as well as give."

"And to do that, you need a bath?"

"Oh, no. It's completely unnecessary. I just like fucking guys in bathtubs. There have to be some perks to the job."

"Will it go into your report?"

"None of this will go into my report. I need to know that you're as good as they say you are, and I need to convince myself that you can keep your mouth shut when necessary."

"And open when necessary."

"From this point on, you report directly to me and my appointed agents. Do you understand? You do not discuss the mission with anyone else."

"Understood." I still had hold of his cock, and was gently stroking it. I wanted it inside me.

"Radek, you can take that towel off now. See that, Dan? He's hard again."

"Yes, I see."

"Whom shall I fuck first? You or him?"

"Me."

"You'd better suck it then."

He raised his hips slightly, and held his cock perpendicular. It was wet and soapy, but that didn't matter. I had to get into a cramped position with my knees jammed under my chest, but I managed. I ran my tongue over his massive dick, from the piss slit all the way down to the balls, immersing my face in water, coming up dripping, eyes stinging, then down again. And then, at further risk of dislocating my jaw, I took him into my mouth and did my best. Judging by the hardness, he enjoyed seeing me try.

Radek was standing idle, but not for long. Reeve

grabbed his wrist, pulled him over and stuck two fingers inside his ass, with nothing in the way of preliminaries. He was still lubricated from our fuck, and didn't seem to mind Reeve's roughness. In fact, he put one foot on the rim of the bathtub to give better access, and lowered himself onto Reeve's hand. His cock—small in comparison to Reeve's—bobbed up and down, slapping against Reeve's hairy forearm. Occasionally Reeve leaned over and kissed Radek's dick, even sucked it a little. My cock, crushed between thigh and ribcage, was feeling left out.

"We'd better get on with this," said Reeve, clearing his throat. Judging by the way his cock was expanding in my mouth, he was close to coming. He stood up, the water gushing off his body, running off the end of his cock as if it were a faucet. The ever-attentive Radek handed him a towel. I unfolded myself and stood, limbs wobbling and aching.

"Get him dry and bring him into the bedroom. I assume the condoms are in place."

"Yes, sir."

Reeve went through, sawing the towel across his broad, hairy shoulders, like a guy at the gym after a tough workout. Radek rubbed me down, and managed a quick suck on my dick to make sure I was at maximum hardness.

"What's he like?"

Radek understood the question. "Very hard." He squeezed my ass. "But good. You'll like it."

He led me through to the bedroom. Reeve was stretched out on the bed, one arm crooked behind his head, the other hand stroking his dick. He had rolled a rubber on it; sheathed, it looked even bigger. This was the real test. Whatever the job had in store for me, Reeve needed to know I could accept a challenge. Mind you, the job wasn't in the forefront of my mind. My ass had taken over the thinking duties, and it just wanted to get filled.

"Lubricate us."

Radek filled his palm with gel, and slathered it over Reeve's shaft. Then he worked it into my ass. I was as ready as I would ever be.

"Go ahead, Dan," said Reeve. "All yours."

I jumped on to the bed, threw my smashed leg over his waist and, facing him, positioned his cock at my hole. I took a deep breath, pressed down to get the head into me and then, on the basis that a short pain is better than a long one, allowed gravity to carry me downwards until Reeve's prick was deep inside me, filling my rectum. Reeve watched my face, monitoring the pain. I held his gaze, resisted the urge to cry out, and concentrated on relaxing every muscle in my body. When I was ready, I started moving up and down. It still hurt, but it was starting to feel good. My cock was oozing a steady stream of precum on to his hairy belly.

"Am I going to have to do all the work?"

"You can if you want to," he said.

The idea of riding him to orgasm was appealing, but now that Radek had told me that Reeve was a hard fucker, I wanted to meet the challenge.

"What's your favorite position when you fuck Radek?"

"Doggy position. Him on all fours."

"Then that's what I want."

"If you're sure. Get off, then."

I dismounted, and knelt on the floor, ass in the air, arms braced. Reeve wasted no time in getting back inside me.

"This won't take long."

"Just as well, probably," I said between gritted teeth. The sensation of his dick pile-driving into me was fantastic, but I couldn't endure it for long. I rested my forehead on my forearms and pushed back against him, meeting his thrusts. Drops of sweat fell from his head to my back. I dared not touch my cock in case I came; it was hard enough taking him when I was insane with lust, but it would be impossible once I'd shot. Reeve picked up the pace, holding on to my hips and slamming into me, both of us panting like athletes.

Finally, he came. Jesus, did he come. Some men like to stay still while they're shooting, the sensations too intense to allow for much movement. Not Reeve. He fucked me even harder, trying to punch his way through to my intestines. Resistance was futile, not to mention painful. I had to let go of everything and become a passive recipient. At last he bellowed, rammed his dick as far as it could go, and emptied himself inside me. He collapsed on my back, pressing me on to the floor; it was like trying to do push-ups with a 180 lb. weight on your spine.

We lay there until I was having difficulty breathing. Reeve rolled off and pulled out. The condom was bulging with spunk.

"You're a good fuck, Dan."

"Now you know."

"Did you come?"

My cock was soft. "No."

"Do you want to?"

"Of course I fucking want to."

Reeve lay down on his stomach and got to work on me, taking my cock in his mouth until it started to grow. He was good; no teeth, not too sloppy. Soon I was fully hard again. The obliging Radek squatted over my face and let me eat his ass. It didn't take long before he was shooting a second load over my chest.

I pulled out of Reeve's mouth and blew my load over his handsome face.

We lay in a sweaty, sticky heap for a while.

"Run another bath, Radek," said Reeve. "We have the room until tomorrow morning. Colonel Stagg—or should I say Mr. Cooper—does not have to be anywhere in a hurry."

I tried to get up and reach for the tissues.

"Oh, before I forget—the sample."

Radek picked up a clear plastic bottle from the bedside table, unscrewed the top, and handed it to Reeve. There was a small spoon attached to the lid, which he ran over the jizz on his face.

"For our records, Mr. Cooper," he said. "A DNA sample. Always useful."

"Was that what all this was about?"

"Officially, yes. And now work is over."

04

Greg Cooper boarded the fast train to Manchester at Euston Station the following afternoon. All that was left of Dan Stagg was in a small plastic specimen bottle, destined for a government laboratory somewhere. My new life was contained in a buff envelope marked CONFIDENTIAL, which had been my constant study since Reeve finished fucking Radek and me in the small hours of the morning.

Cooper's CV had enough parallels to my own to make it easy enough to master. Personality-wise, he was Dan Stagg without any redeeming features—and God knows there aren't many of them—and with a Neanderthal attitude towards women, people of color, immigrants, Muslims, the disabled, you name it. In other words, much like the guys I grew up with. All I had to do was think like them and there I was, Greg Cooper.

I had the carriage to myself. First class, early afternoon, nobody to disturb me except the train crew making their way up and down, checking tickets, offering drinks. None of them interested me.

I read and reread Cooper's file: my instructions were to destroy it as soon as I arrived in Manchester. I'm used to operational briefings, I can assimilate information quickly, and forget it just as quickly when the objective is achieved. I went over my schedule: I was to go straight to the rented accommodation that had been secured for me—"don't expect anything too fancy," Reeve had warned—and get my face known in the local community. I had permission to entertain to my heart's content; I was, in effect, licensed to fuck. After a couple of days I would attend a big boxing match in the city center, promoted by Alan Vaughan. That was to be my entrée to his circle. I felt excited, as I always do at the start of a mission—and this time there was the added attraction of a new start, a new identity, no one to know how badly I fucked my life up. Start again. Fail again, no doubt, but fail in a different way.

There was something else I had to get to grips with: new tech. I'd been issued with a set of miniaturized tracking devices, so small they would be undetectable within the human body, little silicon-encased beads about the size of a pinhead, smooth and practically invisible. Taken orally, they would stay in the system for up to seventy-two hours before being excreted. Inserted anally, they would be good until the subject's next dump. Each device had a unique code, which would enable my controls at MI6 to log the whereabouts of specific subjects, provided I supplied them with relevant digits. All I had to do was get the tracking devices into the subject, at either end. They picked their man well. If there was anyone who could stick things in young men's mouths or asses, it was Dan . . . I mean, Greg Cooper.

That was all I had, apart from a phone and an encrypted email address. No firearms. Dan Stagg felt naked without a firearm. Greg Cooper would have to get used to it.

The train arrived in Manchester on time. Posters advertising the fight were plastered all over town.

Alan Vaughan presents
UNDEFEATED CHAMPION CRAIG LUKAS
vs.
UNDEFEATED CHALLENGER KIERAN MCAVOY
for the
Regional Light Heavyweight Title

But it wasn't the words that caught the eye so much as the photograph of two oiled, muscular bodies that could have been straight off a porn website. One, larger, in the foreground, was dark, Mediterranean-looking, perhaps in his late twenties, with the perfect sculpted body that so many young men aspire to. The other was a puggy-looking redhead with a furrowed brow and close-set eyes, milky-white skin over his muscles. Individually they were hot; as a team, they were irresistible. Craig Lukas, I knew, was Vaughan's star fighter, a charismatic mix of an Albanian father and a Welsh mother, known for his fiery temper and nightlife antics as much as for his boxing. He was a regular fixture in the sports pages, but under Vaughan's management he appeared almost as often in the showbiz sections, out and about with a string of beautiful women, always ready with a quip and a brag, the perfect cocky alpha-male showman. Obviously I wanted to take him down a peg or two, pin him to a mat in some grungy gym and teach him to love cock, but that's my standard response to any handsome face.

It was with the Lukas-McAvoy fight that I was to begin my infiltration of Vaughan's operation. If MI6's suppositions were correct, high-profile title fights like this were the tip of a large, lucrative iceberg. Hidden from sight was a network of prostitution, pornography, blackmail, and God knows what else, the profits of which were finding their way to some very nasty people in the US, the type of assholes who believe every conspiracy theory they're fed and who will back up their delusions with bombs. Operational details were vague: Reeve simply gave me the time and place of the fight. How I ingratiated myself with Vaughan, how I investigated the business, was up to me. It had to look spontaneous, accidental. Reeve was convinced the Vaughan and his inner circle were secretly gay; my sexual prowess, confirmed by Reeve's "tests," was my entrée. A complete lack of morality should do the rest. There was no depth to which Greg Cooper wouldn't sink, even at the cost of his life.

I'm no fan of professional boxing—the guys are attractive, but the razzmatazz and hype make it too much like entertainment for my tastes. I take martial arts and other legitimized forms of violence seriously, as a means to an end, something that might save your life and end your opponent's. All this bouncing around in silk robes and fancy shorts is a foolish distraction. In a way I prefer wrestling, which everyone knows is just two guys pretending to have sex. But there are millions of people out there for whom boxing is a big deal, and by the look of it a good percentage of them had descended on the arena on the outskirts of Manchester when I turned up for the Lukas-McAvoy fight. All human life was here: pimply kids in hoodies and baseball caps, probably with an ounce of weed in their pockets, women old enough to be their grandmothers, in head scarves and overcoats, wealthy-looking men in flashy suits with beautiful women on their arms. And around these, there was a sea of men—just regular men, in their twenties upwards, dressed in the same drab, ill-fitting clothes, clutching messenger bags and backpacks and programs, all of them living out some fantasy in which they too became champions of the world.

Somewhere in this 20,000-seat venue was my first point of entry to Vaughan's heavily protected world. I surveyed the crowd exactly as I would survey occupied territory, looking for the weaknesses, the vantage points, recognizing the rhythms and customs of the people, learning to fit in, to pass without notice, to gain trust, and to betray it. There was plenty to look at. Boxing has always attracted the kind of guys I like—fit and full of bravado, in need of discipline, easy to break. And for once, I had professional reasons to look, as well as personal ones. As Reeve had pointed out, I was licensed to fuck, if that was how I was going to effect entry to Vaughan's inner circle. I needed to find a suitable subject and then pump him—for information, of course.

I hung around the outer fringes of the crowd. There was the usual nonsense going on in the ring, a lot of crowd-pleasing announcements from the referee, an overweight bald man in a tight shirt and bow tie, and a lot of women in bathing costumes parading around for the slavering dogs in the front rows. I was more interested in the comings and goings from the dressing rooms and offices, hoping to catch a glimpse of Alan Vaughan and his entourage, to identify anyone with access to all areas. I couldn't see Vaughan; presumably he was backstage with his Craig Lukas, psyching him up for the fight. I don't know much about the ethics of boxing—if there are any—but I've always found it strange that managers and promoters are often one and the same person. Presumably Kieran McAvoy had been handpicked to lose, and would no doubt go home with a nice wad of cash in his pocket for allowing Lukas to knock him out in the fifth round.

There was a guy with a clipboard running in and out of a door marked STAFF ONLY at the side of the bar. All I could see inside was a brightly lighted corridor leading to a flight of stairs, perhaps to the hospitality suite. He was talking into a cell phone and looked every inch the harassed minion. He was about nineteen or twenty, dark hair and brown skin, Indian or Pakistani origin, I guessed. There were a lot of Asian men in Manchester, and a good number of them under this roof. This one was short, wiry, possibly a fighter himself from the look of him, a good frame for martial arts, light and quick and strong. At the moment he was in a menial job, running errands. A junior figure in the Vaughan operation, an intern even, paying his dues for a chance to get into the ring. In other words, exactly the person I needed.

I let him come and go a few more times. The first fight was due to start in about fifteen minutes. I positioned myself in his path, caught his eye a couple of times. He noticed me. The third time, I nodded and said

"All right." He smiled, I smiled. This carried on a little longer, until at last I said, "Any idea what time the main fight begins?"

"Nine o'clock," he fired back. "There are two warm-ups."

"You going to watch it?"

"Of course. We're all here to support Lukas."

"Hometown hero?"

"Not quite, but I work for Alan Vaughan. His manager."

"Ah, Alan Vaughan. The big man."

"Yeah." The boy smiled. "He's great." He had a curious accent, the local Manchester drawl with a few odd vowel sounds and cadences I recognized as southeast Asian.

"I've heard a lot about him."

"He's the big man."

"Good employer?"

"The best."

"Does he pay well?"

He looked down at his shoes. "Yeah, I mean I'm like a volunteer at the moment." As I suspected. "But if I do well he's going to give me a chance to fight."

"Boxing?"

"Kickboxing. Bit of karate too."

"Where do you train?"

"Gym in Moss Side."

This meant nothing to me, but I nodded anyway. "Good instructors?"

"Yeah, pretty good."

"But you could do better, right?"

He shrugged. "I can't afford it."

"I could help you out, maybe. I'm looking for work."

"I told you, I can't afford a trainer."

"I'll give you some sessions for free if you can introduce me to people who might be able to give me some paid work. I've only just arrived here."

"American, right?"

"Yeah."

"What you doing in a shithole like Manchester then?"

I couldn't really say "I was sent here by the CIA," so I said, "Looking for a fresh start. Things got a bit too hot for me at home."

"I might be able to introduce you to Mr. Vaughan."

"Does he employ trainers?"

"Yeah, course. They're the best in the business." He looked despondent, gazing over at the ring, the bright lights reflecting in his big brown eyes. "Not that I ever get a chance to work with them."

"Why shouldn't you?"

He shrugged. "I don't know. I've won all my bouts. I'm good, but I'm not good enough."

"Then you need to get better."

"How?"

"Here." I scribbled a phone number on his clipboard. "I'll give you an honest opinion. If you're any good, I'll train you."

"Really?" He looked like a puppy that's just been promised a walk in the park. "Why would you do that for me?"

"Everyone needs a helping hand."

"You're cool." He looked at his watch. "I'd better get on. Mr. Vaughan needs me to check up on all his guests, make sure they've got their access passes and drinks tokens and stuff." He had a bunch of lanyards and laminates hanging off one wrist.

"Okay. What's your name?"

"Oz. Short for Osman."

I grabbed his hand and squeezed. "Hi Oz. I'm Greg. Greg Cooper."

"Okay, Greg, nice to meet you. Oz Rafiq." I didn't let go of his hand; he started to look nervous. "So, I really should be. . ."

"Can you tell me where the bathroom is?"

"What?"

"The toilet. I need to piss before the fight."

"Oh, it's over there somewhere." He waved towards the bar.

"Yeah, but they're really disgusting and crowded. Can't you let me into the private ones?"

"No, mate, I'm not allowed."

"Just give me a pass. I'll give it back."

"Okay. But I'll have to come with you."

"Make sure I don't cause any trouble?"

"It's just the rules, Greg. I'm not saying you'd do anything."

"Come on then, Oz. Show me the way."

The arena was getting busy, people pushing past us as they made their way to their seats, hands full of plastic glasses of beer. On the other side of the private door, everything was quiet.

"Just come through here." He held open another door, and suddenly we were in a warm, carpeted area, low lights, the distant hum of voices. "The press room is just round the corner. I think they're doing photos or something. Toilets are down here."

I followed him through the door with the male symbol on it. Two tiny urinals, a hand basin, and a cubicle that was barely big enough for an adult to turn around in. "Thanks, Oz. I won't be long." I stood at the pisser, undid my pants, and flopped my cock out. I was going to have to produce something to give myself credibility. I closed my eyes, thought about waterfalls, and managed a short, steady stream.

"Suppose I might as well go too, while I'm here. Don't know when I'll get another chance." He was beside me, just as I had hoped, pulling the elasticated waist of his track pants down, hauling out a decent-sized dick. With all the crap he was carrying—clipboards, laminates, and so on—he had to manage it with just one hand. He pushed his hips forward and pissed a little against the porcelain. I'd finished, but was making very certain I'd shaken off all the drops. Oz glanced down at me; I was on the way to being half hard, and it looked big. Distracted, he let the clipboard slip from where it was held under his arm; in trying to catch it, he splashed piss over his pants.

"Oh, shit. Sorry."

"It's okay. You didn't get me." I didn't put my cock away, even though there was now no reason for me to have it out. Oz stepped back from the urinal and started brushing himself down. "Here, let me help." I took the stuff he was carrying, and held it for him, making sure I didn't block his view.

"Thanks Greg. Fucking hell. What a mess."

There was an electric hand dryer on the wall, the sort with a directional spout. "Come here. Stand under that."

I hit the button, and Oz tried to angle the damp patch on his pants towards the hot air. He was too far away, and in trying to wriggle around into the right position he exposed his furry brown ass. My dick was getting hard in earnest now.

"You need to get closer."

He stood on tiptoe, even jumped up. "I can't." The wet patch was a very visible dark gray.

"Here." I put my arms around his waist from behind and lifted him so the hot air was blasting straight on to the affected area, flattening the black hair on his thighs like wind blowing through corn. Coincidentally, this position also brought my cock into contact with his ass. I braced my legs and held him, making sure he could feel my growing hardness.

"That's . . . oh . . . that's great . . ."

"We're nearly there."

"Yeah. Just . . . just keep going a bit . . . longer . . ."

A bit longer and I'd have been slipping my cock into him, and he knew it. But when the worst of the wetness had disappeared, I lowered him to his feet. He was rock hard, sticking straight up, and he tried to bend over to conceal it. I didn't bother.

"It's okay, dude. Nothing to be embarrassed about. Look." I smacked the underside of my cock a few times, made it bounce against my belly. "Guys get stiff all the time, right?"

"I know . . . it's just . . . I mean, some people are like . . . you know . . ."

"Uptight about it? They're assholes. It's cool. You're cute. You have a nice ass."

"Oh, I . . . er . . . yeah . . ."

Poor kid was so horny and mortified and confused I thought he was going to cum on the spot. But that wouldn't do. I had to keep him keen. I stuffed my hard dick back into my pants, and buttoned up. He looked heartbroken.

"You better put that away before someone comes in. Here." I grabbed hold of his cock, squeezed it hard, and pulled his pants up over it. "Now think about your mother. That usually does the trick."

He stood like a stunned cow, hands hanging by his sides.

"Come on, Oz. Wake up." I gave back his stuff. He frowned, and tried to pull himself together. "You've got my number, right? Now, let me go watch the fight."

"Oh . . . okay."

Poor kid needed to cum so badly, and he'd felt my dick rubbing against his ass, and nothing would be right in his world until I'd fucked him. That was just how I wanted him. Mission accomplished.

"Call me, and we'll fix up a proper training session."

"Yeah."

"And put in a good word for me with your boss. I need a job."

"Okay."

I moved towards the door. Oz looked as if he was going to start crying. "Oh, for Christ's sake. Come here." I grabbed him by the back of the neck, pulled him in, and kissed him hard on the mouth, pushing my tongue in. He staggered back against the wall and I pressed on, thrusting my groin against him. "You do what I say, and I'll fuck your sweet ass until you can't stand up." I let him go. "Call me, Oz."

I left him to compose himself, and made my way out to the auditorium.

The fight was about to begin. I found myself a seat at the back, where I could watch the crowd as much as the boxers. The ringside seats were taken up by Vaughan's guests, local dignitaries, a few people that looked like minor television personalities, and assorted young men who could have been fighters, soldiers, or hustlers. They were all young, attractive, and dressed in the uniform of their class, sweatshirts, jeans, and sneakers. If this was representative of his inner circle, I was more than ready to penetrate it.

The fight was impressive, in its way. Craig Lukas undoubtedly had talent as well as looks. I've known guys with great-looking bodies who crap out after five minutes of cardiovascular activity; Lukas's muscles were not the display-only type. He was constantly moving, dancing around the ring, punching, dodging, and although he was shiny with sweat by the end of the first round it was clear he was only warming up. The crowd adored him. He had the charisma that marks out a champion, a kind of grace that can transform a bloody fight into something almost beautiful.

His opponent, Kieran McAvoy, was shorter, stockier, with sturdy thighs and massive shoulders, pale skin, and dark red hair. He wasn't much of a looker—his nose was flat and crooked, his eyes on the small side, his ears protruding—but I've never been one for the pretty boys. Even the homely ones look great with my cock in their mouths.

It was quite clear that McAvoy never stood a chance. At best he'd been chosen as an opponent who was totally outclassed by the champion—at worst, he'd been paid to throw the fight. Even if money hadn't changed hands, it was worthwhile for an up-and-coming boxer to be matched against one of Vaughan's stable—it gave him profile and exposure, and may have been the first move towards McAvoy himself being accepted into the Vaughan family. I would make it my business to find out.

Watching him taking the blows from Lukas's merciless right hook, watching the dark blood spotting his pink-and-white chest, I was already planning a visit to the dressing room for a bit of post-fight counselling.

Lukas won after four rounds. McAvoy was down on his hands and knees, blood dripping from his nose to the canvas as the referee counted him out. Lukas's triumph was everything I knew it would be: jumping around, posing for photos with the beautiful girls in bikinis who reappeared in the ring, lifting the trophy belt, kissing it, kissing his own biceps, the full show. Alan Vaughan climbed over the ropes to congratulate his champion, and got the biggest cheer of the night. Lukas may have won the fight, but Vaughan was the gatekeeper to a world of money, fame, and women, the world that Craig Lukas inhabited and that Kieran McAvoy, slumped on a stool with a towel pressed to his nose, did not.

I ran quickly towards the door through which McAvoy's team was disappearing, and tagged on the end. I must have looked the part; nobody challenged me for ID.

McAvoy's trainer was a fat-bellied old geezer who smelt of cigarettes; little wonder the kid was a loser. His manager, who should have been giving him a pep talk or at least comforting him, was busy on his phone. I guess he was arranging how to spend his share of the loot. McAvoy sat on the bench, towel pressed to his nose, head down, the picture of defeat and despondency. I busied myself picking up wet towels, mopping the floor, wiping the mirrors. Nobody ever notices the cleaners. After a few minutes, manager and trainer drifted off, presumably to enjoy Alan Vaughan's hospitality, leaving McAvoy alone, sweaty and bloodstained in his satin shorts.

He started unlacing his boots, lost in his own thoughts.

"Want me to run the shower for you?"

He jumped. "Sorry man. Didn't see you." An Irish accent. "That would be great, yeah, thanks."

"You took a beating out there." I fiddled with the shower controls.

"Nothing I can't handle." The first boot was off.

"You could have done a lot better."

"Yeah?" He looked up at me and scowled. "Who says so?"

"I say so." The water was hot now, steam already billowing out into the room.

"Tonight wasn't the night." Both boots off, and now he was peeling the socks down. His legs were covered in golden fur, his feet large and pale.

"You'll never succeed in this sport if you throw fights."

He stood up, naked but for the shorts—yellow and green, that cheap satin that clings to the skin. He was angry, his face turning red, and he was showing more fight than he had in the ring. "What the fuck is that supposed to mean?"

I shrugged. "You tell me."

"Who are you? What are you doing in here?"

"Call security and get me thrown out if you want. But I'm the man that can turn you into a winner."

He started to say something, but changed his mind.

"You going to have this shower?"

"Okay, okay." He turned his back on me, and pulled down his shorts. The view was inspiring: white marble, sculpted, sweaty. The bloody towel covered his crotch when he faced me. "So who are you?"

"Greg Cooper." I held out a hand; he thought about it for a second or two, then shook it.

"And what gives you the right to barge in here accusing me of cheating?"

"Nothing. But I know what I saw, and I know what you can achieve if you're allowed to."

He threw the towel on the floor and stepped under the jet of hot water. His cock was small and almost retracted, as is often the case after a fight, resting on tight, rose-pink balls. Above it was a mat of red hair. He got himself wet, rinsed off the blood, and started lathering his hair, his big, square hands making slippery patterns over his face.

"I was outclassed tonight is all."

"Crap."

He laughed, smiling through a mask of foam. "You've got all the answers."

"You weren't fighting back, you were just waiting for the end. Did they tell you which round to go down in?"

His hands were working under his armpits now, wetting the red hair, then over his chest and down his stomach. He had not a single tattoo to spoil him.

Obviously I was hard again, but I made sure it wasn't too visible. I couldn't scare him off.

Under the hot water, McAvoy was relaxing both physically and mentally. It was probably a relief to have someone to talk to other than those assholes who mismanaged him. And there's nothing like a hot shower after a bruising fight. What he really needed now was a massage, of course, but this wasn't the place for that.

"Let me ask you a question," he said, washing between his buttocks. "What qualifies you to judge my performance tonight?"

"I'm a black belt in various martial arts. I was a trainer in the US Marines for many years. I boxed myself for a while. I know what I see."

"And you think I can do better?"

"I know you can, and so do you."

"Yeah, you got that right." He'd moved around the front now, soaping up his genitals; I was glad to see that he paid attention to these matters. "But it's not as simple as that, is it?" His cock was slightly bigger now; it was never going to be large, but at least he was relaxing with me.

"It should be. Two guys get into a boxing ring and they fight until one of them wins."

"I used to think that too. But, well . . ." He was rinsing the soap off now, almost ready to get out. I feasted my eyes, in case this was the last time I saw him naked.

"How old are you, Kieran?"

"Twenty-four."

"And I'm twenty years older than you. But you seem to be the cynical one."

He frowned, and turned the water off. The room was quiet. I handed him a clean towel. He didn't attempt to conceal himself as he dried. Boxers aren't bashful; they spend so much time being paraded about like animals I guess they shed their inhibitions. "I want to be better," he said, "and I'm just waiting for a chance to . . ."

"What? Fight an honest fight?"

He shrugged. "I need better management."

"You mean Vaughan."

"Who wouldn't want to be managed by him? He's the best."

"He's the most successful. The richest. That doesn't mean he's the best."

McAvoy looked worried, glancing towards the door. He lowered his voice. "What's that supposed to mean?"

"I've heard he's a crook."

He didn't deny it. We looked into each other's eyes. "We can't talk about that here."

"Afraid you're being spied on?"

"Don't be daft," he said, but he lacked conviction. "Anyway, what can you do about any of this? It's all very well giving me advice, but it means nothing without the opportunities."

"Well said, Kieran. So, why don't you get dressed, and we'll go for a drink."

"I don't fucking drink!"

"Okay, I'll have a drink, you can have a glass of milk."

At least he was smiling as he stepped into his shorts— brightly colored trunks, neon orange and green, as tight as could be. "Go on then. I've got no other offers."

"Where are you staying?"

"They're putting me up in a B&B."

"Come over to mine, then. It's a short cab ride away." He looked hesitant. I took a gamble. "I'm also a physical therapist, by the way, if you need any help with that hip injury."

"How do you know about my hip injury?" He placed his hand on the right side of his pelvis, and pressed.

"Because I have eyes to see with. Your stance is unstable. What did you do?"

"Pulled something in training."

"I'll take a look at it, then. You coming?"

He pulled on a sweater and a denim jacket, slung his kit bag over his shoulder. "I must be bloody mad," he said, "but I'm coming. Just . . ." He glanced around, lowered his voice. "Don't let Mr. Vaughan see us leaving together."

05

The apartment went well with Greg Cooper's
cover story—a man down on his luck, transient, off-
radar. It was small, anonymous, cheaply fitted-out. At
least it was clean and quiet; MI6 had taken care to find
somewhere that wasn't overlooked, where I could hide
away, one of twelve "executive studios" that failed to
sell to executives and were snapped up by greedy land-
lords. The kind of place where contractors are put up by
stingy employers, or husbands rent when they've been
kicked out by their wives. Most of the units were unoc-
cupied. Perhaps MI6 had bought them all, and kept
them empty. There was a tiny entrance hall, an elevator
serving the four floors, and that was it.

As an operational base, or fuckpad, it was perfect.

Kieran chatted away in the taxi, no sign of nerves.
Perhaps he was used to being picked up by men. We
talked about muscle injuries and tendonitis all the way
up in the lift, and it was only once we were inside the
apartment that I laid a finger on him. As he was pulling
his tracksuit top over his head, and was temporarily

blinded, I pressed my thumb into the small of his back, just above the right buttock, the point between the gluteus maximus and the latissimus dorsi (my knowledge of anatomy isn't entirely restricted to cock and ass). Kieran yelped, muffled by his clothes, and I pushed him gently down with my other hand on his shoulder.

"That's the place, isn't it?" His ass was sticking out nicely as I rubbed in widening circles with my thumb.

"Yes. Ouch."

"You need to get that looked at properly."

"Like I have time and money for that." He was struggling out of his top, his face red, lips swollen, a vein standing out in his neck.

"And when it's bad you feel it right down the thigh and into the knee."

"Sometimes up in the shoulder too. I don't know what the fuck I've done."

"You've torn a muscle. Everything's tensing up. All the connective tissue." I was improvising a bit here, but I've spent enough time under physical therapists to have picked up the jargon. "You should be resting it, not fighting. What is your manager thinking?"

"He said it would get me in with Vaughan . . ."

"Bullshit. It just gives Vaughan's boy an easy victory. You'll never be respected if you let people do that to you."

"But how will I ever get a chance?"

"Kieran," I said, pushing him down a little further, digging my thumb into the hard muscle of his buttock, "a boxer has to do most of his fighting out of the ring. It's not just about gloves and glory and all that bullshit. It's about saying no to people who want to exploit you, and recognizing when someone is trying to help you."

"Like you, you mean?"

"Maybe. But you've no reason to trust me."

"Then why . . . ah! Shit!" I'd just given his ass a particularly hard thrust.

"Sorry. Go on." I continued rubbing.

"Why are you wasting your time on me if you don't want to help me?"

"There could be a thousand reasons." And the most obvious one was swelling inside my pants right now, eager to take over where my thumb left off . . . "I could be trying to spy on Alan Vaughan, for instance."

"Well you picked the wrong man if that's what you're after."

"I might think I could make some money out of you."

That touched a nerve. "What the fuck does that mean?"

"Relax, relax." I let him stand up; he was starting to go purple in the face. "I mean, your trainer might pay me to treat you. Or I could poach you from him, set up as a trainer myself. Become a manager. Rival to Vaughan. What do you reckon?"

"I don't know." He looked sullen; something I'd said had touched a nerve.

"Hell, for all you know I brought you up here to fuck you."

He didn't bolt for the door. In fact, he more or less ignored the remark.

"I'll be honest with you, Greg." The false name still jarred on me sometimes, especially in a sentence containing the word *honest*. "My boxing is going nowhere. I'm having to work crappy jobs just to afford my trainer. If I don't make it soon, I'm going to have to chuck it in."

"Then you really are a loser."

He shrugged and sighed. "Maybe I am. I just don't want to end up like one of those guys who are nearly thirty and still fooling themselves that they have a chance."

"Yeah. Poor old bastards."

"I shouldn't have let Vaughan persuade me to throw the fight. But it was a chance. He said if I showed him I could do what I was told, he might take me on. No more training fees; I'd be working with his people, everything paid for, part of the team."

"What does that mean, exactly?"

"Have you seen the kind of lives his guys have? Jesus, Greg. The cars, the clothes, the women. They're like celebrities."

"What do they have to do for all that?"

"They have to be great boxers." His guard was up. "Obviously."

"Is that all?"

"What the fuck does that mean?"

"Oh, I heard rumors about some of the other businesses Vaughan has an interest in."

"Like what?"

I wasn't going to show my hand too soon, so I improvised. "Property development. Nightclubs."

"Well, he's a tycoon, isn't he?"

"So they say."

"He's generous to people who work hard for him."

"You mean the boxers?"

"Yeah, yeah." I'd wrong-footed him. What did he know, or suspect, about the Vaughan operation? How far had he been drawn in? "That's right."

Was he already working for Vaughan? If MI6 was right, there was any number of jobs for a young man of Kieran McAvoy's obvious talents. I had a way of finding out. I'd track him.

"Anyway, we're not here to talk about Alan Vaughan. He's all I've heard about since I set foot in this country. Fuck that. I'm a solo operator." Kieran didn't need to know that Oz was trying to get me a job with the great man. "I can help you, if you want to be helped. I can improve your fitness and technique, and I can work on your mental attitude as well. I was in the US Marines for over twenty years."

"For real?" He looked like a kid at the movies. "Wow."

"Calm down. It's not as exciting as you think."

"But did you fight and stuff?"

"Of course I fucking fought. And killed people, as that's what you're going to ask next. With guns, and knives, and my bare hands." I put one hand very gently around his throat. "That's what I did for a living."

He half-whispered "Jesus" as I let my hand stroke his throat. The ginger stubble crackled.

"Before we get on to all that, I can help you with this injury." I released him. "Come into the living room. I've got a sofa that will do as a massage table." I racked my brains as to what to use for oil; I didn't even have a bottle of cooking oil in the cupboard. I had lube, of course. That would have to do. And it would help me to slip a tracking device into him . . .

I ushered Kieran ahead of me, taking a good look at his broad shoulders, freckly neck and round ass. The room was warm, thank God. "Just take your clothes off and throw them on a chair. I'll be right back." The lube was in the bedroom, with extra towels. When I got back, he was in his underpants, perched on the arm of the sofa. I pulled off my sweater and squirted some lube into my palm. "Make yourself comfortable on your front. I'm going to have to get a proper table." I spread the lube over his back, fanning it out across his shoulder blades then down towards his glutes. "I can feel a lot of tension right through the posterior chain. Are you stretching properly?"

"Probably not. There's never time. Ahhh . . ." All the breath left his body as I pressed down on his lower back.

"That hurt?"

"A bit. It feels great."

"Good. Tell me if it's too hard." I carried on working on his back, enjoying the resilience of the muscles, the smoothness of the skin. I know enough about massage to convince a boy like Kieran. And he wasn't about to argue with a marine. "I'm going to lower these." I tugged at the waistband of his underpants; he didn't complain. In fact, he raised his hips slightly, so I could pull them down to his knees in one move. I'd already seen his ass, but now I had time to study it. I'm not big on descriptions, as you've probably noticed; I'm not the poetic type. It was a young boxer's ass. He was an Irish redhead. It was right in front of me on a bed. You supply your own descriptions. I'll just tell you what I did.

I shot more lube into my hands, rubbed them together, and laid one on each buttock. Kieran flinched slightly; perhaps the lube was still cold, but I'd soon warm it up. I made circular movements across the smooth surface, parting the cheeks on each outward sweep, exposing the pink hole. It was clean, and slightly damp.

"How does that feel?"

"Yeah . . . good." I couldn't see his face, which was buried in the pillow.

"I'm going to work on your hamstrings. You've got a lot of tension there."

"I've always been tight."

I moved down to his meaty right thigh, pressing with my thumbs along the twisted cables of muscle. "No wonder you're getting injuries. These are like solid steel. You need to start doing yoga or something." Inspiration struck. "I'm going to give you a series of stretches to do."

"Okay."

I pushed his thighs a little further apart, enough to get a good view of his balls. How full were they? When were they last emptied? Was he one of those fighters who abstains from sex before a match? But he was young: the tanks fill up quickly when you're twenty-four. I carried on working down to the crook of the knee. Kieran was shifting around slightly on the bed, as if something was making him uncomfortable; I hoped it was his stiffening cock. I'd soon find out.

I switched to the other leg. "Ah, this one's a lot better." There was no difference at all, but I had to sound like I knew what I was doing. "Why are you getting so tight in the right side?"

"Dunno."

I worked back up the buttock to the base of his spine. "Look," I said, pressing with my thumbs, "this is where the problem is."

Kieran raised himself on his forearms, craning his

neck to see what I was pointing out. His chest and upper abs were visible now. "What?"

"Just here and here." I applied pressure on either side. "Top of the glutes, bottom of the back. I think you've torn something on this side"—thumb in on the right, which made him wince—"and the muscles all down the back of your leg are tensing up because of it." It had the ring of truth. "On this side"—thumb on the left—"the muscles are far more flexible. I'm going to show you a few stretches."

In the process of massaging him, I'd managed to work his underpants down to his ankles; it was a simple matter to discard them altogether, before he got any stupid ideas of putting them back on.

"Roll over and I'll show you what I mean."

You can see what I was doing. Most adults with half a brain could see what I was doing. It's fair to assume that Kieran wasn't completely naïve. His cheeks were flushed. "It's . . . it's a bit embarrassing."

"What is?"

"You know, when you get a massage. When someone touches you, you can . . ."

"For God's sake, Kieran. I was in the marines for twenty years." I'm not sure what that was supposed to mean, but it worked. Kieran flipped over on to his back, exposing a very hard cock that pointed straight up towards his belly button. "I'll take that as a sign that I can still give a good massage."

He propped himself up on his elbows, a position which emphasized his abdominal muscles. His cock showed no sign of getting softer. He couldn't have failed to notice the bulge in my pants; it was practically visible from space.

I picked up his right leg, one hand behind the knee, the other on top of his thigh. It was slightly sticky from the lube. "Now, we're going to pull the knee in towards the chest, just to the point where you feel a stretch. If it hurts, stop." I guided the leg up and back into a position that not only exposed Kieran's hole but also pushed his cock over. It throbbed. There was a drop of precum at the end. "You hold it there for a count of ten." I pushed gently and held him in position, enjoying the warmth from his naked body. "Then you rotate the thigh outwards." I moved his leg out to a sideways position, pressing down on his left shoulder. "Keep the upper body in contact with the sofa as much as possible. Now, where do you feel the stretch."

Kieran reached down and touched himself on the inner thigh. "Right here."

"Okay. That's good. Now you hold it there for a while, and straighten the leg." I pulled him down. "And repeat. Up towards the chest and hold, out to the side and hold, release and straighten. We can pick up the pace a little once you get used to it." I rotated his leg a few more times, watching his hard little cock bouncing around with every move. "How does that feel?"

"Fantastic."

"Good, good." We were in that gray area between seduction and sex, when both parties realize what's about to happen but haven't yet taken the first definite step, when you could just about still pretend we were talking about physical therapy and massage rather than what I was doing to his dick and ass. "Now, let's work on the left leg as well." I switched to the other side of the sofa. "Knee to chest, now out to the left, and straight.

See, much looser." I pressed down on his chest, feeling his hard nipple against the palm of my hand. "That's it. Good boy. See how your abs contract when you pull in towards the chest?"

He looked down. "Yeah."

I shifted my hand lower. "You've got excellent core strength." I caressed his stomach, missing his cock by half an inch, rubbing some of the juice into his belly. Kieran moaned. That was it: we'd crossed the line. We were having sex. "Now let's see if we can do both legs at the same time."

"Like this?"

He pulled his knees back and held them close to his chest.

"Exactly like that." I positioned myself at the end of the sofa, grabbed his thighs, and pulled him towards me. My groin was right above his open ass. I leaned forward, pressing against his legs with my torso. My rigid cock, still inside my pants, found its target. I rubbed it up and down.

"Want that?"

"Yeah." He was looking over to one side, eyes half closed, voice indistinct.

"Look me in the eye. Do you want me to fuck you?"

He did as he was told. "Yes please."

"Good. Don't want anyone saying I forced you."

He scowled, as if he was about to say something—but this wasn't the time for interrogation. Afterwards, perhaps, when we were resting between "treatments," there might be some revealing pillow talk, but now I just got on with the job.

"You been fucked before, Kieran?"

"Once or twice."

"You like it?"

He turned his mouth down. "'S'okay."

"This'll be better than okay. I'm going to teach you to love it." I leaned forward so his knees were practically on his shoulders, and kissed him on the mouth. He wasn't expecting that, but after a moment of hesitation he started kissing me back. I put one hand under his head, and with the other squeezed his ass.

Kieran kissed passionately, devouring my tongue, as if he was starving for affection. I know all too well how that feels. For a moment I let myself forget operational considerations, and returned the kisses as well as I could.

He broke away first. "Stop!" he said, his mouth wet with saliva, rubbed red by my stubble. "I'm gonna come!"

I stood up; there was a dark patch on my gray T-shirt from the juice that was leaking out of Kieran's cock. "Not so fast, buddy. Calm down."

He uncurled his legs and sat up, his face on a level with my crotch. "Can I see it?"

"Sure." I pulled my pants down, lifted my cock and balls over the waistband. I was fully hard.

"Jesus Christ."

"What?"

"It's fuckin' big."

"You'll cope."

"I dunno . . ."

"I know what I'm doing. Now let's see how much of it you can get in your mouth."

He looked up at me, his brow furrowed, his eyes wet,

as if he couldn't quite believe this was happening to him. Someone's been mistreating this boy, I thought. Parents back in Ireland, maybe, or his trainer and manager here in Manchester. Alan Vaughan, perhaps. I'd give him some sugar, and he'd surely come back for more.

"Go ahead. It's all yours."

That was all he needed to hear. He grabbed my pants and pulled them down, exposing my hairy thighs, then took the base of my cock between thumb and forefinger and pulled it towards his lips. They opened, and the head went in. I encouraged him by caressing the bristly back of his head. It was tempting to shove right down his throat, watch him gag, but for once I was feeling merciful. And I had a feeling I'd get more value from Kieran if he was in love with me. I let him take me inch by inch, at his own pace. He'd obviously done it before, because I didn't get scraped with teeth, but he didn't have the slick facility of the accomplished cocksucker. I like the newbies. I like the surprise on their faces when they realize they *can* take it, that it actually feels good, that they want it.

By the time he was half way down the shaft, Kieran was pretty much all mine. He was going to make the most of every moment we had together, and then he'd be hanging around me in the hope of getting more. I hoped that I wouldn't have to let him down, that I might manage to salvage something out of the operation without either of us getting killed. But seeing as I was about to turn him into an unwitting spy on the Vaughan operation, that seemed unlikely. Oh well, let's enjoy ourselves for now, before I plant the tracker in him. Let him suck and get fucked and feel that he's wanted, desired, loved. Because for the next hour or so, he will be.

He took it all, despite a bit of gagging, then closed his eyes and started to suck up and down, his cheeks hollowing on every upstroke, his lips being pulled outwards. I tugged his ears, stroked his jawline, his eyelids, rubbed his short ginger hair. And I made very sure that his hands kept away from his own cock. He was going to come when I was ready for him to come, with my cock inside him to seal the deal.

I could feel my own orgasm starting after a while, so I pulled out and stripped off. Kieran watched, taking in every detail of my beaten-up, hairy body. When he saw the scars on my leg, he bit his lower lip. "What happened to you?"

I wasn't allowed to tell him the truth; this could give suspicious minds a link back to Dan Stagg and the attack in Baghdad. A cover story had been supplied, and I was fluent. "I had a bit of a disagreement with a land-mine in Somalia. Got me four months in the hospital."

"Jesus." He ran his fingertips over the deep, bluish scar that runs up my thigh. "Does it hurt?"

"Yes, sometimes. But it's okay. It didn't kill me."

"Thank God." He kissed my leg. "You're so brave, Greg."

"I'm no hero." I'm not even Greg, I thought. "I was stupid."

"Is that why you left?"

"It's one of the reasons. We'll talk about it another time. I've got other things on my mind right now."

"Yeah?" He took hold of my cock and squeezed. "What might that be?"

"Your ass."

"Okay." He started licking my dick again. "I'm as ready as I'll ever be."

"Bend over the sofa. Ass in the air."

I got myself rubbered up, and worked lube into his hole. As soon as my finger entered the tight little ring, he was groaning. I reached around and touched his cock; still hard. Better get on with it. We were both so horny that entry was a swift, businesslike affair, none of that careful inch-by-inch stuff that you have to do with unconvinced virgins. Kieran had been fucked before, and this time he wanted to do it right. He knew how to relax. Perhaps he'd learned the hard way, with men who didn't give a shit whether he enjoyed himself or not.

Once I was all the way in, pressing my lower stomach against the base of his spine, I paused and waited for him to start moving. You know when a guy who's impaled on your cock starts moving backwards and forwards, basically doing the fucking for you, that he's ready to take whatever you've got to give. It didn't take long; Kieran was thrusting back into me, looking over his shoulder with a quizzical expression.

I answered him by starting to fuck. Slowly at first, so he could appreciate just how long my cock was, all the way out, all the way in. He sighed, rested his head on his forearms, and tilted his pelvis to the perfect angle, allowing me maximum penetration into his guts. There was no point in thinking of other positions to fuck him in. This was perfect; one of the greatest unions of penis and anus I've ever experienced. Plenty of time to experiment later, but for now this was the fuck we both needed. Both of us were going to come pretty soon.

He started first, moaning so loud that MI6's decision to place me somewhere without neighbors made a lot of sense. "Fuck me, oh, fuck me Greg, fuck me harder," he babbled in his Irish accent, and that tipped me over the edge. I pounded into him in the ruthless, machine-like way I've perfected over many years in the military, and came so hard I almost blacked out.

Afterwards we lay in bed together, his head on my chest, listening to the traffic swishing along wet streets. We slept. I woke a couple of hours later with his hand on my rock-hard cock. I quickly guided his head down under the sheets and let him suck me off.

Two orgasms inside Kieran had cleared my head enough to start thinking about work again. "Your turn," I said, and got him on his back, legs in the air, while I started playing with his asshole. It was a simple business to implant the tracking device; he never suspected a thing. It sat on the end of my finger like a tiny bead, held in place by lube, and then, carefully, I pushed it into his rectum. The silicon coating, according to the tech boys, would help it adhere to the mucous membrane inside his ass. Only a really massive dump, or a serious case of diarrhea, would dislodge it until its adhesive qualities wore off and it was passed, undetectably, into the toilet.

As covert surveillance operations go, this was one of the most enjoyable.

I got three fingers inside Kieran's silky ass and jerked his stiff cock until he came over his ridged stomach. We slept again, while from deep inside him inaudible signals were sent all the way from my obscure little Manchester apartment to receivers in London, to be shared with intelligence agencies on both sides of the

Atlantic, bringing down a criminal terrorist network, saving lives, punishing wrongdoers.

That was one hardworking ass.

06

The next day I got a call from Oz, sounding very pleased with himself. "Mr. Vaughan wants to meet you! I told him all about you and he says he might be able to use you! Isn't that great? We might be working together! He's very happy with me, says I've shown real initiative."

Normally I'd be happy to have an eager little puppy like Oz chasing after my cock, and obviously I was happy to stick it to him in any way that was necessary to the operation. I'm a professional in these matters. But things were complicated now. Despite my best efforts, I was growing fond of Kieran McAvoy, the defeated Irishman, the victim of some deal between his manager and Vaughan. He hadn't given anything away, and I was careful not to ask too many questions, but I was sure Kieran was being exploited and abused both in and out of the ring. It crossed my mind that he was a double agent, that Vaughan knew exactly what I was up to and had baited the trap with Kieran. In this game of bluff and counter-bluff, anything was possible.

The meeting was arranged for the gym in Moss Side, an ugly suburb of Manchester that was dotted with boxing clubs and gyms, the traditional escape route for local kids who are never going to make it through school. I know what these places are like: I've trained in them, worked in them, screwed in them. They're not much different on either side of the ocean. City Fitness had the same tired, badly designed street frontage, a cheap-looking Perspex sign screwed over a blacked-out window, a glass door, a dirty buzzer panel, everything covered in grime and graffiti.

The interior told a different story. Beyond the filthy lobby there was a newly decorated reception area with subdued lights, charcoal carpets and white walls, and an attractive young woman with neat blonde hair and flawless makeup presiding over a gleaming desk. "Mr. Cooper?" she said, in an Eastern European accent. "Mr. Vaughan is expecting you. Please follow the corridor all the way to the end of the gym, and you'll be met at the second set of doors."

The corridor ran along a glass wall, etched with images of weights, feet, and arms, anything that said "fitness." Beyond it were ranks of gleaming machines, treadmills, rowing machines, recumbent bikes, resistance equipment, and ten or fifteen fit young people of both sexes working out to the music that came from the DJ in the corner. City Fitness was not a book you could judge by the cover. The interior must have stretched across two or three units knocked together, and the conversion looked like the work of a serious architect. Vaughan liked to keep his investments discreetly hidden.

At the end of the corridor, doors led into a fully-equipped boxing gym; it was empty and dark at the moment, but I could make out the ropes and punching bags in the gloom. Further along, another set of doors was marked PRIVATE. I was looking for a button to press when they were opened from within.

"Greg!" It was Oz, of course, with a huge beaming smile, clapping me on the back, pulling me into the inner sanctum. "Great to see you mate! Mr. Vaughan's really looking forward to meeting you. Thanks for coming. Means a lot. How have you been?" Poor kid was almost mounting my leg.

"Okay, Oz. Thanks for the warm welcome. Now, where do I go?"

"I'll show you." He knocked on a door, grinning like a fool. A voice from within said "Come."

'It's Greg Cooper, Mr. Vaughan. Here he is, just like I said . . ."

"Show him in." Oz practically bowed as I passed him. "And now leave us alone." He looked crestfallen, as if he was about to wet himself.

"It's okay, Oz," I whispered. "I'll see you later. Thanks for everything." That sent him away happy.

Vaughan's desk was in front of a large window looking out onto trees and a courtyard, further evidence of his architect's ingenuity. The office was brightly lit, beautifully designed, and to an impressionable young athlete, I imagine, overwhelming.

"Mr. Vaughan."

I couldn't see him properly, just a large silhouette standing up behind his desk.

"Mr. Cooper. Or should I say Captain Cooper."

I stepped towards the desk and took the outstretched hand. I could see him now: taller than me, broad shouldered, heavily built in a well-tailored blue suit, thinning dark hair artfully cut and combed, a heavy-featured, jowly face, charismatic rather than handsome. Late forties, fifties.

"You've been doing your research. But I'm a civilian now."

"I take an interest in the people I work with. I like to know what makes them tick."

The benign employer, or blackmailer.

"And what about you, Mr. Vaughan? What makes you tick?"

"Money. Success. Putting something back into the world."

"That's very admirable." Bullshit, of course. "Looks like you're doing pretty well."

"Oh, this is nothing much. It's a convenient operational base. Please, take a seat."

There were two black leather sofas; I chose one. Vaughan paced.

"I hear you were at the fight."

"That's where I met Oz."

"Oz. Yes, Oz."

"Nice kid."

He stopped, turned, looked at me. "What did you think?"

"Of the fight?"

"Yes, of course."

I was being interviewed, clearly. This was not the time for pussyfooting. "It was crap."

He scowled. Was I about to be thrown out, or beaten

up by Vaughan's goons? I assumed he had some. "You noticed."

"Yeah, I noticed. But don't worry. Most people are taken in."

"Just as well." He sat down on the other sofa, facing me, leaning back, legs wide apart, the standard alpha male pose. I wondered how many of the boys had knelt before him. "Lukas is a good fighter."

"Is he?"

"He can be. He used to be."

"But now?"

"He's greedy. He's lazy."

"No discipline."

"Something like that. He wants the rewards without the hard work. And he has trouble with the concept of loyalty. That's something that you, as a military man, would understand."

"I guess so. But as I'm sure you know, I was thrown out of the military."

"And why was that, Greg?" We'd dispensed with "Mr. Cooper," but I wasn't going to start calling him "Al" just yet.

"I'm sure you know."

"I'd like to hear it from you."

"I said some things that you're not allowed to say any more, apparently. Stuff that everyone says—it's just that I got caught saying it. And I was stupid. I didn't apologize."

"Why should you?"

"Because that's the game you play in the US Marine Corps these days. It used to be a decent job for a man. Now it's . . ." I shrugged. "I don't know. It's not the world I grew up in. Been in the corps since I was eighteen. The world's changed, and I guess I didn't get the memo."

"The world is what you make it, Greg."

"Yeah. If you have money."

"I have money."

"I can see that."

"Do you need a job? Oz said you might."

"Sure. This isn't a social call."

"I like you, Greg. You don't beat about the bush."

"Perhaps I should learn to. I might still have a career."

"You can have a career here, if you want one."

"Doing what? Sweeping floors and picking up wet towels? No thanks, I've done that."

"As a trainer. As part of my team."

"What makes you think I'm any good?"

"Your record speaks for itself. You've worked all over the world. You've trained a lot of guys in unarmed combat. You're a master of several martial arts."

"Okay. But you promote boxing. That's showbiz."

"Boxing is just part of what I do."

This was what I'd been waiting to hear. "Oh?"

"We manage fighters in all sorts of disciplines. We need someone to coordinate that. And to be honest, we need someone who can bring a bit of military efficiency into the operation."

"You mean someone who isn't afraid to kick asses."

"That sort of thing."

If Vaughan had really done his homework, he'd know that kicking wasn't the only thing I did to asses.

"So, do I get a tryout?"

"We can discuss the details later."

"You're very trusting."

"You come highly recommended."

"By Oz?"

"He's been raving about you."

We locked eyes and had one of those unspoken conversations that went something like:

What did he tell you?

He said you have a big dick.

Is that part of the job?

It could be.

Do I get to fuck the boys?

Yes, if you're discreet.

Like you?

Like me.

"That's nice to hear," I said out loud. "I always try to make a good impression."

"Okay." Vaughan stood up, businesslike again. "I have to do a magazine interview. There's a photo shoot. I hate photo shoots. But hey ho." He shook my hand again. "That's show business."

"I don't know how you stand it."

"Because, Greg, the rewards are very, very great. I'm going to hand you over to Tom Jackson. He's my right-hand man. He's fully briefed. It's been a pleasure to meet you."

And he left, the door closing silently behind him.

Any idea I may have had of snooping was quickly dismissed; I was alone for less than twenty seconds.

Jackson was definitely not a boxer. You don't get to keep a face that pretty if you're fighting regularly, not even if you're winning. The young man in the expensive suit who came into Vaughan's office, carrying a black leather portfolio, looked like a model. Light brown hair swept up into a modest quiff, great skin, perfect bone structure. A little too perfect for my taste. He reminded me of Jody when I first met him—a conservative, suit-wearing version of Jody, but the same kind of attention to detail, the same consciousness of his looks. It said a lot about Vaughan's tastes.

"Mr. Cooper. I'm Tom Jackson, Mr. Vaughan's PA."

Piece of Ass?

"Nice to meet you, Jackson. Vaughan said you'd take me through the details."

He took off his jacket—he was wearing one of those tailored shirts that seem to cling, wrinkle-free, to every contour of the body—and we sat. "Initially, we'd like you to work with some of the new, up-and-coming fighters, see what kind of results you can get with them."

"And if I pass that test?"

He looked me in the eye and smiled. "Then we'll move you on to other areas of the business."

"What areas might those be?"

"Mr. Vaughan has a lot of different projects."

"Sounds interesting."

"But he's very particular about the people he works with."

"You mean, he has to trust you not to talk."

One perfectly-shaped eyebrow went up an inch. "You could say that."

"And I come from a military background. What does that tell you?"

"That you understand the importance of . . . discretion."

"Secrecy, we'd have called it."

"Secrecy, then."

"And you know all his secrets, do you, Mr. Jackson?"

Jackson smiled. He had perfect white teeth, and rather prominent, sharp canines. "Mr. Vaughan trusts me."

"He says you're his right hand. Must keep you busy."

"It does."

"What about his wife? Does she know his secrets?"

This shook Jackson's composure a little. "Mrs. Vaughan concentrates on family life, and runs a lot of the charity work."

"That sounds like something from a press release."

He allowed himself a short, silent laugh. "Perhaps you will meet Mrs. Vaughan one day."

"Will I like her?"

"Mrs. Vaughan is a wonderful lady."

My turn to laugh. "I just bet she is." Turning a blind eye to Vaughan's boys, his criminal empire, happy to enjoy the profits without asking too many questions. I'd seen photos of her—an elegant, beautiful woman in her forties, spends a lot of time in salons and spas, outsources the childcare to professionals, goes to the right restaurants and openings with Vaughan, a perfect disguise. . .

"Now, I've got some documents for you to sign." He laid out papers on the coffee table. "Usual stuff. Terms and conditions."

"What's this?"

"Nondisclosure agreement."

"Meaning what, exactly?"

"That you won't talk to the press, or anyone outside the company, about Mr. Vaughan's business affairs."

"Is it legally enforceable? I mean, what happens if I talk? I lose my job—so what?"

Jackson frowned. "It is not a good idea to break these rules, Mr. Cooper."

"That's a threat."

"That's not what I . . ."

"You mean that Vaughan punishes who steps out of line."

"You're putting words into my mouth."

"Uh-huh." I let the silence hang for a while. Jackson was getting fidgety, which I enjoyed.

"Will you sign?"

"Let me read them first." Of course I was going to sign; that was the whole point of the job, and I didn't have to worry about the legal implications. But I wanted to make him sweat a little. I'm sure most of the people on the payroll were way too eager to sign their lives away, only to discover, like Oz, that Mr. Vaughan didn't always follow up on his promises. I made myself comfortable and read the papers, occasionally letting Jackson see that I didn't like what I was reading.

After a while I said, "Okay."

"Ready to sign?"

"I'm ready. We both know that this isn't legally enforceable. But I want to work for Vaughan, and if it makes him feel happy to have my name on a document, it suits me."

"Thank you."

"Just a minute, buddy. I have questions."

"Right." His voice sounded tentative, unhappy, as if no one had ever asked questions before. Vaughan obviously expected blind obedience.

"First of all, tell me about Craig Lukas."

"What about him?"

"Vaughan doesn't seem happy with him. Am I supposed to do something about that?"

"We'd like you to train him."

"Boxing?"

"Mental discipline."

"You mean, I convince him that if he doesn't do as he's told, I'll break his bones."

Jackson's eyes were wide. He didn't deny it.

"And another question. Who am I allowed to fuck around here?"

"Well, really . . ."

"Come on, let's not pretend I don't know what's going on. I'm gay. I guess you're gay. And Vaughan is . . ."

Jackson's pale blue eyes were goggling in panic, the pupils tiny.

"Vaughan is married," I said, and laughed. "Understood. But there's a lot of hot boys around here, and I want to know if I'm going to get the sack for fucking their asses."

"Provided you are discreet, we consider that to be a private matter between adults . . ."

"Thanks for the permission, Jackson. You just let me know if I'm poaching in the wrong wood. I guess some people are definitely off limits."

He thought a while before he replied. "As I say, provided everything is discreet. . ."

That answered my question. Jackson officially "belonged" to Vaughan, but he'd be up for a fuck provided the boss didn't find out. Good news; I couldn't think of any other way of getting a tracking device into his tight little body.

"I'll bear that in mind. Thanks." I squeezed my dick through my pants. "See, I need a lot of sex."

Jackson cleared his throat. I don't think he'd met anyone as crudely direct as Greg Cooper. He was used to being wooed and pursued in a more civilized way. "Now, if you don't mind, perhaps we could have a signature?"

I'd tortured him for long enough. I stood right in front of him so my crotch was at face level, and held my hand out for the papers. He was sweating slightly as he handed them over, a dark patch under his armpit. "Okay, Jackson. Give me a pen. I'm sure everything is in order. Because after all, why would you try to screw with someone who can kill you with his bare hands?"

"Quite." He clicked a ballpoint pen and handed it to me.

"There you go." I signed "G Cooper"—I'd been practicing. "Now, I need to get laid." This wasn't strictly true, after my night with Kieran, but I was horny enough to make it convincing. I stroked the bulge in my pants. Jackson stared, licked his lips, cleared his throat. "Any suggestions?"

He lowered his voice. "This is not a good idea. Not here."

"Then where?"

He was about to come up with a suggestion, but his phone rang. I wouldn't be at all surprised if the room was bugged. "Hello, Tom Jackson. Oh, hi. Yes. Yes, absolutely." He turned away from me, avoiding the distraction between my legs. That suited me; I went up behind him, put my hands on his hips, and pressed my groin against his ass. He didn't miss a beat, just carried on talking on the phone.

"Yes, everything's ready for tonight. Everyone's been briefed, and I've checked with the venue. Of course I'll be there."

I pushed against him; he braced himself and pressed back. Reaching a hand around, I found out that he was as hard as I was. I stroked him gently through his pants.

"They're all ready. Yes, it's all arrived, no problem. I think so, yes. Oh, yes, it's a very good one, I think. Yes. Yes."

I couldn't hear the other side of the conversation, but I was sufficiently master of myself to realize that something important was going down tonight. My main objective was to get Jackson "on side," however terrified he was of Vaughan. From the way he was pushing his ass into me, and the way the veins were standing out in his neck and forehead, I seemed to be winning. I grabbed his balls and squeezed; he went up on tiptoes, gasped a bit but disguised it as a cough, and managed to wind up his phone call without losing his cool.

"You fucking bastard," he said, with a smile on his face.

I span him around so our cocks were pressed together, my hands on his ass. "You going to suck me off?"

"Not now."

"Okay." I let him go. "But you're going to, some time, and it had better be soon. I bet you're good at it."

He said nothing, but looked cocky.

"And I bet you're a great fuck as well."

"Mr. Cooper, I'm going to have to leave you now. Take time to read through the papers. You'll see a few things on your schedule."

"And what about this?" I grabbed my dick, which was genuinely rock hard and in need of attention.

"You'll think of something," said Jackson. "Of that I have no doubt."

Oz was waiting for me. "So? Are you working here now?" He was bouncing up and down on his feet, like an excited five-year-old.

"Yeah. I've signed up. I'm on the payroll."

"That's fantastic, Greg. Thanks mate. Really, I won't lie, I'm pleased about that."

"Okay, buddy. Calm down. It's just a job."

"Yeah, but it means that Mr. Vaughan has some respect for me. He listens to stuff that I say."

"Good for you, Oz."

"So, when can we start training?"

He looked so eager to please, and I was still hard, so I said "Well, I've been looking at my timetable, and it says I'm free to use the facilities till five o'clock. That gives us a couple of hours."

"For real? You're going to train me now?"

"Sure, why not? Let's see what you're made of." We were walking back along the glass-walled corridor by the side of the gym.

I took him through a basic half-hour fitness test: ten minutes on the treadmill, fast enough to get him breathless and sweaty, then a mini-circuit of chin-ups, push-ups, planks, and burpees. He was in great shape; more interestingly, he obeyed every command without question, always trying to do a little more than was asked of him. I kept it businesslike; we weren't alone in the gym, and there were plenty of people watching the new trainer. Oz loved the attention; obviously this marked his new status within VaughanCorp. When I was finished, I held Oz's wrist and checked his pulse against the clock on the wall. "Now I'm going to take you somewhere quiet," I whispered, "and you're going to suck my dick for me."

He looked at me with those big brown eyes, sweat running down his face, and I swear his pulse quickened. "Okay, Greg. Sure. Yeah." He picked up his towel and was halfway out of the gym before I'd taken a step. Eager—or just obedient? There was something about the ease with which Vaughan's boys—Oz, Kieran, Jackson—could be seduced that was making me suspicious. I may have a high opinion of my own sexual attractiveness—there aren't many men out there who can resist Dan Stagg's dick once it's pointing in their direction—but these were hot young athletes who could be fucking people of their own age, not someone twenty years their senior.

In a while, if things went according to plan, I would know more. I had a tracking device inside Kieran, and soon I'd get one into Oz. It could only be a matter of time before I had sufficient access to Tom Jackson's holes to get him bugged as well.

Then, it was up to the Global Positioning System, and some backroom boys down in London, to supply me with the data about where these boys were going. I'd work out the rest.

Oz was waiting for me at the door to the changing

rooms. Was he seriously intending to have sex in here? It wasn't particularly busy, but there were people coming and going, presumably not all of them interested in seeing me shove my dick into Oz's handsome face.

"Do you want me to have a shower first?"

"I don't care. You're going to need one afterwards anyway."

"Oh, right. Well, shall we just, you know, go ahead and . . ."

"Lead the way."

He was more than eager; he was organized. Consulting my tastes. Putting the customer first.

"There's a sauna that's pretty quiet."

"Where else?"

"Disabled toilet."

"I don't want to fuck you in a toilet."

"Or we could go through to one of the private rooms."

That's what I was waiting for. "Sounds nice. I've never been to a gym with private rooms."

"They're for Mr. Vaughan's special guests. He gave me a key." He showed me a swipe card he'd been keeping in his pocket. "Look."

"Show me the way."

Oz led me through a door that looked like a cupboard, along a short passage to another door that he opened with the keycard. Inside it was a room about twelve feet by ten, big enough for a large leather divan, a couple of chairs, and a hand basin mounted in a black wood cupboard unit. In other words, a fuckroom from a very upmarket sex club. The floor was carpeted, the lighting subdued, the walls painted dark red.

"Very nice," I said. "You entertain a lot of clients in here?"

"I've never actually been inside one of these rooms before. It's good, isn't it?"

"Yeah. Perfect. Now take your fucking clothes off. Don't be shy. I've seen it before, remember?"

He was naked within ten seconds, hard dick standing up against his furry belly. I put my hands on his ass, pulled him towards me, and kissed him hard on the mouth. His knees buckled, and he kissed me back with equal force. These boys aren't getting enough love, I thought. They're getting fucked plenty, but that's it. No affection. Strange that a heartless bastard like me should be talking about love, but as an operational strategy it had its uses. A hard cock gets you a certain amount of loyalty, but if you show love to the love-starved, you have a slave for life. That's how cult leaders get started.

"Now you're going to show me if you can suck cock as well as the stuff you do in the gym. Think of it as part of your training. You're in charge. This"—I squeezed my hard dick through my pants—"is all yours."

Oz wasted no time. He dropped to his knees, got one hand inside my waistband, and hauled my cock out. His lips encircled the head and started moving down. By the time he'd reached the thickest point of my shaft, about half way, I'd decided he was good. By the time his lips were disappearing into my bush, I'd decided he was excellent. Plenty of practice. Almost professional.

"Good boy," I murmured, rubbing a hand over his brush-cut black hair. "Suck your daddy's dick. Come on. Make me feel good." He looked up at me with those big brown eyes, his brow furrowed, and came right up to the head again, teasing the ridge of my glans with his lips, tickling me underneath the pisshole with his tongue.

"Now look," I said, "we have a bed, and we have privacy. Do you have to be anywhere?"

He let go of my cock. "Not for a while," he said, wiping his mouth with the back of his hand.

"Okay. Let's enjoy ourselves." I pulled off my shirts and pants. "Lie down."

He threw himself on to the divan, bouncing a little, and I straddled his thighs, letting my balls drop down on to his stiff prick. In that position, I could run my hands over his firm, hairy torso and pinch the nipples that were sticking up through the fur. Oz squirmed, but I had him pinned. I shuffled further up his stomach and chest till my dick was resting on his dimpled chin. He opened his mouth, pulled his head forward with one hand, and let me fuck his mouth.

He didn't even gag.

Okay, let's see if his ass is as good as his mouth.

"There are condoms in the cupboard," he said.

"It's okay. I prefer to use my own."

"You brought some?"

"Of course. I've been wanting to get inside you ever since I saw you."

"Oh, Greg. Fuck me, man. Please. I mean, fuck me because you really like me."

"Of course I fucking like you. Do you like me?"

"I . . . I really . . ." He was preventing himself from saying "I love you," but the point was made.

"I thought maybe you were doing this because Vaughan told you to."

He said nothing, and didn't look me in the eye.

"It's okay. I'm happy either way."

"I owe him so much. And he's been very good to me."

"Yeah, right." I could just imagine Vaughan's technique: find young men with no career prospects, low self-esteem, and a small amount of talent, establish yourself as a kind of despotic father figure, and they'll do anything you tell them to do. What was Oz's story? Why was he so desperate to follow orders? I'd find out, after I fucked him.

I rubbered up, took a fingerful of lube and pushed it deep into Oz's beautiful asshole, taking care to lodge the tracking device as far up as I could. A good fucking would just push it deeper; that was the theory, anyway. I'd soon find out if it worked.

He took it beautifully, from the rear, on his side, on his back and, finally, on top of me, working himself to an orgasm that sprayed all over my chest and even hit me on the face. I scooped it up and put my fingers in Oz's mouth, forcing him to taste his own jizz as I shot my load deep inside his guts.

He kept me inside him for as long as he could, then reluctantly climbed off. We were both sticky and sweaty, and the leather covers of the divan were going to need a good hosing down; presumably Vaughan had staff for these jobs. Perhaps Oz would be back in there with a mop and bucket later on. For now, we lay together, feeling the jizz drying in our body hair, sticking us together like Velcro. He curled up against me, seeking warmth, his head on my shoulder. I caressed his face, kissed him on the forehead. Bet he didn't get that from Vaughan and his associates.

We shifted around a bit, and I felt something digging into my thigh; Oz was hard again. I reached around, took hold of him, and stroked him gently while our tongues joined inside our mouths. He came quickly, groaning as if in pain.

Oh, to be young again. I was only just beginning to get hard before it was all over.

"You okay?"

He snuggled in closer, reluctant for this to be over. "Yeah."

"Come on." I sat up. "We'd better get out of here. They'll be wondering what we're up to."

"I suppose so." We pulled apart, the sticky hairs on our bodies pulling painfully. "I wish we could stay like this, Greg."

"Me too." I took hold of my cock, hard again now. "I want to fuck you again."

"You can! I mean, I don't know if I can come again, but I'll take it . . ."

"That's okay, Oz. Let's keep it for another day. When you get some time off, maybe you could come over to my place for the weekend."

"You mean it?"

"Of course I fucking mean it. What does it look like?"

He was on his knees sucking me again before I had time to object. I let him feed for a while, then stood up.

"That's enough for now. Come on. Let's hit the showers."

"Please, let me . . . "

"Cool it." I spoke firmly. Oz looked as if he might cry. I took him by the shoulders. "It's all right, buddy.

I'm not going to disappear. I'm here for you." You and Kieran, I should have said, but I could only concentrate on one at a time. Although two at a time . . . the thought was not unwelcome. Oz and Kieran fighting over my dick. Could be arranged. "I think you need someone to look after you, Oz."

He shrugged, and wiped his hands on a towel. "I'm okay."

"No you're not."

He put the towel over his face. He was crying, but I wasn't going to draw attention to it.

"Never let them see you're upset. Greg Cooper's First Law. Okay? I'm here now. I'm going to look after you."

"For real?"

"For real." And at the time, I meant it. But looking after Oz was going to be more difficult than I expected.

And a lot more dangerous.

07

Keeping in touch with MI6 was a simple matter;
I emailed them from my phone on a secure, encrypted
server, and they acknowledged receipt. As soon as I got
back to my apartment, I submitted the serial numbers
of the tracking devices, and a code name for each of the
subjects. These were chosen from a list of randomly-
generated words, so that I was not tempted to give them
nicknames reflecting identifiable characteristics. The
email read:

> 1400021 WARDROBE
> 1400022 PANOPLY

Completely incomprehensible if intercepted. Trackers
1400021 and 1400022 were currently lodged deep
inside the rectums of Kieran (Wardrobe) and Oz
(Panoply), and for as long they stayed there they would
give us some insight into the workings of the Vaughan
operation. Perhaps we were barking up the wrong tree,
and Wardrobe and Panoply would spend their time

at home or in the pub or at girlfriends' houses. But I doubted that.

The acknowledgement came back, carefully designed to look like spam, and quickly deleted.

It was seven o'clock in the evening. I lay on the bed, dozed for a while, and then read through the documents Jackson had given me.

A plastic document wallet contained a printed spreadsheet headed CALENDAR. My name was peppered throughout the squares, thoughtfully high-lighted in yellow, with the words "training session," "physio," "staff development," "interview."

I was going to be busy, it seemed, even if this was a probationary period.

And shit! Today, 8:00 p.m., "interview."

It was 1950 already. I was out of the house and running up the road in less than a minute. I arrived at City Fitness out of breath and five minutes late.

Another flawless Eastern European receptionist buzzed me through.

The man who met me on the other side was obvi-ously not one of Vaughan's chosen companions. He was older than me, well into his fifties, about five foot six, overweight, with poor posture and gray hair badly in need of cutting. He was wearing a shapeless beige fleece, baggy combat pants, and dirty trainers. He had a camera slung around his neck.

"Greg Cooper? I'm Bill Brett. You've probably heard of me."

I shook his hand; the nails were dirty, and too long. "Sorry, I've not been here for long. Good to meet you, Bill."

"The photographer." He added a note of interrogation, as if by jogging my memory he'd help me to recognize his reputation.

"Uh-huh."

He scowled. "Well, as you'll soon find out, I'm one of the most sought-after camera artists around at the moment. My work appears on websites all over the world."

"That's great, Bill." I couldn't think of anything to say. "I love photography."

This didn't satisfy him. "So you're Mr. Vaughan's new discovery, are you?" He looked me up and down. "I don't see what all the fuss is about."

Maybe the fact that I could snap your cervical vertebrae with one blow? Maybe the fact that at least three of Vaughan's boys want this dick? "Neither do I," I said. "Now, what are we here for? It says 'interview' on my calendar."

"Oh, you looked at the calendar, did you? I was beginning to wonder."

"Sorry about that. It won't happen again."

"Mr. Vaughan expects punctuality and professionalism."

I said nothing.

"Come on, then." He bustled off down the corridor and up the stairs. I hadn't explored the upper levels of City Fitness yet. "We're in the studio." Studio? What kind of operation was this? "They're waiting for us."

"Who?"

Brett stopped and turned. "Seriously? Has nobody briefed you?"

"I think that's probably your job."

He was about to say something rude, but the look on

my face stopped him. "Okay, okay. Every couple of weeks we interview new guys who come to us through the website. They're looking for experience as personal trainers or boxers or whatever. We assess their abilities and explain some of the opportunities that we can offer them."

"And what's the camera for?"

"Mr. Vaughan runs a highly successful elite modelling agency."

"What kind of modelling?"

"Fitness, mostly. Some of the boys get into fashion and lifestyle."

"That's amazing."

"Yes." He looked me in the eye, trying to figure out how much I knew. "So our job is to talk to them, discuss their ambitions, and take a few test shots. I pride myself on being able to spot raw talent."

"Good for you."

The studio was a large, airy room with mirrors at one end and windows all down one side. At one time it must have been used for exercise classes; now it was full of photographic junk, tripods, lights, backdrops. At one end, sitting together like nervous schoolchildren waiting for the headmaster, were three young men.

"Good evening, good evening, I'm Bill Brett, great to meet you." Brett briskly shook their hands and busied himself with technical matters. He made no attempt to introduce me.

The candidates looked exactly like the kind of guys who join the military—young, restless, directionless. No self-respect, no respect for others. Military discipline soon deals with that; perhaps that's what Vaughan wanted me to inject into his boys, as well as my penis.

"Do you have your CVs?" I barked.

They looked at their shoes.

"Have you submitted your CVs?"

"Yeah," said one of them, a tall, long-limbed black guy, "I sent mine on email."

"And you two?"

They made noises that I interpreted as "yes."

"Lesson number one. When you're going for an interview, you take a copy of the paperwork with you, in case, like today, you're asked for it. Lesson number two. You stand up straight when you meet your potential employer, you look him in the eye, and you speak in an intelligible manner. Understand?"

There was some shuffling of feet and glancing around. These boys were even more useless than the recruits I'm used to dealing with. But all of them were good-looking. That, I assume, is why they'd been called in. But what else did they have in common? Why, out of the thousands of young men out there desperate to break into sport, modelling, the big time, had Vaughan chosen these three?

"While Mr. Brett gets set up over there, I'm going to ask you a few questions." I pulled up a chair. "Please, sit down. So, names first of all. From left to right. Go."

"Joshua," said the black guy.

"Jared," said the next one, who was Asian.

"Dakota," mumbled the third, who was white. Something for all tastes, I thought. Clever Vaughan.

"What?"

"Dakota." He sounded angry and defensive. "All right?"

"Is it real?"

"Yes. My mum's idea."

"It's a perfectly good native American name. And a great aircraft as well. Dakota. Okay, I'm Greg Cooper. I work with Mr. Vaughan."

Brett scowled. I think he expected me to sit in the corner and keep quiet while he processed the boys. As far as I was concerned, he was just the photographer. It's always a good idea to take control early. Makes reprisals harder.

"I guess you're all involved in combat sports in some way?"

Joshua and Dakota nodded. Jared glanced around, looking frightened.

"Go on."

"I'm . . . I don't . . . I mean, I play football really."

"To what level?"

"Local leagues."

"And you two?"

"Boxing," said Joshua.

"Kickboxing," said Dakota, "and a bit of judo."

A few more questions established that they were all unemployed, all worked out at least five times a week in a gym, two of them lived with family while the third (Dakota) was in his own apartment. Their ages ranged from eighteen (Jared) to twenty-one (Joshua). Yes, they all wanted to work for Mr. Vaughan, they'd like to be managed as fighters or used as trainers, and they all liked their chances as models. They had, they said, sent in photos, as requested. Presumably Brett was keeping those to himself.

"And what about school? Any of you still in education?"

They shook their heads.

"Any qualifications?"

There was a lot of glancing around. "I got some GCSEs," said Joshua. The others said nothing.

"Well, there's only so much you can learn at school. I learned everything worth knowing in the marines. Think you can learn?"

They nodded eagerly. I saw an eagerness for orders, a hunger for attention, that I recognized in my younger self.

I waited till Brett was out of the room before asking, "Have any of you been in foster care? Or come from broken homes?"

"Yeah," said Joshua. "My parents left me with my nan. I still live with her."

"I live with my mum," said Jared. "I never knew my dad. She doesn't talk about him. If I ask her she goes fucking mental."

"I was in care till last year," said Dakota. "My father was in prison for most of my life. My mum's a junkie."

My hunch was correct; all three from broken homes, emotionally vulnerable, easy to manipulate. Coincidence? Probably not.

Brett was back, his ears practically waggling. "We'll continue this conversation at another time. I think our cameraman is ready. Brett?"

He didn't like the role I was pushing him into—a service provider, a technician. He was obviously used to running the show.

"We'll take you in order of age, oldest first. That's you, Joshua. Leave your bag there, and take off that hoodie. Bill, are you shooting stills or video or both?"

"Both. Now if you could just . . ."

"So, stand over there, Joshua, in front of the back-drop. Let your arms hang by your side. You look terri-fied, man. It's just a camera. Bill's not going to bite you. Get into stance."

Once he was taking orders, Joshua was a lot more relaxed. He dropped into a boxing stance, bouncing on the balls of his feet, hands up protecting his face.

"Now I want you to go through a shadowboxing routine. I'm going to call out some sequences and I want you to follow them. Okay?"

"Yeah."

Bill tried to put his foot down. "This isn't how we do it. Mr. Vaughan wants . . ."

"We're doing it my way today, Bill." He glared at me, looking for the courage to fight. "Okay?"

"He's not going to be happy."

"Ready, Joshua? Give me jab right, jab right, hook left, jab right. One-two-three-four."

He was quick and responsive; the technique was good, not perfect. "Keep your elbows up on the hooks, and turn in on the back foot. One-two-three-four. Now switch stance. Hook right, hook left, jab left, uppercut right. . ."

We carried on with a few changing sequences until Joshua was sweating, and very much at his ease. Brett, I was glad to see, was snapping away. No more complaining.

"Good. Now, skipping."

"I haven't got a rope."

"Fake it."

Joshua took direction well—that, surely, would be of

interest to Bill Brett. He mimed skipping, simple jumps, then some fancy footwork, even pretending to cross the rope over.

"Let's get your shirt off. See what you're made of."

Joshua grabbed the hem of his T-shirt and pulled it up over his head. What he was made of, it seemed, was solid muscle, no fat, and a smooth skin that gleamed where it was wet with sweat. Not content with a six-pack, Joshua had an eight-pack.

"And back into stance . . ."

I took him through the shadowboxing and skipping again, shirtless. Under the heat of the lights he was getting even sweatier, streams of it running down his chest, dripping off his nose.

"That's enough. What kind of underwear have you got on?"

"Trunks."

"Okay. Take your pants off."

"Huh?"

"Your trousers, I mean. Sorry. I forget I'm in a foreign country sometimes."

This made the boys laugh, and they all looked rather starry-eyed. I was learning that British guys are impressed by Americans with a service background. Comes from all those movies and games, I guess. I intended to exploit it for all it was worth. Joshua, at any rate, found me easy to obey. He was pulling his tracksuit bottoms over his trainers. His underpants were lime green with an orange waistband and piping. The look was completed by white tube socks and white trainers, as if he'd bought the outfit direct from a gay porn website.

"Now we're going to do some stretches. Shoulders first—arm across your chest, that's it." I took him through a full body stretch, showing off his muscles to the camera; he was relaxed now, and enjoying himself, moving his hips to the rhythm of some music in his head.

"You're a natural, Joshua. You done any modelling before?"

"No, man. Not me."

"I think we can safely say that you'll get a good deal of work out of this. What do you think, Bill?"

"Yes, now if he could just . . ."

"Okay. Stand with your hands behind your head. And flex the abs for me. Crunch 'em down. Good man. Getting this, Bill?"

The photographer grunted in reply, but kept shooting.

"Now hook your thumbs in your waistband and pull it down a couple of inches. That's it. Right down, just above your dick. You're smooth. Do you shave?"

"Yeah. That okay?"

"It's fine. Now turn around. Show us that ass. Great stuff. Very nice. Just pull 'em down a bit, perfect. Right. You're done."

He stood up. It was impossible not to notice that he was getting hard inside those lurid shorts, but that could wait. I don't know what Bill Brett's method was, but I was not going to risk scaring these boys off. They were already making themselves vulnerable to exploitation. Could I protect them as well? Or would that blow my cover? If I turn out to be one of the good guys, will Vaughan dispense with my services—or, worse, figure out who I'm really working for?

"Dakota, you're next. Kickboxing and judo, right?"

"Yeah." He ambled into position, ran his fingers through his hair, every inch the cocky pretty boy he was. But scratch that surface, and he was the most vulnerable of the lot. "Want me to strip?"

"All in good time. You seem very relaxed in front of the camera."

"I am. Done it loads."

"I see. What sort of stuff?"

"Bit of modelling. You know."

"No, I don't."

"Er . . . like fitness stuff, body stuff . . ."

"Nudes?"

"Yeah, once or twice. It was a laugh."

"I see. What else?"

"Bit of webcamming."

"For money?"

"Yeah. Why not?"

"Nothing wrong with that. I'm very much in favor of nudity."

"So what do you want me to do?"

Run away from here and never come back. "Take your shirt off. Show us your body."

He stripped slowly, making sure that Brett was capturing every angle, finally scrunching up the shirt and throwing it on the floor. He had a wiry body, the pale skin covered in tattoos.

"That's a lot of ink for someone your age."

Dakota ran a hand down his chest and stomach, looking at the camera all the time. "I started young."

"Tell us about them."

"I got that one," he said, pointing to a badly-executed bird in flight on his left pec, "for my fourteenth birthday.

This"—a date in Roman numerals over the ribs on his left side, must have hurt like hell—"was the date that my mum tried to kill herself."

"And what about the name down your arm?"

"This?" He pointed to something in curly script on the inner part of his left forearm. "This is my daughter's name, okay?"

"I can't read it."

"Kayleigh. She's two now."

"Okay. And how's she doing?"

"I don't see her."

The air was leaking out of his balloon, so I changed the subject. "So, kickboxing. You done many fights?"

"Yeah, at club level."

"And you want to go further?"

"Of course. That's why I'm here, right?"

"Show us some moves, then. No, no, take your pants off . . . I mean your trousers off first."

"I'm not wearing anything underneath."

"Okay. I'm sure we can find you something. Bill—do you have a jock or a thong or something?"

"I expect so." Brett was more compliant now that I was getting results for him. He grabbed a holdall and started rummaging through what looked like someone's laundry: vests, T-shirts, underpants, socks. All clean, I hoped. "Here you go." A classic Bike jockstrap in black. "Try that for size."

"Should I change somewhere?"

"It's okay, Dakota. You're among friends. Brett won't take any pictures till you've got it on."

"I don't mind." Dakota pulled his light gray pants down and kicked them off. He was semi-erect, and he had a lot to show. He must have been making a good income from the webcams. Brett, Joshua, and I stared openly. Only Jared seemed uncomfortable, looking at his feet, at the ceiling, anywhere but at Dakota's big prick. After what seemed like about a minute, Dakota stepped into the jockstrap. It framed his ass beautifully. I was hard now as well; that made at least three of us. Brett was crouched over his camera, and Jared had his bag in his lap.

"You show that ass on webcam?" I asked.

"Course I do. People pay to see it." He turned to show his butt to the camera. Brett got busy.

"Worth every penny. Now do some squats for me. Deep ones."

Dakota executed a perfect squat, and in the process showed the camera his tight pink hole.

"Very nice," I said. My voice sounded gruff, and I had to clear my throat. "What do you think, guys?"

Joshua was sitting with his legs stretched out, massaging the bulge in his pants; he hadn't bothered to dress again. Jared, on the other hand, had his knees clamped together and a look of panic in his eyes.

"I . . . I think I'm in the wrong place . . . I just remembered . . . I've got to . . ."

"You got an appointment elsewhere, buddy?"

"Yes. I'm sorry."

"Off you go. Hey, thanks for coming. Don't worry. It's not for everyone."

Jared scampered out of the room as quickly as his feet would carry him. Brett looked furious; I wondered if Jared now posed a security threat. But I didn't think he'd go to the police. No offense had been committed.

"And then there were two," I said. "You guys both cool?"

"I am," said Dakota, his hands on his hips. "What about you, man?"

"I'm good," said Joshua.

"Enjoying the show?" I asked.

"Yeah. Nice." Joshua rubbed his cock. Brett was having trouble deciding which way to point his lens.

"Okay, Dakota," I said, "let's see that ass again. Push it towards the camera. Hold it open. That's it. Now, run your finger around it."

Dakota did exactly as he was told while Brett snapped away. The tip of his finger slipped inside his ring, which got a "yeeeah" from Joshua. Dakota knew exactly how to turn men on.

"Now stand up. Let's see how hard you are."

Whoever invented the material that Bike jockstraps are made out of deserves a Nobel Prize; the mesh fabric of the pouch is soft and stretchy enough to allow a hard cock to stand straight out from the body. Dakota was not only fully erect, he was also oozing precum right through the pouch, a messy silver patch on the waffled black cotton. He posed like a professional, pushing his cock this way and that, tensing his muscles, running his hands up and down his tattooed torso.

"Okay. Lose the jock."

Dakota peeled it down over his hips and thighs, and a big, meaty cock bounced free, with a pearl of precum dangling from a silvery thread.

"Rub that over the head."

He did as he was told.

"Now taste your fingers."

There was no longer any pretense that this was a fitness shoot. Dakota had taken it straight into porn territory. Brett moved in for close-ups, while Joshua got his dick out of the leg of his underpants.

"Shall we get the two of you together now?"

"Why not?" said Dakota, licking his lips.

Joshua stepped back in front of the camera and slung an arm around Dakota's shoulders. He was a good six inches taller. Dakota rested his head against Joshua's neck.

"What you want us to do?" asked Joshua.

"Take hold of each other's cock."

They crossed arms over their stomachs, black hand grasping white dick, white grasping black.

"Just hold it there while we get the photos. Come on, Brett, do your thing. Try and get it in focus."

Brett hated me for my snotty attitude, but loved me for getting the boys to do things he could only dream of. If he'd asked them to get hard or fool around they'd have kicked his ass. But some of us inspire obedience. Joshua and Dakota stroked each other, staring intently down at their cocks.

"How about kissing?"

I expected this to be the line they wouldn't cross, but far from it—it seemed, from the eagerness with which they locked lips, that they had been waiting for permission. They made out with a passion that went far beyond porn, turning to face each other, chest to chest, their cocks pressed between their muscly abs, buttocks clenching as they thrust, hands everywhere. Dakota was on his tiptoes.

"That's enough, now. Take a break."

They unglued themselves unwillingly, and stood there not knowing what to do with their hands, their cocks. Brett occupied himself with lights and lenses.

I took Joshua and Dakota back to their seats, gave them bottles of water.

"You're doing well, guys."

Joshua wiped his mouth. "Thanks, man." His cock, like Dakota's, was still hard.

"Is this what you were expecting?"

He shrugged. "Kind of. Maybe. I don't know."

"What about you, Dakota?"

"Fitness modelling usually means porn."

"Ah. The voice of experience."

"I don't mind. It's good pay."

"And what about your family and friends? What will they think?"

"I don't fucking care," said Joshua. "They won't see it anyway."

"And you, Dakota?"

"Bit late for me to start worrying about that. My girlfriend doesn't exactly like what I do, but she's happy enough to spend the money."

"You got a girlfriend?" asked Joshua, scowling. "Shit, man, I thought you were gay."

Dakota shrugged. "I'm up for whatever. What about you?"

Joshua grabbed his hard dick and squeezed. "What does it look like?"

"Want me to suck it?"

"Yeah. Course."

Dakota got down on his knees, and was about to make a start when Brett interrupted. "No, no, no! For

God's sake, what are you thinking? Get them in front of the lights!"

He had a point; I'd been so absorbed I'd temporarily forgotten my role as exploiter and abuser of emotionally needy young men.

"Come on, guys. Let's do it for the camera."

"I'll suck," said Dakota, "but I won't fuck."

Joshua looked disappointed.

"Not on camera, I mean. If you've got a place . . ."

"I live with my nan."

"And I'm not allowed visitors after ten o'clock. It's . . . well, you know. One of those hostel type places."

"You'd better come back to mine, then," I said, but not loud enough for Brett to hear. "Right, Joshua, you stand there. Dakota, get on your knees and make love to that thing."

He did as he was told, with enthusiasm and efficiency. Joshua's knees were buckling. "Are you about to come?" asked Dakota, squeezing Joshua's tight balls.

"Yeah."

"Right." He stood up and wiped his mouth. "That's your lot."

"But . . . but . . ." stammered Brett, obviously hoping for the money shot.

"This is an audition, right? You already got more than you expected, didn't you? If you want more, we need paying."

"But if we're pleased with what you do today, you may get a chance to . . ."

"I've heard it all before," said Dakota. "A chance to what? Be one of Vaughan's fighters? Get some legit modelling gigs? Pull the other one, mate." He started dressing. "This is porn, and if you want it, you pay for it."

The situation was getting tense. Time for Captain Cooper to take control. "You've got what you need, haven't you Brett? Good. We'll be in touch. Put your clothes on, boys, and I'll take you back down to reception."

We were out of the studio in less than a minute, leaving Bill Brett, the foremost camera artist in his field, swearing under his breath.

"Meet me in half an hour in the pub at the end of the road," I said. "And try," I said, pointing to the still-huge bulge in Joshua's pants, "not to get yourselves arrested."

"Mr. Vaughan's not going to be pleased when I tell him about this," Brett said when I went upstairs to say goodnight. "He likes the way I do things. We have a good little operation going here."

"If you don't like the way I work," I said, "that's fine. I'll just make sure we're not put on any jobs together in the future. I'm sure I can find another photographer who does. I'll ask Vaughan to keep a lookout."

Brett flinched when I moved. I had established the power of fear over him—fear and lust. Perhaps he wasn't interested in me, but he was interested in what I could make the boys do.

"It's been a pleasure," I said, slapping him rather too hard on the back.

Vaughan wasn't around; presumably he was playing the family man, or holed up with Tom Jackson in a luxury fuckpad somewhere. No doubt Brett would report to him as soon as he could. Let him. I was confident that he'd like my style.

I hid myself away in the bathroom, checking for

CCTV, and accessed my emails. Already a list of coordinates for WARDROBE and PANOPLY had come up; postcodes, addresses where possible. At no point had they been in the same place at the same time—but they had both been moving around. Busy. Working?

I would investigate that tomorrow. Now it was getting on for ten o'clock, and I had two very horny young athletes waiting for me down the road.

I'd take them home and let events take their own course.

You don't need me to describe the mechanics of the night. Joshua and Dakota, twenty-one and twenty, horned up past the point of no return, and Captain Greg Cooper, over twice their age, happy to help out if needed.

We had a bedroom, a bathroom, a living room, a kitchen, plenty of floors and mirrors, and we made full use of them for several hours until they left, after kissing just inside the doorway, at seven in the morning.

08

Vaughan disappeared for a few days, and as I
hadn't managed to shove any electronica up his asshole
I had no idea where he'd gone. MI6, however, had ways
of tracking persons of interest that did not involve
penetration, and my encrypted email quickly told me
that he'd flown to Miami. It was up to me to find out
why. Given the secrecy that ruled VaughanCorp, you
might think this would be impossible—but such is the
power of the penis, I had not one but two ready sources
of information very close to the man himself. Bill Brett
had started out hating me, but the day after the photo
shoot it became clear that he now regarded me as an
enabler.

He greeted me at City Fitness with "Hey, Greg!"
and a pat on the back, as if coercing two young men to
have sex in front of the camera made us best buddies. I
played along; Greg Cooper was not as squeamish about
these things as Dan Stagg. Dan had no problem about
killing people in a combat situation, but exploiting the
young and vulnerable stuck in his craw. The unpleasant

Captain Cooper, he of the racist attitudes and the nothing-to-lose outlook, didn't care.

"Hey, Bill. How did the pictures come out?"

"Really nice." His voice sounded croaky, as if he'd been up all night poring over his computer screen. I'd been up all night variously fucking Joshua and Dakota, but Brett didn't need to know that. He could suspect, of course. That would be useful. "I'll show you if you like. There are some great ones of his . . ."

"It's okay, man. I'm not big on pictures. I prefer the real thing."

He dug me in the ribs with his elbow, and I fought back a desire to thump him in the mouth. "I bet you do." He licked his lips.

"Is the boss around? I need to speak to him."

"Not today."

"Of course," I said, pretending that I was party to Vaughan's plans, "he's off to Miami, isn't he?"

It was a gamble—in fact I was nowhere near being trusted with this kind of information. But Brett was blinded by lust, and instantly believed that Vaughan confided in me. "That's right. Cutting through a lot of red tape for the Craig Lukas fight."

"I didn't realize he was going so soon. You're obviously much more in his confidence than I am." *Which Craig Lukas fight? Why Miami? What red tape?* I knew that direct questions would get me nowhere, but flattery and misdirection might succeed. "It's ridiculous that they're putting up so many difficulties, but hey—that's America for you. Take it from me." Guesswork—but I could well imagine the problems a British promoter would face trying to break into the US circuit.

"He'll sort it out. He's got good lawyers over there."

"He'll need them."

"Don't worry. Mr. Vaughan is very good at smoothing out little problems. I don't know how he does it but . . ." Brett snapped his fingers. "Poof! They just disappear."

"I wish I had that power."

"Maybe you do now. You're part of the team. It'll be useful for Mr. Vaughan to have an American on board."

"I guess so. I can be his fixer when we go over for the Lukas fight."

Brett sighed. "Lucky you. I don't get to travel. Anyway, I've got websites to update . . ."

"And I've got training to do. See you later, buddy. Let's get a beer sometime, go out and pick up some boys."

Brett made a snorting sound like a pig at a trough, and trudged up the stairs to the studio, presumably to upload last night's photos. Evidence for a Vaughan-Porn operation was mounting.

My second informant was the fuck-ready Tom Jackson. Now that the cat was away, I hoped that the mouse would play—although not right away, as I needed a few hours to recover from last night. It turned out that, while young athletes very much enjoy fooling around with each other, what they both wanted was hard cock up their asses. And with two greedy bottoms in the bed, it was fortunate that there was one well-hung top to give them both what they needed.

Thinking about those tight holes and ripped bodies was making me stiff again, so I entered Jackson's office with something for him to feast his eyes on.

"Morning, Jackson."

He looked as cool as a cucumber in his fitted shirt and tight pants, his hair perfectly parted, his face freshly shaved. Oh, how much better he'd look soaked in piss and splattered with cum, perhaps with a massive dildo in his ass. See? I was beginning to think like Greg Cooper. Perhaps Greg Cooper has always been there. Perhaps death has set him free, and Dan Stagg will never come back.

"Ah, Greg. Good to see you." He was sitting at his desk, tapping away at a laptop.

"Busy as ever, I see." I stood near him, trying to be as distracting as possible.

"Yes." He didn't tell me to go away.

"What you doing?"

"At this very moment? VAT returns, if you must know."

"And what's a VAT return?"

"Accounts for the taxman. You'd call it sales tax, I think."

"You're quite a little expert, aren't you?"

"I'm a qualified accountant."

"Vaughan didn't just hire you for your looks."

Jackson closed the lid of the laptop before I could get a look at the figures. "Is that meant to be insulting, Captain Cooper?"

"I'm just saying you're cute as well as smart."

"Thank you." He folded his arms across his chest; biceps bulged in the white cotton. "I got the job on the strength of my professional qualifications."

"That's right, baby." I squeezed his arm. "The rest is just a happy coincidence."

Jackson smiled. He was more relaxed with Vaughan away. "Maybe my looks gave me an edge."

"I don't see many women in Vaughan's workforce."

He arched a perfect eyebrow. "No, you don't."

"One or two use the gym, but that's about it."

"Mr. Vaughan doesn't handle female boxers."

"I'm sure he doesn't."

"But City Fitness is open to anyone."

"It has to be, by law."

Jackson shrugged. "I suppose so."

"And it looks good. More . . . normal."

"Did you want anything, Greg? Because I really need to get this finished before lunch."

"Yeah. I want to fuck you." Was Dan Stagg ever that crude? I couldn't remember.

"I know that." Jackson looked very pleased with himself.

"You're a cool customer."

"I am."

"You won't be when my cock's inside you."

"Very sure of yourself, aren't you, Greg?"

I squeezed my dick. "Yep. Pretty sure."

"And what makes you think I'll let you fuck me?" He impersonated my accent on the last two words, and pushed his chair back from the desk, stretching out his legs. From the bulge in his pants, he was enjoying this foreplay as much as I was.

"Because I can see it in your eyes."

"And supposing I'm not the type that cheats?"

"Cheats on who?"

"Come on, Greg. You seem to know everything about me."

"You mean Vaughan? He's married."

Jackson smiled; there was something catlike about

his expression, his hooded eyes, his fine bone structure. A cat in heat, maybe. And like a cat, he'd only let himself be stroked on his own terms. Boys like Kieran, Joshua, Dakota, and Oz were like dogs—they came when bidden. Jackson was not going to be so easy. But Pussy would get his cream, of that I was certain—splattered right into his handsome face.

"Nobody's perfect, Greg."

"Not even you?"

He waggled his head from side to side, as if weighing up the answer. "The jury's out on that one."

"I look forward to the verdict. When's he back?"

"Mr. Vaughan? Day after tomorrow."

"Long way to go for a short time."

"It's tough at the top."

"Why didn't he take you?"

"He doesn't need me on this trip."

"You mean he's got someone to fuck out there?"

Jackson scowled, and moved his chair back to working position. "You're very crude."

"I'm a marine."

"So I noticed. And to answer your question, I don't know the details of Mr. Vaughan's private affairs. Sometimes I accompany him on business trips, if he needs my services."

"Services. Right."

Jackson laughed, thank God. "Oh, go away. You're too distracting."

"You need distracting."

"With that?" He placed his hand over my cock.

"You know it." His hand rested there, applying a slight, rhythmic pressure. "Want to suck it now?"

Jackson removed his hand. "As I say, I've got work to do." He was still smiling.

"What time you finish?"

"I should be done by four."

"I'll leave you in peace." Jackson's face was flushed—he was as horny as I was, probably more so, considering his age and my exhausting night. I moved towards the door. "Oh, by the way, are you going over for the Lukas fight?"

"What, to Miami?"

"Yeah."

"I hope so. I mean, if it comes off."

"I thought everything was moving ahead. That's what Vaughan told me," I lied. "I mean, he's started publicizing it, hasn't he?" Guesswork: I knew nothing about the time frame or the business strategy.

"Absolutely. But you know what it's like. Don't count your chickens. Many a slip. All that sort of thing."

"Is it Lukas? Is he the problem? I'm seeing him later today. Maybe I can help."

"Oh, Lukas is always a problem. He's a prima donna. Always wants more money, better fights, more publicity, and then when he gets what he wants . . ." Jackson shrugged. "He's not the most mature person I've ever worked with, shall we say."

"But he's not going to blow a chance to break into the American circuit, is he? That's where the money is."

"He knows that. And I think he'd like nothing better than to stay out there after the Miami fight, and wash his hands of us."

I stood up, making sure my cock was still visible. "Ungrateful little shit. I'll knock some sense into him."

"Calm down, Rambo. Mr. Vaughan has everything under control."

"You hope."

"What do you mean?" Jackson looked suspicious.

"If everything works out at his meeting in Miami."

"It will. It's just, you know, red tape."

"Immigration stuff, you mean? He could have sorted all that out at the embassy."

"Thank you, Greg. If I need any advice, I know where to come."

"Okay. I'll pick you up at four." A final squeeze to the dick. "Bring a toothbrush."

I had half an hour to kill before I had a personal training client; I wondered idly if he would be as fuckable as the rest of the Vaughan entourage. Or would it be one of the female members whom Vaughan encouraged as camouflage, or window dressing? Were they part of the operation? How far did he cast his net? Were they the bait in the trap?

I found a quiet stairwell at the back of the building to compose an email to control in London. Unencrypted, it read:

Please check any criminal records or other reason why boxer Craig Lukas may not be able to enter or work in USA. Also any fiscal or other financial factors that would limit Alan Vaughan's ability to work/conduct business in USA. Please list any websites owned by or otherwise connected to Alan Vaughan.

My inbox contained further details on PANOPLY

and WARDROBE. Panoply had ceased transmitting at 0615 this morning at a new address, suggesting that Oz had either had a good shit or a very rough fuck. Wardrobe (Kieran) was still transmitting, but had been in the same location since 0800. Lazy, or possibly dead. Maybe someone found out he'd been giving it away. Maybe a client took things a little too far. The thought nagged at my mind.

I had his number, so I called him.

"Oz. It's . . ." Shit! I nearly said *Dan*. "It's Greg. You okay?"

"Yeah, good man. Sorry. I'm still in bed."

"Get up, you lazy bastard! Shouldn't you be at work?"

"I've been at work all fucking night, man. What do you want?"

"I just want to see you again, that's all."

"Hey, that's nice." His sleepy voice sounded inviting. "You could come and join me in bed."

"You want to get fucked again?"

He laughed. "Maybe later, okay? I need to give it a rest."

"Sore ass?"

"Something like that."

"And how's your cock?"

"Hard, now I'm talking to you."

"Me too."

"Want me to jerk off on the phone? I can do Skype."

"Get some sleep, Oz. You need to look after yourself."

"I need you to look after me, Greg."

"Okay." Shit. Feelings are not useful. "I'll see you

later, dude." I hung up before I said something I'd regret. Damn these boys for reminding me I was still human.

I went outside, jogged around the nearby park a couple of times, avoiding syringes and dog shit, and returned to City Fitness with a soft cock and a clear head, ready for my client. Fortunately for me, it was a straight middle-aged man with a waistline bigger than his age, who liked talking about fitness more than he enjoyed doing the exercises. I put him through a basic circuit class; he did about thirty percent of what was asked. He left sweaty and satisfied.

It was nearly noon; time to get out into the streets.

Thanks to a selection of untraceable credit cards I was able to hire a car with a GPS navigation system and work my way through the addresses where Panoply and Wardrobe had been traced in the last twenty-four hours. Some of them I could dismiss without further investigation: their homes. But the others needed to be looked into.

Particularly one—a large, detached house in a quiet residential cul-de-sac in the well-to-do suburb of Trafford. Nothing remarkable about it: big back garden, what looked like a swimming pool, some mature trees. Google Earth told me that much. MI6 told me who lived there, of course: Richard Everett, a businessman in his sixties, married with children and grandchildren, unblemished record, big donations to charity, etc.

Nothing remarkable, except for one thing. Both Oz and Kieran had visited the address during the tracking period. They were there, together, for just over an hour and a half, between 2200 and 2330 yesterday.

Jackpot.

I planned a route that took in the four addresses that my implants had produced. A round trip in good traffic would take me about forty-five minutes. That gave me time to stop at each location, observe, record.

Not that I really needed to go. I'm no Sherlock Holmes, but a process of deduction led me to one inevitable conclusion. What could possibly take Oz Rafiq and Kieran McAvoy, two beautiful and sexually compliant young men in the orbit of Alan Vaughan, to a series of private homes in the Manchester area? And why would they both go to the same place? Drug dealers? I ruled that out: nothing suggested Vaughan was involved in pharmaceuticals. Oz and Kieran were delivering something else. They were part of a chain of supply and demand into which newcomers like Dakota and Joshua were entering.

They were whores.

Both of them were beautiful, and very good at sex: I could vouch for that. Both of them were connected to Vaughan; Oz worked for him, and was ambitious as a fighter, while Kieran was still on the outside, being lured in with the promise of opportunities to come.

A business model suggested itself to me.

Vaughan and his scouts (Brett? Jackson?) identified suitable young men from the gyms and boxing clubs in the area. They were given to understand that their sporting talents might gain them entry to Vaughan's charmed circle, and the money and acclaim that came with it. Equally, they were offered the emotional and social support that was lacking in their lives: these were all men from insecure and troubled backgrounds who would be drawn to an authoritative father figure like

Vaughan. They were lured sexually as well; some of them, I guessed, were already gay, but in other cases Vaughan exploited the natural sex drive of men in their late teens and early twenties and turned it to his commercial advantage. Fitness modelling quickly led to porn. Some, like Jared, were wrong for the job, and easily dismissed. Others like Oz were being used as bait or rewards within the Vaughan system; I had no doubt he'd been thrown in my way in order to reel me in. And now it seemed that Oz and others like Kieran, who proved themselves compliant, were being pimped to wealthy clients in the area. And if they complained? Vaughan withdrew his offers of support. Perhaps he went further than that. Perhaps he blackmailed the boys: after all, he'd have photographs and maybe surveillance footage of what they'd been prepared to do for him. He probably had the same on me—maybe that room that Oz took me to was fitted up with spycams. Maybe he was blackmailing his clients as well, getting the boys to gather material on some of Manchester's most successful businessmen and sports personalities, the men that lived in those big mansions out in Trafford, who entertained one of two of Vaughan's boys while the wife was away. . .

Vaughan had excellent relations with the press, who reported whatever he wanted them to report, and kept well away from his private life. How did he secure their support? By paying them off with other, juicier material. Perhaps he counted editors and publishers among his client base.

If any of this seems far-fetched, just think about those irreproachable media personalities who played the publicity game for decades before it was discovered that they'd been sexually abusing children all along, paying the press and police off at every turn. Pushing vulnerable young men—adults, let us not forget, however immature—into pornography and prostitution might not seem quite such a grave offense in comparison. Dan Stagg would have disapproved. Greg Cooper was content to fuck as many of these young men as possible, protect them from further harm if he could, and to play Vaughan's game in the interests of the mission objective. It was Vaughan's business empire I was interested in—the details of how he got his money and, more importantly, the uses to which he put it. If it turned out that the CIA and MI6 were right, that he was funding extreme right-wing groups in America by exploiting the tight asses and hard cocks of these young athletes, then that, and that only, made it wrong enough for me to care.

The addresses fitted the theory: big, expensive houses that boys like Oz and Kieran could have no possible connection to. They weren't visiting parents or grandparents. Neither of them practiced a trade, other than the obvious one. I had no evidence of what went on behind these doors, but I had a working hypothesis. All I had to do now was find how payments were made, where they were hidden, and where the funds ended up.

First-person testimony from the boys would answer half the question. MI6's access to private financial records might fill in the gaps. But I was going to need to penetrate deeper into this operation for my evidence to be worth anything.

I returned the car, and took the precaution of wiping my fingerprints off it. If one person can use tracking technology, so can another, and I was pretty sure that Vaughan had insider dealings with the local police. If he found out I'd been visiting these addresses, my cover would be blown.

Back at home I switched on my laptop and worked through four website addresses provided by control in London in response to my request. Further confirmation of my theory. The first was innocuous enough, a fitness/fashion website featuring photos of young men in sportswear, sometimes topless, flexing muscles and furrowing brows, with information about their age, sport, ambitions, likes, and dislikes. Interested clients could hire these models through the website, which would charge a modest "agency fee." It implied that the clients would be PR companies, events managers, fashion editors and the like, and that the website was a gateway for young men to break into the modelling business.

The second site featured some of the models from the first, but this time all pretense of modelling sportswear had gone. Photo sets and videos were released twice a week, showing the boys stripping down, posing nude, and getting hard. Both Oz and Kieran featured on this one.

The third site took things a stage further, with models masturbating and shooting for the camera, sometimes posing together, touching each other, a little light oral.

The fourth and final site was hardcore.

Each of the three porn websites had a "contact us" feature, which promised to pass messages on to the models, but was presumably used as the starting point for further business arrangements.

None of the sites made any mention of Alan Vaughan.

Bill Brett had been busy. The content went back four years; the most recent updates were from two days ago. An update, featuring Dakota and Joshua, must be imminent.

There was no response to my request for information on Craig Lukas's immigration status. Perhaps there was nothing to tell. I would try and find out.

My appointment with Craig Lukas came under the heading of "training" in my calendar, but there was very little that I could teach the champ. He made it clear from the moment we met that he resented me, and believed himself to be a god. I instantly suspected cocaine use.

I wasn't going to get a tracking device in this guy, however much I might want to; Lukas was a big, hefty fellow with a meaty ass that needed pounding just as badly as his ego. But unless he surprised me, and bent over in the showers, I was going to have to use other methods.

He warmed up with a skipping rope; he had all the fancy moves, crossing the rope over, doing double jumps, and so on, that men of his type take such pride in. God, I wanted to trip him. "So, what exactly is the point of this?" he said, after keeping me waiting for over five minutes.

"We're going to work on your flexibility."

"There's nothing wrong with my flexibility. Fuck that."

I said nothing. Lukas executed a few more flashy moves, but finally got his feet tangled up. He was furious.

"Jesus fucking Christ. I'm not in the mood for this bullshit." He moved towards the door.

"You will stay put, and you will do as you're told."

"Or what? Fucking jerk. . ."

He didn't get much further, because I hooked a leg out from underneath him with my foot, turned him as he fell, and caught him with my forearm against his windpipe.

"Care to run that by me again?"

Lukas's struggles just increased the pressure until he could hardly breathe. I waited for the fighting to subside, then dropped him to the floor.

"What the fuck? I should have you done for assault." He started coughing.

"Go right ahead." I held out my phone. "What's the emergency number here? 999, right?"

He gasped the word "twat," but didn't attempt to retaliate.

"On your feet, champ."

He pulled himself up, red-faced and sulky. "You're a fucking psycho. You know that?"

"Oh, yes, I know that all right. And so do all the people I killed in active service. I'm sure that was the last thought that went through their minds. Greg Cooper is a fucking psycho."

"What do you want?"

"To work on your flexibility."

"Do you normally do that by choking people?"

I was about to say that choking people was part of my repertoire, but the time was not yet right. I didn't know whether Lukas was part of the underside of Vaughan's operation, whether he'd worked through the ranks by peddling that meaty ass around the luxury homes of the greater Manchester area. For all I knew he could be nothing more than a legit boxer, unaware of Vaughan's grassroots business activities. But he was Vaughan's only visible weak spot, a thorn in his side who was making demands that the boss was not happy about. He was too valuable for Vaughan to lose—but how would they keep him on side? What power did they have over him? Had Craig Lukas made a name for himself on Vaughan's websites before his boxing career took off? Was there other, more private material? Were they keeping him quiet with blackmail?

I put him through a stretching routine, the kind of thing I warm up combat trainees with. If you're using your arms and legs to kill people, you need to keep strength and flexibility in perfect equilibrium: too much of one, and you lose the other. Boxers, especially those at the heavier end of the spectrum, tend to lumber around like carthorses. I noticed it during the McAvoy fight; Lukas was as stiff as a block of wood, and if the relatively supple McAvoy had fought at the top of his abilities he might have won. I could, of course, testify to McAvoy's flexibility in other areas, not to mention his excellent control of the gag reflex.

When Lukas was forced to admit that he might actually learn something from me, his defenses dropped. He was still an arrogant little shit, but at least he was giving me information.

I plied him with questions about the forthcoming Miami fight. He was excited, and indiscreet.

"Yeah, you see I could make a real killing in America, right? I've had loads of agents and promoters from over there getting in touch, offering me all sorts, and not just boxing. I could get into TV, acting, there's even someone talking about doing a reality show about me, you know, coming to America, winning fights against the odds, that sort of thing. It's great."

"You'd do well out there. You've got the right kind of attitude. You believe in yourself."

"Yeah, well you got to, right?"

I let him ramble on for a while, then when he paused to take a breath I asked, "And will Mr. Vaughan go with you? I understand he has ambitions in the US as well."

"Oh, that." Lukas scowled. "Yeah, that's what he says. But I'm not sure it's right for either of us." He lowered his voice. "Between you and me, I think I've kind of reached the end of the road with Vaughan. He's holding me back."

"What do you mean?"

"Oh, nothing bad." Lukas didn't trust me yet. "He's a brilliant manager and the best promoter in the UK. I just think that if I'm going to make it over there, I need someone who's, like . . ."

"Big time. And Vaughan is small time."

He thought that over for a while. I corrected his hamstring stretches, pushed him gently into position, enjoyed the feel of his tight leg muscles.

"Do you really think that? That he's small time?"

"Of course he is. He makes a lot of noise over here, but in America they'd eat him alive. Besides, I wouldn't be too sure that he'll be allowed to work in the States."

"What do you mean?"

I didn't want to come straight out and say "he's being investigated on a serious criminal matter." "I understand there's a lot of red tape that needs to be sorted out."

"Yeah. That's why he's in Miami now. It's just permits and that."

"Yours, or his?"

"I don't know. I guess I need a work permit or something."

"You don't have a criminal record, or anything that would prevent you from entering the US?"

"Fuck no."

So much for Vaughan's cover story: he was obviously taking care of other business over in America. Terrorist business, if the CIA was right.

"And what about the money?"

"What money?"

"Does Vaughan pay you well?"

"He keeps me on a retainer. A fucking small retainer. He says the prize money is being invested in my future."

"What does your contract say?"

"You better ask my lawyer."

"I will."

"But you're working for Vaughan, right? He's got you to ask me all this stuff to find out what I really think of him."

"You have no reason to trust me."

"That's right."

"And yet," I said, "you do trust me. Or you want to."

Lukas scowled; his thick black eyebrows and a heavy beard growth made him look like a cartoon villain.

"Okay," I said, "let's leave it there and carry on with the stretches. Get into a high plank . . ."

"Are you queer?"

"What?"

"You heard me." His voice was low, but not hostile. He stared at his feet.

"Yes, I'm queer. I like to fuck men. Why do you ask?"

"You're one of his lot, then."

"Meaning what?"

He glanced up, presumably to make sure that I wasn't about to get him in a chokehold again. "They're all gay, all of Vaughan's lot."

"And what about you, Craig?"

"I've got a girlfriend."

"And Alan Vaughan's married. You wouldn't be the first famous sportsman to go out with a string of beautiful women because he's gay."

"Yeah?" Maybe this was news to Lukas. "Well I'm not. I like women." I said nothing. "I do! Jesus, what do I have to do to prove it?"

"Stop trying, that would be my advice. And if you're really straight, ask yourself why you've surrounded yourself with gay men. Like you say, everyone on Vaughan's team, including me, is queer."

"But you were in the marines, right?"

"Right. And you can imagine how many men I got to fuck. I was like a kid in a candy store." I was in full Greg Cooper mode. "New recruits will let you fuck them just to get ahead. Senior ranks will let you fuck them because they've learned to love it. Yeah, Craig, it's a man's life in the Marine Corps."

"Christ," he said, and swallowed hard.

"I'm good at it too." I let silence fall for a while. "Even better than I am at fighting."

"That so."

Lukas nervously rubbed his knees, then cleared his throat.

"Look, mate, I'd better get moving. I've got a photo shoot in an hour. Got to get washed and shaved and all that."

"Photos? What sort of photos?"

"Publicity stuff for posters and that." It sounded innocent enough; perhaps Lukas really didn't know about Vaughan-Porn.

"Go on then. Make yourself beautiful. And we have more work to do, okay?"

"Agreed. I'm as stiff as a fucking board."

Not, sadly, the kind of stiffness I'd have been interested in, but at least he'd signed up to the program.

"And if you ever need to talk, Craig, if you need any advice—well, I'll do my best to be an impartial listener."

"Bullshit."

I shrugged. "I know it's a leap of faith."

He opened his mouth to say something, then thought better of it.

"Thanks for the offer, mate." Perhaps he was going to report me to Vaughan for insubordination or espionage or something. Who was spying on whom?

I let him go to the showers without following, however much I wanted to see that thick-set, hairy body. Lukas, if he was to be of any use, had to be won over slowly.

Besides, it was half past three. Half an hour before Jackson got off work. And my balls were nice and full again.

09

Getting inside Tom Jackson's ass was not going to be easy. Jackson was not like the rest of the lost boys. Jackson was a well-balanced, intelligent young man with healthy self-esteem and no obvious signs of emotional distress. He was using Vaughan every bit as much as Vaughan was using him. He knew Vaughan's secrets, and in return for absolute discretion he could pretty much name his price. One word from Jackson and the whole Vaughan empire would be blown to pieces. He must be one hell of a fuck. I intended to find out.

I was in reception at four o'clock sharp. Jackson kept me waiting for twenty minutes, then came out of the office looking as crisp and clean as the moment he'd walked in. He was on the phone, acknowledging my presence with a nod of the head. You'd never have known this was a fuckmeet. I like these little games. I like the guys who pretend they don't want it. It makes the conquest sweeter. I like to look into their eyes when the last bit of pretense melts away. And then, when all dignity has been fucked out of them, they show me the truth. Yes, Tom Jackson, in your tailored shirt and your ass-hugging slacks, I will break you down.

I was hard. I stood up and let him see. He glanced down, then up, nodded as if he'd been reminded of a business appointment, and continued his conversation. It was dreary stuff about venues, insurance, security . . . I tuned out, and watched his ass as he leaned against the desk, sticking it out at me, reminding me of the prize. It worked. My mouth was watering as I thought of how good it would taste when I ate him out before sticking my dick in him . . .

"Okay, Greg. Are you ready?"

I must have looked more than usually stupid as I came out of my daydream. "Huh?"

"Let's get out of here." He put on his jacket.

It was dark in the street, the air full of dirty drizzle.

"Where are you taking me?" he demanded.

"What?"

"Are we going for a drink? It's too early for dinner." He looked at his watch: stylish, steel, expensive. "Well?"

"Where do you live?"

Jackson ignored the question. "I suppose you don't know Manchester very well yet. At least, not the kind of places I would like." He looked me in the eye. "Unless you've been well briefed."

That gave me a shock. I acted dumb. "The only places I know are the Manchester Arena, City Fitness, and the pizza place near my flat." What the fuck did he mean, *briefed*? Was he on to me? The idea flitted across my mind that he, too, was a mole in the Vaughan operation. Surely someone would have warned me. I raised my guard, while trying to look stupid and horny. "If you're hungry, I'll buy you a pizza after I fuck you."

"Oh, Greg, Greg," he said, in a mocking voice, "if you think I'm going back to whatever dump you call home for a shag and a takeaway, you are very much mistaken."

"Then what?"

"If you want easy meat, call Oz. He's desperate for you to fuck him again."

"You know about that?"

"Everyone knows about that. Oz can't keep his mouth shut."

"So, I fucked him. Is that a problem?"

"Not at all. That's what he's for."

"And what are you for?"

Again, he ignored me. "A word of advice. If you're going to work your way through the staff list, try to be discreet."

"Discreet? Me?" I squeezed my cock. "That's not my strong suit."

"I just mean that if you do things that you might not want the rest of the world to find out about . . ." He left the sentence unfinished.

"I don't give a shit who knows. I gave up worrying about that a long time ago."

"What about your family?"

I was about to say something dramatic like "my family is dead to me" but then I remembered I was Greg Cooper, not Dan Stagg, that I had a family not only back home in the States but also over here in the UK. Remember my English grandfather? My dossier contained all sorts of details that I had committed to memory—but Tom Jackson's ass had pushed that information to the back of my mind. I'd have to watch myself. The mission comes first, however deep undercover I go, however much I let myself become Greg Cooper. There's a divorced mother living over here, separated from my American father fifteen years ago. There's a half-sister in college I'm supposed to be in touch with.

"Thanks for the reminder, Jackson. Sometimes I let my cock do the thinking for me."

"That's fine for the Ozes of this world," said Jackson, "but now you're upgrading."

Of course—he's done his homework, reading the fake news that Ethan Oliver and his CIA buddies have been meticulously planting about me. He knows all about former USMC Captain Greg Cooper, his successes and his catastrophic failures. That's why I'm here, in the Vaughan camp. They see qualities that may be useful. I have a role to play in their plans. I'm not just a trainer and a useful piece of dick; I'm a headstrong racist with no visible morals and a talent for killing. Did Jackson know about Vaughan's involvement with the extreme right? Did he know what Vaughan was involved with in the US? Maybe not. But Jackson was smart. He could follow the money, and he could figure out—better than me, probably—that there were inconsistencies in Vaughan's accounting. Where did all the black money go? If anyone knew, Jackson did. This was why I was going to fuck him into submission. I would break him down until he was so addicted to my cock that he'd go into withdrawal when I withdrew. He'd tell me anything. This was a strategic fuck.

"Okay, man. I'll be guided by you. Where does a guy like Tom Jackson like to be taken?"

"That's more like it." He looked me up and down. "I don't suppose you have a suit, do you?"

"Of course not."

"What about your marine uniform?"

"You don't get to keep it when you're thrown out. It's not fancy dress."

"Shame."

"But I'm still a marine underneath."

"So I've seen." He smirked. What had he seen? Photos? Surveillance footage?

"So, where should I take you?"

"Is it too early for cocktails?"

Dan Stagg would have said something dismissive about cocktails, and suggested a beer in a blue-collar bar, but Greg Cooper was eager to please. "It's never too early for cocktails. I'll be on my best behavior."

"Not for too long, I hope," said Jackson, flagging down a taxi. Soon we were speeding through the drizzle to the city center. I put my arm along the back of the seat, allowing my thumb to brush the neatly clipped hair at the back of his neck. He didn't move away. In the enclosed space of the cab I could smell his fancy aftershave.

We arrived at our destination: a busy bar, customers coming and going, standing outside smoking, all of them well-dressed, smart casual, stylish haircuts. All of them men.

"A gay bar?"

"Of course a gay bar, Greg." Jackson tutted and rolled his eyes. "Where do you think I go when I'm off duty? Church?"

"Okay, okay." I followed him inside, watching the nods and smiles of greeting, fielding the appraising glances. "Hey, do you bring all your boyfriends in here?"

"You're not my boyfriend, Greg."

"Not yet." I took a handful of ass. He didn't push me away.

"Confident, aren't you?"

"Shouldn't I be?"

"Let's find out. Hi, darling," he said to the barman, a pretty little blond with a diamond stud earring. "Two sidecars, please. We'll be over there somewhere."

No money changed hands. I presumed that Jackson had an account, the bills settled by Vaughan.

"Right." He settled into a chair, loosened his tie and ran a hand over his immaculate hair, parted at the side in a precise line. A services haircut, as interpreted by an expensive salon. "I feel like I'm playing truant."

"I won't tell."

"I don't normally socialize with colleagues."

"I'm honored."

"You interest me, Greg."

"You interest me, Tom."

The drinks arrived. Jackson made chit-chat with the waiter, who kept glancing at me as if waiting for an introduction. None was forthcoming, and he disappeared.

"They're all dying to know who you are, Greg."

"Let 'em die."

"Mr. Vaughan wouldn't be seen dead in a place like this."

"Of course not," I said. "He's straight, isn't he."

Jackson wet his pretty pink lips in his drink, raising his eyebrows in reply.

"I'm not," I said. My voice was gruff; I had to clear my throat. Damn Jackson and his poise; he was making me nervous. He was too much in control of himself, and of me. I swigged my drink. Cocktails aren't my thing, but I was glad of the liquor.

"So, Greg, tell me all about yourself."

"What do you want to know? You've done your research."

"Like, why are you here?"

"In this bar? You know why."

"I mean in England. Particularly in Manchester."

I shrugged. "I'm one of those drifters you see in movies. Rides into town, nobody knows where he comes from . . ."

"But really, why?"

"I needed a fresh start."

"Because of what happened."

"It's not nice to see yourself all over the media as a racist and a thug."

"Even if you are?"

"You can't say anything these days without getting into trouble."

"So you came to England, hoping that we don't read the same news that you read at home."

"Something like that. Was I wrong?"

"Who knows?"

"You know everything that goes on."

"Someone has to. And that's why I'm glad to have this talk."

Shit—had he really brought me here just to talk? I'd assumed we were having a couple of aperitifs before the main event. Time to regain control of the situation.

"Okay. I'm listening."

"Do you mind," said Jackson, lowering his eyelids, "if I ask you a couple of direct questions?"

"Fire away."

"Did you come to the Craig Lukas fight because you wanted to get a job with Mr. Vaughan?"

"It was one of the reasons, yes."

"And did anyone tell you beforehand that we might be looking for new people?"

"No. I just assumed that a man like him could use a man like me."

"Why?"

Careful, Dan. "Alan Vaughan's the biggest promoter in the UK."

"Is he?"

"He's certainly one of them."

"Who else did you consider approaching?"

Damn it. That wasn't included in my briefing. "Okay, I'll be honest with you. I wound up in Manchester because . . ." Think quickly, Dan. "I got involved with a guy in London. I followed him up here. I thought . . . Well, it doesn't matter what I thought."

"You don't seem like the type to go trailing around after guys. I rather thought it would be the other way round."

"Usually is."

"What was so special about this one, then?"

Now, the kind of guys that Dan Stagg usually falls for are sweet, sexually voracious young men like Will, and Mark Williams back in Iraq . . . I had a sudden stab of pain around the heart. What would Greg Cooper do? "He was rich."

"You're a gold digger."

I shrugged. "A man has to eat."

"And what happened?"

"He disappeared."

"In a puff of smoke?"

"On a plane from Manchester airport. Without me."

"Oh, dear. You didn't play your hand well enough."

"I should learn from you, right?"

"What's that supposed to mean?"

"How to hold on to a man. You've done pretty well with Vaughan."

"If you think I'm going to give away trade secrets, you're very much mistaken." Jackson smiled his Cheshire Cat smile.

"I'm sure you're worth every penny."

Jackson sipped his drink. "I couldn't possibly comment."

"Don't worry," I said. "I don't want to know the details. I'm sure you're the best fuck in town, and I'm equally sure that you know way too much about Vaughan's business operations for him to let you go."

"He has complete trust in me."

"Even when he's out of town?"

"Going for a drink in my favorite bar isn't exactly a crime."

"True." I managed to look him in the eye. "And is that what we're here for?"

"What could you be talking about?"

I leaned towards him, and lowered my voice. "You

know perfectly well what I'm talking about. I want to fuck you up the ass."

He feigned surprise, and hand fluttering to his chest. "Oh! Captain Cooper!"

"Don't act the queen with me. It doesn't suit you."

That ruffled his feathers—which was my intention. "Fuck off." He knocked back the rest of his drink. "I don't take that kind of crap from anyone."

"Suit yourself. This place sucks." I stood up. "See you at the office, Jackson."

"Sit down, for God's sake. People are looking." He was flustered.

"Let 'em look."

"Okay, okay. I'm sorry." Jackson put his jacket on. "Let's go. It was a mistake to bring you here."

"I know what you're up to, Jackson. Vaughan told you to wiggle your ass at me, then do a bit of detective work while my guard's down. That's okay. I'd do it myself if someone like me turned up in the organization. Extreme vetting."

"It's not like that."

"Oh, sure." I walked towards the door; Jackson followed. "Thing is, Jackson, I can get laid without too much trouble. I can do without the interrogation. I did a lot of that kind of thing myself, you know, except in the marines it involved actual torture."

People were eavesdropping. Jackson hustled towards the door. Outside in the chilly street he said "Stop, Greg, please. I didn't mean to be a wanker."

"Really."

"I do like you." He was looking at his feet, passing cars, the sky—anything but me. I waited. "I just . . . the thing is, we have to be careful. There are aspects of all businesses that might be open to misrepresentation."

Time to show my hand. "Like porn websites."

"You know about that?"

"I'm surprised I'm not on them."

Jackson laughed nervously. "Perhaps you will be one day."

"Or do you just keep that footage in case I step out of line?"

Now he glanced up at me. "What's that supposed to mean?"

"I'm not sure yet. Surveillance cameras, I'm guessing. That's why Oz took me into that room. Am I right?"

Jackson said nothing. I started walking down the street, away from the crowds. Jackson caught up with me.

"Why are you so interested, Greg?"

"Did you think I was just some dumb hunk? I'm a military man, Jackson. We notice things. And you may think you're very clever and discreet in this operation, but it's wide open. Any asshole with a basic training in intelligence could figure out what's going on. I'm surprised the police aren't all over you."

"Really?"

"I guess they're part of Team Vaughan as well."

That shut him up. We walked on in silence for a while.

"So," I said, "where do we go now?"

"Depends what you want to do."

"You know what I want to do, Jackson. I want to fuck you. That's why I'm here. I don't want to discuss Alan Vaughan's business methods, and I don't want to listen to your attempts at detective work. I want to stick my dick inside you." I walked faster; Jackson had to jog to keep up.

"All right! I get the message. You don't like being questioned. But listen for a second . . ." He put a hand on my arm, pulled me to a halt. "You have to see it from our point of view."

"Our?"

"I work for a very important man."

"He's just a boxing promoter."

"He's very influential."

"You mean he has power over a lot of people."

"And I need to protect my own position."

"What position is that, exactly?"

"As an employee."

"So do I."

"I'm Mr. Vaughan's PA, and that means I have operational knowledge of all areas of the business."

"All areas?"

"Yes."

"Even the criminal ones?"

"I'm not supposed to discuss anything outside the office."

"What do you think I'm going to do? Run to the cops?"

"No." He was right there: I was going to run to the intelligence services.

"Even United States Marines know a bit about the commercial side of sex. We have to supplement our incomes somehow." This wasn't entirely untrue; I know a few grunts who have sold it, even a few who were stupid enough to model for porno. "And Alan Vaughan isn't the only gay man in the boxing world." Jackson opened his mouth to say something. "Okay, okay, he's not gay, he's married, let's take that as read. But I've come across a lot of men in that world who are there for the boys as much as for the sport. Empires have been built on it. I could name, what, four or five world champions who have fucked their way to the top. They're not gay either. They're famous. They're married. But they use what they've got, and there are plenty of men out there buying."

I was making this up as I went along, but Jackson seemed to be lapping it up.

"Let's just forget all this for a while, shall we?" said Jackson. "We can go back to my place if you like."

"Suits me. But promise me, no more questions."

"I'll try."

Jackson's apartment was on the 14th floor of a new tower block right by the waterfront in Salford Quays. No wonder he was protective of his status in Vaughan-Corp: this place must have cost a fortune, far more than a PA in his twenties had any chance of earning. Presumably it belonged to Vaughan, in fact if not in name. It didn't take us long to get naked and into the king-size bed. Once he shut up and took his clothes off, Jackson was a much more attractive proposition. His body was perfectly designed for the pleasure of men: firm, sculpted, smooth skin, a round ass, and a stiff cock that curved upwards like a banana. No wonder he ensured Vaughan's patronage. We'd been making out for twenty minutes, kissing and sucking, when I started to get my fingers into his asshole.

"I . . . I don't get fucked."

That stopped me in my tracks. "What?"

"Mr. Vaughan doesn't like . . . that stuff."

"You are kidding me, right?"

"No. We don't do it. He's kind of . . . fastidious about it."

"Fastidious?" I burst out laughing. "You cannot be serious."

Jackson hid his face in the pillow. My fingers were still applying gentle pressure to his tight little hole. I reached underneath him to check he was still hard. He was.

"What do you do, then?"

"I suck him."

"Yeah, of course. Go on."

"I . . . show off." He was gently pumping into my hand.

"Is that all?"

"Sometimes he gets me to do stuff with another guy."

"And he watches? Or joins in?"

"Mostly watches."

"Is he impotent?"

"No. I mean, he comes. But he's kind of . . . I don't know. Repressed."

"And what about this ass, then? Does that never get anything?"

"I use toys on myself."

"With him, or on your own?"

"On my own. Mr. Vaughan doesn't like . . . he's very squeamish about . . . you know."

"Shit."

He stopped pumping. "Yes."

"Okay." I let go of his cock and ass, and rolled away. "Well that's really killed the moment, hasn't it?"

"Sorry." He sat up, red-faced and crestfallen. "Not what you were expecting, am I?"

"What do you mean?"

"I'm not the cocky little fuck you thought I was."

"Perhaps not." I put a hand on his thigh. "I like you better for that."

"Really?"

"I thought Tom Jackson was a bit too good to be true."

"Thanks." He shifted across the bed and lay next to me, stroking my hairy stomach. "The truth is, I'm not actually that experienced."

"Are you for real?"

"Before Mr. Vaughan I didn't really have boyfriends. One or two guys of my own age that I fooled around with, but . . ."

"Please don't tell me that you've never been fucked."

Jackson moved in closer, and buried his face in my armpit.

"Christ. A virgin."

We lay like that for a while, each waiting for the other to start. I lost patience first.

"Okay, baby. I'm going to take it slow. Are you sure you want it?"

"Yes."

"You know it's going to hurt, right?"

"I don't care." Jackson's hand was on my cock, bringing me back to full stiffness. "I want you inside me, Greg."

"I'll take it easy. If it doesn't work out, I'll stop." *Like hell*, I thought. "And you mustn't worry about Vaughan. He doesn't own you."

"He does."

"He can't even fuck you. Why do you stick around?"

Jackson spoke in a small voice, half-buried in my hairy pit. "He's very generous."

"And you know what that makes you?"

"Yes." He was breathing heavily. "You don't need to tell me."

"Shall we just do what we came here for?"

In reply, Jackson worked down my chest and stomach and started sucking my cock. I reached around and played with his ass; the idea of taking his cherry was working its usual magic. I know it's predictable, but I've always taken great pleasure in showing guys what they've been missing.

"Ready?"

"As ready as I'll ever be," said Jackson.

"Hold it. Let me get condoms."

"Oh. Right."

Did he seriously think I was going in bareback? I'd have to watch myself around Vaughan's boys. Their need for sex outstripped their understanding of health issues. I'm old-school: I don't mess around. Condoms every time.

I rubbered up—Jackson watched with fascination, and couldn't stop stroking the thin, stretched latex—then got two fingers, a large blob of lube, and a minute hi-spec tracking device inside his silky rectum. He moaned and squirmed, precum drooling out of his cock in a thick silver thread. If he wasn't ready now, he never would be. I pushed him down on his back, scooped up his legs behind the knees, and pressed my cock into position. He looked good, all tensed definition, his tits hard, his balls tight. Even his perfect hair was a bit messed up, which made my dick throb. Better get inside him.

It wasn't easy. Even going slow, he was tight. I told him over and over to relax, but the pain made him clench and tighten. Eventually I was in. Jackson's eyes were screwed up, his jaw like a vice, and his dick shrivelled to an acorn. This would not do.

"Want me to stop?"

He said "no" through gritted teeth.

"Come on. This isn't fun for you." It wasn't great for me either; it felt like I was fucking a bag of rocks.

"Give me a minute, Greg. I . . . I want it. Please. Don't take it out now."

I stayed inside him, gently stroking his legs, reaching forward to run my fingers over his face. He kissed them, slipped his lips around them, sucked them. I murmured "good boy, good boy" a few times, and that had the desired effect. The clamp around my dick loosened, and the blood started to return to Jackson's cock. It shifted and started to lengthen. He moaned a couple of times, feeling the pleasure rather than the pain. After a couple of minutes he was fully hard, and starting to move against me.

We didn't need words. I fucked him slowly at first. There was a look of intense surprise on his face. I would have laughed, but I didn't want to spoil things again.

It didn't last long. Jackson was whimpering, crying out, and finally his hand went to his cock and started to jerk it. Ten seconds later, thick jets of cum were squirting over his tight belly and chest. I pushed myself in to the hilt and emptied my balls into the condom. Fireworks were going off behind my eyelids. My toes were slipping on the carpet, I was pushing so hard.

We stayed like that for a few minutes, unwilling to break the spell.

It hurt him when I pulled out, even taking it as slowly as possible. The tracking device must have been embedded half way up Jackson's digestive tract, I thought with satisfaction.

We got into the bed and I held him while his breathing slowed. I thought he was sobbing at one point; I said nothing, just held him tighter, kissed his jaw, and stroked his stomach. We slept for a while, and when I woke he was sucking my cock.

10

I was due in work at seven for a personal training session. That was four hours away. I walked home. I needed to clear my head. What I thought would be a slick, heartless fuck turned out to be something much more complicated. Now it was Jackson I wanted to rescue from a life of sexual servitude. I pictured Vaughan as a self-loathing, impotent sadist, Jackson as the butterfly caught in his web, and me as the knight in shining armor . . . My metaphors were as mixed up as my brain. I was falling in love with everyone I fucked. Oz, Kieran, Joshua, Dakota, Jackson . . . Luiz in the hospital, Reeve and Radek at MI6, even Ethan Oliver, the CIA agent who I hadn't laid a finger on . . . What was happening? Surely the main point of Greg Cooper was that he didn't give a shit about anyone except himself.

You'll be nodding your head at this point and saying "But Dan, you just went through a near-death experience, you lost someone you cared for, this Mark Williams you've mentioned a couple of times but seem reluctant to talk about, you're experiencing post-traumatic shock, you should not have been sent on this mission so soon."

Well, congratulations, smart-ass. You're right. USMC, the FBI, the CIA, and MI6, all those letters and numbers who controlled me, had thrown me into Vaughan's world like a lighted match into a can of gasoline. Maybe that was their intention. Maybe my emotional instability is what they wanted—not my prowess at killing and fucking. I wouldn't put it past them. Let's set up an explosive situation and see what comes out of the wreckage.

I was brooding over this as I walked through the quiet city. All I had to do was throw my cell phone into the canal and that was the end of it. Dan Stagg, Greg Cooper, off radar. I could keep on walking, get on a plane, go anywhere, be anyone I wanted to be. Okay, they'd catch up with me sooner or later: for all I knew, they had a tracking device in me, perhaps in one of the bits of metalwork that held my smashed right leg together. I'd be lying in bed with some twenty-year-old in Fiji or China or Greenland or some tiny fucking rock in the middle of the Pacific Ocean, and there would be a knock on the door, they'd reel me back in, not because they needed me but because when you know too much you can never, ever escape . . .

I was walking fast, talking to myself in the rhythm of my footsteps, Oz, Kieran, Joshua, Dakota, Jackson, Luiz, Oliver, Reeve . . . Try it. It makes quite a nice little sing-song rhyme. Over and over, until other thoughts were crowded out, and I arrived at the apartment with a clearer head.

I logged on to my secure email account and registered the new tracking device up Jackson's butt (code-name: TABLECLOTH). There was email in my inbox that contained orders. Heavily encrypted and bristling with code words, it translated as:

Intelligence sources point to November 12 as likely date of focus activity. Target unconfirmed military base New Hampshire. Check against subject's known itinerary. Security code highest.

November 12. Today was the ninth. Three days away. And where was Alan Vaughan—the "subject"? Supposedly in Miami, finalizing plans for the Craig Lukas fight. But his real whereabouts? Unknown to me, and presumably unknown to the intelligence services. Nobody had a tracking device up Vaughan's ass, and it sounded as if he had slipped past the watching eyes of homeland security. In short, he could be anywhere, talking to anyone.

Jackson would know the official itinerary, and after last night I was pretty sure he'd share it with me. It could be checked and verified. If Vaughan had gone off radar, we'd soon know.

I was in the shower when the intercom buzzed. I wrapped a towel around myself and answered.

"Greg? Oh, thank God. Let me in, please. It's Oz."

Oz was wired, hands shaking, pupils too big. If you'd seen him walking down the street you'd have thought he was some kid coming home from a nightclub. But I knew enough about Oz's nocturnal activities to suspect a different scenario. He stopped in the hallway when he saw me, glancing around as if he wanted to run.

"It's okay buddy. Come on in."

I didn't ask how he knew my address. Perhaps he accessed my file at City Fitness. Perhaps he'd been stalking me. I got him into the apartment and locked the door.

"What's wrong?"

"Greg . . . fuck . . ." He wiped his hands over his face, as if he was getting rid of cobwebs. "I'm so fucked up . . . Shit . . ." He laughed, a high, nervous cackle. "I'm off my fucking face."

"What have you taken?"

"G."

"How much?"

He danced around on the balls of his toes like a fighter, hands up to protect his face, hissing through his teeth.

"Oz. Oz!" I grabbed his wrists. "Stop it. Come and sit down." His skin was clammy. Should I call an ambulance?

He went limp, letting his weight fall against my body. The towel started to slip. "Oh, man . . . That feels nice . . ." He started kissing my chest, rubbing his stubbly face against it. "Are you going to fuck me, Greg? Please. I really want you to fuck me." He was slurring a bit, and there was a lot of saliva coming out with the words. I've done some bad things in my time, but fucking guys who are likely to slip into a coma wasn't about to be added to the list. I got him to the sofa, where he slumped on his side and started snoring. I know enough about party drugs to realize it's not a good idea to let people fall asleep. I pulled Oz upright and sat with an arm around his shoulders. My towel was long gone.

"Oz, listen to me. Open your eyes. That's it. Now look at me. Try to focus." His eyes were rolling back in his head. Had he done this to himself, or had someone administered the overdose? How many of Vaughan's boys disappeared? I had heard of at least one. No body, no missing persons report, probably no family or friends to bother. Vaughan chose his boys carefully: the vulnerable, the dispossessed. Oz was the most vulnerable of all. A gay Muslim? Not an easy road to travel. Thrown out and disowned, or brought up in foster care. Cannon fodder for the likes of Alan Vaughan.

"Greg . . . Is that you? Greg!" A big goofy smile broke out on Oz's face. "Oh, it's great to see you, man. How are . . ." His voice trailed into incoherence and he slumped further down, his cheek against my stomach. I grabbed him under the armpits and walked him around the room in a lurching slow dance. He was humming, occasionally speaking, but at least he was not sleeping.

Suddenly Oz's body tensed, his eyes opened wide and he said, "I'm gonna puke." I threw him over my shoulder and made it to the bathroom just as the first trails of vomit were hitting my back. Most of it, thank God, went in the bathtub.

Oz was on his knees, tears were running from his eyes, snot bubbling from his nose. I turned on the shower, washed the puke away, and started trying to undress him. He was still limp, but consciousness was returning. Perhaps throwing up had saved his life. Now he was groaning rather than babbling; pain, I always think, is an indication of consciousness.

He was a mess: as well as the vomit, there was mud and dried blood. He'd fallen over, or been thrown out of somewhere, or been in a fight. Fucked up on drugs, he wouldn't have been able to defend himself.

"Stand up, Oz."

I pulled him to his feet, pulled his T-shirt over his head. He swayed but didn't fall. I knelt, pulled off his shoes and socks, pulled down his pants. There were grazes and bruises on his buttocks and thighs, as if he'd been beaten or dragged across a floor.

Interrogation could wait; first I had to get him cleaned up, and make sure he wasn't going to slip into a coma. A shower was too risky in his condition; I put the plug in the bath and turned on the taps. While it was running I held Oz in my arms. He was cold, his teeth starting to chatter. "Come on. It's okay. You're safe now." Poor bastard; the only comfort he had in this world was a dead man.

I lowered him into the water. He stretched out, sighed, and relaxed. He'd live.

"My head hurts."

"I'm not surprised. What happened to you, Oz?"

"I don't know. I got into a fight." He wiped his mouth with the back of his hand; there was a smear of blood.

"Who did this to you?"

"I don't know." His voice sounded hopeless.

"I don't believe you."

He looked up at me, fear in his eyes. "What?"

"You know what happened, and you know who did it. Tell me."

"I was walking along the street and two guys jumped me. I swear."

"You're not a very good liar, Oz."

"Please, can we just . . ." He lowered himself into the water till it covered his ears.

I waited for him to come up. "So, you were attacked in the street."

"Yeah." He busied himself with soap, washing his face and armpits. "Two guys. Maybe three."

"Did you see their faces?"

"No."

"And where exactly did it happen? Where were you?"

"I don't know. I've . . . had a few drinks."

"You said G."

"That, yeah, that too."

"We'd better call the police."

"No way. That's not necessary. I mean I'm fine, I'm all right."

"You've been seriously assaulted. I'm going to call them right now."

Oz said nothing.

"Do you think you'll be sober enough to give them a statement?"

He put his hands over his face.

"The next person might actually get killed. You don't want that on your conscience, do you? When you could have stopped it."

"Okay, okay!" He was shouting, his face distorted with anger. "I wasn't attacked."

"That's better. Now tell me what really happened."

"I can't."

"I'll tell you, then. You were sent out to a client. One of those rich guys in the suburbs, I guess. You were given some drugs, and things got rough. You were too stoned to do anything about it." I put a hand into the water and felt his legs and ass, where the injuries were. He winced. "Looks like they hurt you pretty bad."

"You know, then."

"What?"

"About the clients."

"Of course I fucking know, Oz. I'm part of the team."

"I thought you were on our side."

I had to be careful; Oz wasn't the brightest of boys, but I couldn't let him know that I was working against Vaughan rather than for him. "We have to protect our assets." I was still stroking his asset under water. I hoped I'd get to fuck him again, under happier circumstances.

Oz looked up at me with big puppy-dog eyes. His dick was stirring; that must have been some seriously strong shit they gave him. "I wish you'd look after me."

"Is that why you came here?"

"I don't know, Greg. I don't know anything anymore." He sounded close to tears. "I thought I was getting into this because it would give me a chance at fighting. But . . ."

"Didn't turn out that way, huh?"

"I just want to . . ."

"What?"

Oz closed his eyes, and whispered. "I want to feel safe."

This was not what I needed. Dan Stagg wanted to take in the little wounded puppy and nurse him back to health. Greg Cooper had no shits to give, and would betray Oz to his employers if he stepped out of line.

"If the client has overstepped any boundaries, I'll take the necessary action." I was improvising, but it sounded convincing. Bullshit comes naturally. "In the meantime, you'd better stay here."

"Can I? Really?"

"I've got to go to work soon. You can hang out till I get back. How are you feeling?"

"Terrible."

"Is the stuff wearing off?"

"I suppose so." Oz's dick was semi-erect, and my hand still appeared to be in the water. "Not completely."

I retrieved my hand and wiped it on a towel. I was still naked, and despite everything I was getting hard too. "Do you still feel stoned?"

"No. I think I puked it up."

"Okay. Get out of the bath."

He stood, I stood, and both our cocks stood as well. Oz stepped out on to the mat, and into my arms. I held him, letting our dicks press together—and that was as far as I allowed it to go. "Not now, dude. We need to get you into bed."

"With you."

"I'll join you later." I held him at arm's length, our cocks reaching out to each other.

"Will you?"

"I promise."

"They all promise."

I thought of all the people that had let him down—parents, teachers, social workers, carers, clients—all the users and abusers, and I was the last in the line. How could I help him, without betraying myself? For all I knew, Oz was bait in a trap.

I stepped away and passed him a towel.

"Dry yourself. I'll find you something to wear. Your old stuff can go in the trash."

I busied myself in the bedroom, and got dressed, despite my cock's attempts to prevent me. I found pants and a sweater for Oz. He could sleep in those. He appeared in the doorway dry, hairy, and fully erect. I threw the clothes at him; the sweater hooked itself over his cock and hung there.

"Put that away, Oz. It's just the G talking."

"It's not, Greg. You know it's not. Please. Hold me . . ."

He held out his arms. Poor bastard.

I moved away, tried to sound angry but had to clear my throat. "Not . . . not now, Oz. You need to rest, and I need to work. I'll be back around twelve. Think you can stay out of trouble till then?"

He put the clothes on. "I suppose so."

"There's food in the fridge. You can make yourself coffee."

"Okay."

"Don't answer the door and don't make any calls. There's nothing worth stealing, by the way." I tried to make it sound like a joke.

"I'm not a fucking thief."

"Jesus, calm down. Now get into bed."

"Get in with me. Please. I just need you to . . ."

We lay on the bed together for a while, and I held him in my arms. He kissed my neck, my chin, he pressed his dick into me, he fidgeted around like a horny cat, and eventually settled. "There you go. That's enough. Now be good, and go to sleep." I got up, kissed him on the forehead, and prepared to leave. My phone was safe in my pocket. There were no incriminating items in the apartment; I carried the tracking devices with me at all times. No printouts, no computers, nothing that could be read or hacked.

I locked the door behind me, already looking forward to getting home in a few hours and giving

Oz—a refreshed, sober Oz—what he so badly needed.

And that was the last time I saw him alive.

City Fitness opened for business at five in the morning, for those early birds who think that an hour of messing around with weights before they sit in the office all day is going to get them fit. By the time I got there at 6:45 the place was buzzing, all the treadmills busy, the music turned up way too high, a lot of grunting and pumping in the free weights area. Jackson was at his desk, picture perfect, not a hair out of place, showing no signs of his sleepless night. His powers of recovery were impressive.

There was no one else in the room so I said, "Morning, hot stuff," and leaned against the wall, arms crossed, pushing my biceps up. Only a few hours ago Jackson had been licking them while I pumped into his hole from behind.

Jackson barely looked up from the papers on his desk.

"Morning, Greg." His voice was neutral, his face blank.

"How are you?"

"Fine."

He was trying to freeze me out.

"Want to get a coffee later?"

He scowled. "I'm very busy at the moment, as you can probably see."

"Running the empire?"

"Something like that. So if you don't mind . . ."

"What's the big event?"

"What?"

"This thing you've been planning for the last few

days, while Vaughan's been away. Not a fight. Something else."

"None of your business."

"Okay." I turned to go. "Suit yourself."

"Although, actually . . ." His tone changed. "Close the door for a minute, Greg."

I did as I was told. "So?"

"I have a problem, and you might be the solution."

"I was last night."

He brushed that away with an impatient gesture. "I have a job for you."

"Go on." Was I about to be pimped?

"Can you wrestle?"

That was unexpected. "Wrestle? What, you mean like . . ."

"Holds, throws, all that stuff."

"Of course I can wrestle."

"Okay." He thought for a while, drumming his pen against the desktop. "You're not busy tonight."

"I don't think I have any plans."

"Good. I need you for a match."

"What's the venue?"

"It's a private event."

"I see. That kind of wrestling match."

"We put on events for some of our valued clients and their invited guests."

"You don't have to bullshit me, Jackson. What's the deal? Some rich guy wants to be beaten up?"

"It's genuine wrestling. Four contestants. Two heats and a final."

"And one of your guys dropped out?"

"That's it."

"Why?"

"That doesn't concern you."

I raised an eyebrow, and waited.

"Okay, Greg. I suppose I have to spell it out to you."

"That might be best."

He lowered his voice. "The winners fuck the losers."

"While the rich old guys sit around and watch."

"Yes."

"That's a bit risky for the Vaughan Corporation to be involved with."

"Stop calling it the Vaughan Corporation, Greg. There's no such thing."

"I keep forgetting. He's just a boxing promoter. A straight, married boxing promoter."

Jackson's professional mask was back in place. "Are you sure you really fit in here, Greg?"

Ah, threatening me with the sack. "No, I'm not."

That took the wind out of his sails. Presumably most of the guys at City Fitness quaked in their boots if they thought they might lose their jobs, and, more importantly, their connection to Alan Vaughan. They'd do anything, swallow any humiliation, for that shot at the big time. Not Greg Cooper.

"The thing is, Jackson, I like to know what I'm getting involved with. If I'm going to be a whore . . ."

"Have you been spying?"

"Spying? Jesus, a child could see it. Vaughan's running a sex ring. That's what the papers would call it, right? Recruiting vulnerable young men, and exploiting them."

"That's not how it is at all."

"Yeah. Right."

I could hear the cogs turning in Jackson's brain. In

Vaughan's absence, he had to make decisions—the boss trusted him enough for that—and right now he was calculating whether or not to take me into his confidence. Was I a security threat? With no leverage in terms of dismissal or blackmail, how could my discretion be assured? What was to stop me going straight to the police? Boys like Oz would never talk to the cops: they had too much to hide. And if they didn't when they first arrived at City Fitness, they soon did. Photoshoots, secret videos, implication in blackmail, drugs, and prostitution . . . It would take a brave man to blow the whistle on all of that. And I knew what happened to those who did. They disappeared.

"It's true that we provide services for some of our investors that might appear . . . unorthodox to outsiders," said Jackson, choosing his words with care.

"You mean boys for rich old men."

He pursed his lips. He hadn't been so fastidious this morning, when he was begging me to come in his mouth. "We prefer to call it companionship."

"I bet you do."

"And if you don't have any problems with that . . ."

"What exactly do you want, Jackson? Let's cut the crap."

"I need to be confident in your . . ."

"Oh, for fuck's sake. You want to know if I'll go to the cops."

"That's one thing."

"Or sell my story to the media."

"That's another."

"Anything else, while we're at it?"

"You won't try any . . . independent transactions."

"Blackmail, you mean?"

He smiled. "Well?"

"I signed a contract, remember? It's all covered in there."

"Then I'm going to have to trust you, aren't I?"

"What will Vaughan say?"

"Mr. Vaughan thinks you're a safe bet."

"And what if he finds out I've fucked his boyfriend?"

Jackson blushed. "He won't find out. Will he?"

"Not from me."

"You put me in a very difficult position, Greg."

"I put you in a lot of positions."

"Very funny." He picked a hair off my shoulder with his fingertips, brushed his hand against my jaw. "You're a dangerous man."

"That's right."

"And I might be making a big mistake."

"You don't need Vaughan. You can do better."

"You mean you?"

"I can't afford an expensive piece of goods like you. But there are plenty of men who can. Or you could just get an honest job."

Jackson hung his head. When he looked up, his face was pale, his brows contracted. "Don't lecture me."

"Oh, Jesus." I kissed him on the lips. "You're hard fucking work, Jackson, you know that? Now, what about this wrestling match? Do you want me to do it, or not?"

"You'd be helping me a lot if you did."

"And who do I have to fuck?"

"There are three other fighters. Kieran, Dakota, and Oz."

I tried not to react when he mentioned Oz. "And who am I replacing?"

"Craig Lukas."

"What? You're fucking kidding me. I didn't think he was on the . . . I mean, in the companionship program."

"All City Fitness employees help out when necessary. And these are very special clients."

"So why isn't he doing it?"

"He's being . . . difficult."

"Really? With this big fight coming up? I'd have thought he'd be eager to please."

"That's why Mr. Vaughan is flying back tomorrow. He's cut his meetings short."

"Does that mean the American fight isn't going ahead?"

"I won't know until Mr. Vaughan gets back from Florida. He will brief me then."

"Florida? Is that where he's been?"

"Yes, of course."

Like hell; he's somewhere up in New Hampshire building bombs with crazy extremists. This doesn't add up. "Who's his opponent, by the way? Anyone I've heard of?"

"I don't remember the name off the top of my head."

"I'm sure it'll come to you."

He was saved further embarrassment by a phone call.

"Yes! Hi, Mr. Vaughan!" Jackson signalled me to stay put. "Yes I have. Yes. Absolutely. He's here right now. No, I'm sure. Do you want to speak to him? Oh, okay. Well, thanks. See you tomorrow. You're welcome. Bye." He ended the call. "Mr. Vaughan is pleased that you're on board."

"And what was he asking? Whether you've done all the background security checks?"

"That sort of thing."

"What do you guys think I am? An undercover cop?"

"We can't afford to take risks."

"Does this mean you trust me then?"

"Mr. Vaughan trusts you, that's all that matters."

"And will I get to fuck you again?"

"Not if you keep your client waiting. Now get out of here, and let me get on with arrangements for this evening."

It was nearly twelve when I checked my phone for messages. Nothing from Oz. Poor bastard must be sleeping it off. I had a few hours to kill: better check up on him. Perhaps, despite my best efforts, he was in a coma.

I took a taxi back to my apartment, my heart beating fast, half expecting to find him choked to death on his own vomit.

"Oz? Oz!" My voice sounded dead in the stillness of the apartment. The empty apartment. Oz had gone, the bed was made, the bathroom clean, the towels dry. There was no evidence of his ever having been there.

11

I tried his phone. A message said that the number was unavailable. I texted him—*call me asap, are you ok, where are you*—but there was no response. With a growing sense of dread, I emailed MI6. Panoply had gone missing. Tracking device obsolete. Cell phone not responding. I gave them the number, in the hope they could work some magic. I did not tell them that I had started to care about Oz. Did someone know that he had been telling me things about Vaughan's business dealings? Last night he'd been beaten and drugged— was that a warning, or a failed attempt at murder? Was it a message to me—this is what happens to people who snitch? Had they come for him?

Why would Vaughan care so much about Oz? How could he be a threat? Had he told me more than I realized?

I racked my brains. Had he said anything about America, or about the Lukas fight? Anything at all that might suggest Vaughan was communicating with terrorist groups in the US? Sure, he told me about the sex work, he turned up at my apartment off his head on drugs, but that was hardly classified information. Jackson himself, the most trusted of Vaughan's inner circle, was recruiting me into the same profession. Perhaps Oz was just the victim of a sex game that had gone too far. He came running to me, and then, when he woke, he tidied up and disappeared. Perhaps he'd run away from all of us—including me. Maybe, by now, he was far away, starting a new life.

But there was another, more compelling theory. Oz, like other Vaughan boys before him, had been disposed of. He was out of control, and that constituted a threat to the whole Vaughan operation. Whatever happened last night, someone had decided to terminate him.

Why hadn't I stuck another tracking device inside him? Oh, shit, Dan, you're a thoughtless bastard. This made me angry for about ten minutes. Then I got myself back on mission.

Time to get ready for the show. Get into character. For Greg Cooper, this was a chance to get some extra pussy and to ingratiate himself with Alan Vaughan. To prove that he was trustworthy, to penetrate the inner circle of the organization. A little light wrestling, which he would easily win, and three holes to fuck. Kieran, Dakota, and Oz—that's what I'd been told, and that was what I must expect. Maybe, despite my fears, Oz would show up.

I sat on the floor and cleared my head. Focus on your goals, Greg. Focus on their holes. I thought about each of the boys, lying defeated on the mat as I pinned them, my cock ready to slip inside them, one after the other, and the faces out there in the dark watching me, wishing they could be me. Kieran, with his pale skin, his freckles, his rose-pink nipples. Dakota, all cocky arrogance until the dick was inside him, then he squirmed around like a cat in heat. And Oz . . . no, Greg, don't let yourself worry, just focus on that hairy ass, the cheeks held open, his eyes closed, black eyelashes fluttering as he feels me opening him up, pain and pleasure on his face . . .

My cock was hard, my mind was clear, and that was the moment when the balance tipped in favor of Greg Cooper. Dan Stagg was dead, wasn't he? Let him stay that way.

I got to City Fitness at five; I was early. Jackson called me into the office.

"Good news," he said. "Craig Lukas is back in the match."

"So you don't need me."

"Oh, yes, we need you. Mr. Vaughan says it's a dream lineup. You and Lukas versus Kieran and Dakota. The audience will love it."

"What about Oz?" Damn: the words were out before I could stop them.

"We bumped him. He was always the weak link in the chain. He's no good at fighting."

Think like Greg Cooper. Don't show concern. "He's a good fuck, though. Very good." Jackson looked nettled by that remark. "One of the best, in fact."

"I'm not the jealous type, so don't try."

"Don't worry, boy. There's plenty of me to go around. You'll always be top of the list." I grabbed his ass and pulled him towards me. "Want a little taste?"

"Are you fucking mad?" Jackson's face was dark with anger, or possibly lust. Either one suited me.

"Okay, okay. What can I do to help? Is there a van that needs loading, or anything?"

"You can help the others get ready."

"What does that involve?"

"You should know better than anyone. Make sure they're washed and . . . you know. Clean."

"Seriously? You want us to douche?"

"You'll find the equipment in there." He jabbed a duffel with his expensively shod toe. "Mr. Vaughan insists that these events are hygienic."

"Fuck me. He's scared of a bit of shit?"

"It's not just him. It's the clients."

"I fucking hate closet cases." Jackson said nothing. "Don't you?"

"I'm not paid to think," whispered Jackson. "Now please just . . . get on with something, and leave me alone."

I went out to reception to wait for my fellow sportsmen, content that I'd found the chink in Jackson's armor. He was growing tired of the lies and evasions of Vaughan's world. Money is a great anesthetic, but like all anesthetics, it wears off.

Kieran and Dakota arrived together, and I sent them off to the bathrooms with their little individual enema kits. Neither of them complained.

Craig Lukas was late. Six thirty, six forty-five, seven o'clock came and went. The party was due to start at eight, and it was a half hour ride out to the suburbs. If Lukas didn't get here soon, we were one man down. An idea occurred to me. I went through to the office.

"Lukas isn't here."

"Oh, for fuck's sake." Jackson was furious.

"Call Oz instead. He'll be fine. I'll make it look real."

"No, no, he's . . . on another job." There was just enough hesitation to confirm my fears: Oz had been removed. "Lukas will be here."

"How are you going to make that happen, Jackson? You going to wave your magic wand?"

"If you don't mind, I have a few calls to make."

I didn't move.

"Private calls." He pointed towards the door. I let him sweat for a minute, then left him to it. He couldn't be calling Vaughan, who was, as far as I knew, in transit over the Atlantic. What was the urgent, secret business? Last-minute party arrangements? Or was there more? Was Jackson deeper into Vaughan's criminal activities than he let on?

Lukas arrived, scowling, hunched, like an angry child. He was wearing a suit and tie, as if he'd just been dragged away from a board meeting. Beads of sweat were shining on his forehead.

I went on the attack. "Where the fuck have you been? You're over an hour late."

Lukas bunched up his fists and lowered his brow, then thought better of it. Someone—I suspected Vaughan himself—had done a good job of persuading him that cooperation would be very much in his interests.

He said "I'm sorry," and stared at the carpet.

"You'd better go to the bathroom, and make it fast." I handed him an enema kit.

"What the fuck is this?"

"You know what it is. Do you want to do it yourself, or shall I do it for you?"

"I won't fucking need it." Ah—he knew the rules, then. Loser gets fucked. He was planning on beating me. But my combat training could whip his boxing any day of the week, and he knew it.

"I don't think our client will be very happy if you shit all over his expensive carpet."

Poor bastard looked as if he was going to burst into tears, but he trotted off to the bathroom like a good boy. Kieran and Dakota looked at me with something like reverence on their faces.

The party was in full swing by the time we got there; nobody seemed to notice that we were late. They were all in the lounge—or one of the lounges, there seemed to be several of them. As we unloaded the gear (crash mats, clothing, towels, oil, a set of scales borrowed from the gym) we could hear them talking, laughing, the braying sound of a large group of men. Captains of industry, successful retailers, senior police officers, football managers: it looked like a Masonic lodge. I glimpsed them through the half-open sliding doors, all silver hair, shiny foreheads, cashmere sweaters and open-necked shirts. There was a whiff of aftershave and cigars, a clink of glasses, the popping of corks. Vaughan knew how to entertain. A waiter in tight black pants, white shirt, and black vest came strutting through the hallway with a tray of empty glasses perched in his upturned hand; I wondered if he, too, was on the menu.

We set up in the dining room. Chairs had been pushed to one end and arranged in a semicircle, and the table was against the wall. This left a large space for the performance. We laid out eight large mats, and dragged the scales into position near the chairs. They were the old-fashioned type with a vertical stand, a horizontal crossbar, and sliding weights. I had been instructed to get them right up at the front, near the audience.

When everything was in place, we got changed in a small room off the main entrance hall. Our outfits were the Lycra wrestling singlets that you're probably familiar with from adult websites: one-piece with integral shorts, so tight that they leave nothing to the imagination. I checked the labels; they were all small. Pulling the shoulder straps up had the effect of pushing the cock and balls into extreme relief.

Kieran and Dakota were clowning around, popping their dicks out of the leg holes, wiggling their asses around; they were more than ready to go out there and entertain. Lukas was finding it harder to get into the party spirit.

"This is fucking humiliating," he said, his Welsh accent more pronounced than usual. "I'm not a fucking whore."

"Of course you're not," I said. "You're not getting paid for this."

Lukas looked confused, his brows contracted. He was kind of dumb, like most boxers. All those blows to the head. He stood there in his shorts and T-shirt, unwilling to make the final change.

"Hey, cheer up," I said, as I stepped into my singlet. My dick was swinging around. "What's the worst that could happen? You get this up your ass."

"Fuck off."

"Oh, it's not so bad. Is it boys?"

Kieran and Dakota grinned and sniggered, waiting for Lukas to get naked.

"What? You've . . . both of them?"

"Yes. Although not at the same time. Yet."

"Jesus." Lukas scowled, as if trying to figure out how that might work.

"Come on, Craig," said Dakota, turning around and waggling his ass towards Lukas, "it's your turn tonight. Better than any pussy you've had."

"Oh, fuck off," Lukas repeated, although he didn't sound too sincere. His eyes followed Dakota's ass up and down, side to side. He licked his lips and cleared his throat.

"And what about this one," I said, taking Kieran's chin in my hand. "Like getting your dick in here?" I rubbed his lips with my thumb, and he started sucking. "Bet you'd like that."

Lukas still looked angry, but his cock told a different story. It was obviously hard, like a rolling pin down his shorts, and getting wet.

"You need some help getting changed? I'm sure the boys will oblige."

He didn't have time to say no before Kieran was on his knees, pulling Lukas's underpants down over his huge, hairy thighs. His cock sprang straight out, precum glistening at the tip. Kieran took the shaft in his hand, looked up at Lukas with those big blue eyes, and started licking the piss-slit. Dakota was rubbing himself through his Lycra shorts, and I was getting hard too.

"Okay, that's enough. Ding ding. End of round one. Dicks away, everyone. Kieran, let it go. On your feet. Lukas." I bunched up a bright red Lycra singlet, and threw it in his face. "Put this on, if you can get that thing into it."

He stripped off his T-shirt. His torso looked fine, the hair clipped close but still covering him from collarbone to crotch. "They won't have any cameras out there, will they?"

"No. This is a private affair. Nobody wants their picture going on social media."

"You sure?"

"Craig, the guys out there have even more to lose than you have, believe it or not."

Eventually, after a lot of wriggling and rearranging, we were all four of us squeezed into our outfits, two red (Lukas and Dakota), two blue (Kieran and me). I went through to the lounge. "Gentlemen, the contestants are ready, if you would like to make your way to the function room."

The event had been well organized. I'd been fully briefed with a running order, even a script. Vaughan knew what his clients wanted, and he trusted me to deliver it. If things went smoothly tonight, I was part of the inner circle.

There was a cheer, and an immediate surge of movement towards the dining room. I ran ahead and joined the guys on the mats. We warmed up with skipping ropes as the audience took their seats. There was fierce competition for the front row, the alpha males banishing the betas to the back.

When everyone was settled, I folded up my rope and stepped to the fore. "Gentlemen, we have three bouts for you tonight, two heats and a final. You will be responsible for deciding the result of each. When an overall winner has been declared, you will decide on the penalties for the losers. May I remind you that the use of cameras and recording equipment is strictly forbidden. If you have not already done so, please leave your phones and any other devices in the trays provided."

There was a certain amount of shuffling, and one or two smartphones were handed over to the waiter. The audience settled.

"But first—the weigh-in."

They cheered. This, I had been told, was one of the most important parts of the show. We were to be lined up, weighed, measured, prodded and poked like the pieces of meat we were.

"First, for the blue team, Kieran McAvoy, twenty-four years old."

Kieran stepped on to the scales, and I adjusted the weights. "Seventy-two kilos, gentlemen. That's 158 pounds. Just over eleven stone."

"Get him naked!" bellowed one of the guys in the front row, a heavyset sixtysomething with a red face and white hair. He'd obviously been enjoying the champagne. The rest of the audience cheered its approval. There were about twenty of them, ages fifty and up, behaving in exactly the rowdy manner that men display in strip clubs.

"You heard him, Kieran. Get it off."

Blushing, he pulled the straps over his shoulders and stepped out of the singlet as the audience roared its approval. There was a sheen of sweat on Kieran's pale skin, and his cock had shrunk to its smallest size. Hands reached out from the front row to touch him; those at the back stood up to get a better view.

"Now, gentlemen, I must remind you to treat the contestants with respect. You will be allowed to touch them"—more cheers—"but if anyone tries to hurt them, I would remind you that I am an ex-US Marine and I'm trained in all the more deadly forms of combat. Okay?"

There was a lot of nodding and clearing of throats.

"Now, Kieran. Step forward, please."

I steered him towards the outstretched hands. Fingertips touched his ridged stomach, his chest, his nipples. The bolder ones reached out and stroked his cock.

"Come and sit on my knee," said the loud, red-faced man. "Let's have a good look at you."

Kieran did as he was told, his ass on the man's knees, his body tilted back. The man ran his hands up and down Kieran's torso and legs, lingering over his cock. Kieran's eyes were closed, his lips parted. He was starting to get hard. Other hands joined in the groping until every part of Kieran's body was being stroked and squeezed. He shifted around, and extended his legs over the neighboring laps, lying back, thrusting his groin in the air. He was now fully hard, and didn't try to push away the hands that were exploring his ass.

"Next, we have Dakota, aged nineteen. Step up to the scales, Dakota." He was bouncing on the balls of his feet, making no attempt to disguise his erection. He couldn't wait to dive in. "Dakota is 75 kilos, 165 pounds." He stepped off the scales, and started stripping before he was even asked. His dick smacked up against his hard belly as he freed it from the Lycra. He worked the front row like a pro; presumably he had plenty of experience. I've seen go-go boys in New York gay bars who were less professional than Dakota. That girlfriend, if she existed, must be mighty broad-minded. He ran his hands down his chest, emphasizing the musculature, and he played with his hardening dick. Everyone was given one brief touch before he moved on, ruffling hair as he went. Kieran, meanwhile, had been lifted by several pairs of hands and was being passed through the air to the back row. His eyes were closed, head back, as he was kissed, licked, fingered, and stroked, giving himself over completely to the experience.

There was hardly any attention left when I announced the third contestant, but eyes turned as I said the name, and Craig Lukas himself stepped out of the shadows. Those who were not actively engaged with Dakota or Kieran gathered around the scales.

Lukas looked drugged. His mouth was slack, his eyes hooded, and he walked forward with a swaying, unsteady gait. He stepped on to the scales, his magnificent body gleaming under the lights. Hands reached out and touched him, stroking his arms, squeezing through the Lycra, even running up the solid length of his prick. Lukas stood immobile, head bowed, arms hanging by his sides, and did nothing to prevent the groping.

"Shall we undress him, gentlemen?"

An affirmative roar.

"Kieran! Dakota! If you could let them go, gentlemen, they have work to do." This was off-script, but I didn't think anyone would mind. The boys needed no further instructions. They stood on either side of the champion, pulling down his shoulder straps, rolling the Lycra down his torso, finally kneeling to pull the garment over his cock and down past his knees. When Lukas's dick finally bounced free there was a gasp, and then silence. It was a mighty big piece, and it throbbed up and down as it swung between his legs. Perhaps because of Lukas's celebrity status within the boxing world, nobody grabbed it right away.

"Now, gentlemen, to business. The first bout is between Craig Lukas for the red team, and Kieran McAvoy for the blue team. Freestyle. The first contestant to pin his opponent three times is the winner. No gouging, no biting, no scratching. And, of course, to make things more interesting . . ."

I took a bottle of baby oil and squirted it all over the mats.

"Gentlemen, take your places. And may the best man win."

There was no doubt, of course, as to who would prevail. We'd already seen this fight in a real boxing ring. I recognized some of the guests from the front row.

The oil made them lose their footing right away, and soon they were grappling on the floor, muscle sliding against muscle, Lukas's dark skin against Kieran's pale skin, hard cocks trapped between thighs, asses pulled open, holes exposed. I circled them, doing an impression of a referee, but really just enjoying the show. The crowd was silent, watching, breaths held.

Lukas pinned McAvoy within two minutes, pressing his biceps to the mat with his knees. Kieran winced in pain. Lukas's big hairy balls were just inches from his face. For all his scowling and complaints, Lukas seemed to be enjoying himself. The cock was half hard.

I split them up, sent them to opposite sides of the mat, and restarted the match. Kieran's pale skin was covered in pink patches where he'd been hit or squashed. His ass was shiny with oil; I wanted to slip a couple of fingers inside him myself.

"Round two!"

This time Kieran was fighting back, whether because he genuinely wanted to win or just to give the customers a good show, I'm not sure. He kept his stance low and used his smaller stature to get under Lukas's feet. It was a good tactic, one I'd have advised myself, and it worked: within less than a minute, Lukas was sprawling on the mat, and Kieran threw a leg across his stomach, working his way up to a straddle position. The oil made it easy for him to slide along Lukas's hairy torso, and for all Lukas's attempts to push himself up with his hands and feet, Kieran clung on. I counted to ten, then shouted "McAvoy!"

They were in no hurry to break off. Kieran was sliding his butt up and down Lukas's hard stomach, and every time he reversed, Lukas's cock came into contact with his asshole. Both of them were erect now. The third and final bout would be interesting.

"Fuck him!" yelled a man in the second row, and there was much cheering and whistling. Men were standing to get a better look. Kieran started to bounce up and down, the muscles in his thighs tensing and straining.

I shouted "break," much to the disgust of the crowd, but we had to keep up some pretense of actual sport. Judging by the precum swinging from Kieran's dick, he was ready to get fucked.

"Gentlemen, this is the clincher. The winner of this match will wrestle the winner of the following match. And then you, the audience, will decide the punishments and rewards."

Kieran and Lukas were at it right away, rolling around on the floor, shoving cocks and assholes in each other's faces, making no attempt to wrestle. This was sex. Lukas grabbed Kieran's buttocks at every opportunity, squeezing them, spreading them, while Kieran tried to get his face in Lukas's groin. Finally Lukas flipped Kieran on to his stomach and lay on top of him, his hard dick disappearing between Kieran's buttcheeks. It was enough for me to count them out and declare Lukas the winner.

The two combatants got up reluctantly from the floor, shining with sweat, oil, and precum. Kieran's cheeks were red, his hair wet, and he looked ready to shoot a load at any moment. I dared not release him to the crowd; one touch and he be jizzing over their expensive knitwear. I directed them to seats on opposite sides of the room, where they could be seen and admired but not touched.

"And now," I said, pulling down the shoulder straps of my wrestling singlet, "bout number two. Are you ready, gentlemen?"

They roared "yes." Most of them preferred their meat young and tender, but there was enough interest in my hairy old body to prevent me from feeling unwelcome. And when I revealed my cock, which was about three quarters hard, my approval ratings soared.

"If you would be kind enough to release Dakota, sir . . ."

Dakota swaggered on to the mat, his prick bouncing with every step. Taking him down would be so easy. I let him get close enough, then shot my foot out, hooked it behind his Achilles tendon, and pulled. His feet shot out from under him and he landed on his ass.

"You fucking bastard," he hissed, and from the look on his face he meant it.

I prowled around him, daring him to get up. It was tempting to get this over with; I could pin him three times in ten seconds if I wanted to, but there was a certain satisfaction to drawing out his humiliation. I like arrogant boys. I like puncturing their balloons and bringing them to a better understanding of their place in the world. That place is on the end of my cock.

"Come on, Dakota," I sneered, beckoning him up. "You can take an old man like me down."

He raised himself to a kneeling position, but I kicked his hand aside and he sprawled again. While he was down I planted my foot up his ass, and pressed my big toe against his hole. The audience laughed. This was the worst thing they could have done. Dakota liked being admired and adored, not humiliated.

He scooted across the slippery mat, and this time I let him get to his feet. His cock, which had been so stiff and proud while his sugar daddy was jerking him off, was small and shrivelled. My hand darted out, grabbed it, and squeezed. Dakota yelped.

I pulled him towards me with my other hand at the back of his neck. "Okay, pretty boy. You're going to do as I say."

He struggled, but even with the oil I held him firm. I moved my fingers from his balls through his legs to his ass, and suddenly lifted him up, cradling him in my arms. I brought his stomach right up to my face, licked along the ridges of his abs, then threw him over my shoulder. Dakota was light, and I could play with him like a doll. If he struggled, he'd fall. I walked around the mats, then rolled him down my arms and on to the floor. The hatred had gone out of his face; he knew he'd better behave himself, or he'd get hurt. I placed a foot on his chest, then slid it up to his throat; a little more pressure and he'd have blacked out. My cock was dripping. It seemed a shame to waste it, so I dropped to my knees, one on either side of his chest, pinned his shoulders with my hands, and positioned my dick so the precum landed on Dakota's lips. He opened his mouth, and looked me in the eye. It was just too tempting to resist. A little shift of the hips, and my cock was in his mouth, fucking him gently, sliding against his velvety tongue.

The crowd cheered.

I withdrew, and pulled Dakota to his feet.

This time I attacked him from behind, slipping my hands up under his armpits and grabbing his shoulders. He flailed around, trying to get a grip on me, but it was hopeless. From there it was easy to go slowly to my knees, pulling him against me all the way, my cock pressed into his ass, his body fully exposed to view. I slipped my left forearm around his throat again, and let my right hand play with his nipples, his belly, and his cock. Despite the pain and the humiliation, or maybe because of it, Dakota was hard again. I stroked him until he was squirming around, close to the edge, his ass practically sucking my dick inside, and then I flipped him over, smacked him down on the mat, and pinned his shoulders with my elbows. His face was pressed hard into the floor, his nose bent out of shape. He struggled to breathe. I let him up before it became dangerous.

The fight had gone out of him now, he didn't know if he was coming or going, whether he loved me or hated me. It felt good. I let him roll on to his back and catch his breath.

The third pin was quick and easy. Dakota got unsteadily to his feet, engaged me in a grapple for just long enough to give him a taste of control before I locked his arm behind his back, twisting so hard he screamed in pain and dropped to his knees. It was easy from there to push him over with my foot, hold him down with my hands on his biceps and, as the final gesture, kiss him on the mouth. His mouth opened, and my tongue went in. He squirmed on the mat, moaning into my mouth, utterly defeated.

Craig Lukas was a worried man as our bout started. While Kieran and Dakota sat aside and rubbed their sore places, well out of reach of the sweaty palms of the audience, Lukas and I squared up across the slippery mats. Of course I knew I would win, unless he got lucky and landed a punch straight to my face—but unless it was a straight KO I could still take him. I could kill him if it came to it, and he knew it. The swagger was gone. He knew he was going to take a beating, and that he would then get fucked in front of an audience. He glanced down at my cock, nervously licking his lips, wiping his brow with the back of his hand, shifting from foot to foot. Psychologically, I'd already won. I took my cock between thumb and forefinger and waved it at him.

"You want it, boy? Then come and get it."

Outside this room Lukas would have punched anyone who said he wanted cock; he was the ladies' man, the eligible bachelor, squiring beautiful models to launches and parties. But now things were different.

Some guys just need to have the element of choice taken away from them.

He tried to grab me by the arms; he was fast, but I was faster. I twisted away, spun on my back heel, and used the moment to rock him off his feet. He was down on the floor, looking up at me from cock level.

"Get up, boy."

He didn't like it, but what could he do? He may have had the looks and the muscles, he was probably ten, twenty pounds heavier than me, but I was in total control.

I had an idea. I put my hands around the back of his neck and jumped, wrapping my legs around his waist. He had no choice but to carry me, his cock rubbing against my ass, my cock pressed against his belly and chest. He staggered a few steps and then, top-heavy as he was, slipped on the mat and broke his fall with his hand. I got my feet to the ground just in time to prevent my full weight crashing on to his ribs. I straddled him, sat down on his cock, and bounced around on it. My dick was doing a dance all of its own. Lukas looked half winded. I grabbed his wrists and pinned him.

I pulled him to his feet and tripped him again, this time pinning him with my cock in his face; he didn't even turn his away, just let me rub it over his lips. One more pin, this time with me on my back, Lukas lying on top of me, immobilized by my arms and legs, and the match was over.

"So, gentlemen," I yelled, sounding like a fairground huckster—a voice I had only used on the parade ground—"what do you want to see first?"

There was a confusion of shouts, with all our names

in various combinations, and the repeated syllable "fuck."

I raised a hand for silence. "Let's start with the losers. Boys, get over here."

Dakota and Kieran stood on either side of me.

"Get down on your knees and suck some cock."

Lukas and I stood side by side, panting, sweaty, hairy, while the two boys knelt in front of us. Dakota got to me first; Kieran took his position in front of Lukas. I caught the look between them, as Kieran cupped the big man's balls and started to lick his shaft. This was more than just a job for them. The old me would have been finding ways to get them out of here, give them some privacy. The new me pushed Kieran around so that everyone could get a good view of Lukas's dick entering his mouth.

Dakota, of course, was sucking like a pro, making sure the audience got all the good angles. All I had to do was put my hands on my hips and concentrate on not shooting too soon.

The audience was quiet now. Some of them were jerking off. This was what they'd come for. The sex show. It felt good being a whore. The thought nearly made me cum. I pulled out of Dakota's mouth, and resumed my MC duties.

"And now, Lukas. On your fucking knees, pal."

He did as he was told, and gave me a barely adequate blow job. Compared to Dakota's skilled slickness, this was strictly beginner's level stuff, but the look of concentration on Lukas's handsome face was enough to keep me close to the edge. I'd teach him, even if I had to lead him around on all fours sucking every stiff cock in the house . . .

"And now for the fucking. Let's see a show of hands, gentlemen. Who wants to see Craig Lukas take it up the ass?"

There was little doubt as to the outcome. Every hand in the place went up. Never underestimate the appeal of a straight man taking it.

"Okay, boys. Get me rubbered up."

"For Christ's sake . . ." whispered Lukas through gritted teeth. "This can't be happening."

I knelt down beside him. "Don't worry," I said, "I'll take it easy. Unless you want it hard."

"Shit . . ."

He looked as if he was going to cry, but his cock was telling another story—stiff as a fucking iron bar, wet and drooling.

Dakota was trying to roll a condom on to me, so I stood up and gave everyone a good view. Lukas positioned himself on all fours.

"McAvoy! Lube him up."

Kieran did his work well; Lukas's ass was open, and I glided in without resistance. Lukas groaned and sighed and gave himself to me.

Fucking him on all fours was great—the view of his back tapering out to his massive shoulders was inspiring me—but the audience couldn't see his face or his cock. I wanted them to see him cum as I pounded into him. So I pulled out, flipped him over, and raised his legs, the quads and hamstrings pumped and heavy. It was easy to push back into him, and now everyone had a clear view of his hairy torso and handsome, superhero face as he took my cock deep into his guts. Dakota and Kieran were spellbound, both of them hard. I could hear groans in the audience; I guess one or two of the guys had cum, which was the kind of ovation I welcomed.

I gave it to Lukas good and hard, and he took every inch. His dick never softened. His arms were above his head, his deep, furry armpits exposed, but at last he could stand it no longer and brought a hand down to his cock and started stroking. I guess that cumming in front of an audience of men while you've got a dick plunging into your ass means that your reputation as a heterosexual is kind of compromised, but Lukas was past caring. He needed to cum, and it only took a few strokes before jets of thick white spunk were feathering out all over his torso.

I kept going until I could stand it no more. I pulled out, whipped off the condom, and shot my load in Lukas's sweaty face. Some of it went in his mouth, some of it hit him on the forehead, some of it rolled down his cheeks and chin. He didn't turn away.

This left the two losers naked, hard, and ready for anything. I felt the time was right for a little audience participation.

"Okay, gents. Who wants to make these boys cum? I'm feeling generous. Two lucky winners get to give them a helping hand." Every hand in the room went up. "Okay, you," I said, pointing to the rich-looking Daddy that Dakota had chosen, "and you." My second choice was one of the younger men in the room, not much older than me, who looked like he could be in the military. Cropped black hair with a bit of silver, a sports jacket, an open-necked shirt, and a conspicuous gold band on the third finger of his left hand. If I'd had to choose one for myself it would have been him, so he'd do nicely for

Kieran. Perhaps later we could work something out, the three of us . . .

The boys went willingly to their appointed partners, sat on their laps, and let hands roam all over their bodies. This wasn't going to take long. Dakota straddled his gent's lap, facing him, and bucked up and down, his hands behind the guy's head. Kieran lay back in the man's arms and let him kiss him and wank him at the same time. He came first, shooting his jizz in an arc through the air, landing with an audible splat on the floor. Dakota made more of a show of his orgasm, leaning backwards, his abs tensed, as the guy milked his dick. The spunk shot over an expensive cashmere sweater. I guess it didn't matter; he probably had a closet full of them at home.

My instructions were to get out of the party as soon as the show was over; Vaughan didn't want the boys giving away any freebies. I herded Lukas and the boys back into our dressing room; we wiped up, dressed quickly, and made for the doors.

And it was just before we left the house—twenty seconds later and we'd have been out of there—that we heard the first shot.

12

The shot was followed by shouts, the sound of a scuffle, then three more shots fired in quick succession. I told the boys to hit the floor, and opened the door between me and the hall, cursing the fact that I hadn't been issued firearms.

The body lay faceup in the middle of the marble floor, blood pooling from a wound in the back. The eyes were wide open, and there was a slight movement around the mouth as the throat struggled pointlessly to draw breath into destroyed lungs. Very soon it ended. The pool of blood grew larger, and the body was still.

It was Oz.

No time to care about that. First of all, secure the situation. There was a gun lying a couple of feet away from Oz's right hand—presumably he had fired the first shot—which I quickly picked up, put on the safety, and pocketed. The shot or shots that killed him must have come from the reception room, judging by the way the body had fallen. There was nobody there, but I could hear movement from beyond the door. Faces peered cautiously from the dining room, where only a minute or two ago we'd been doing a different sort of shooting. They looked terrified, wide-eyed and ashen-faced. Nobody posed an immediate threat. I approached.

Inside the room, people were dispersing quickly. The man who had made Kieran come—the handsome, dark-haired guy—already had his overcoat on, and was closing a briefcase.

"Everybody stay exactly where they are," I said, in the voice I've used in combat situations around the world. "This is a crime scene."

"And who are you?" said the man with the briefcase, cool as a cucumber, his handsome face unperturbed.

"Greg Cooper. Captain Greg . . ."

Before I could give my bogus credentials he cut me off. "Well thank you for your concern, Greg. As it happens, I am a police officer."

I said nothing. A few minutes ago he'd been part of an orgy—not actually breaking the law, but certainly doing things that would not recommend him for promotion. Bringing the force into disrepute, I guess, unless the British police force thinks that jerking off prostitutes in front of an audience is reasonable behavior.

He raised an eyebrow. "Do you want to see my warrant card?"

"That's fine, sir. I'm sure you're in full control of the situation." What was in his briefcase? It looked as if he'd just put something away. Another gun? It was not up to me to confront him. "If you need a witness statement . . ."

"But you witnessed nothing, Captain Cooper."

"I know the deceased."

There was muttering from the crowd. "I think," said the cop, "that most of us know the deceased. Now if you'll excuse me, I need to make a phone call." There was sarcasm in his voice. "I'm sure you understand. Perhaps you will take the other performers home."

What should I do? To intervene too much would jeopardize the mission. On the other hand, someone had just killed a boy I knew, a boy I might have cared about. If this really was a police officer, and if the other guests were prominent businessmen and pillars of the community, then the chances of a cover-up were sky high.

I calculated quickly.

There was more to be done from a position inside the Vaughan organization than outside. If necessary, I could blow the whistle once the mission was safely complete. I would put myself, as well as Kieran, Dakota, and Vaughan, at risk if I challenged him.

I moved towards the door. "Is there another exit, so I don't have to bring them through here?"

One of the other guests stepped forward. "I'll show you," he said, gesturing towards the room where the boys were still hiding. "You can go through the garage."

And so, with the sound of the gunfire fresh in my ears, and with Oz's blood still oozing over the marble floor, I led Kieran, Dakota, and Lukas away from the house without them seeing a thing.

We went back to City Fitness to pick up our money. Nobody spoke much in the cab. Lukas stared out of the window; perhaps he'd seen all this before. Kieran and Dakota huddled together, tense and frightened. This is what happened to Vaughan boys who stepped out of line.

I needed to contact MI6.

Jackson was waiting for me. He, too, looked scared.

"Mr. Vaughan is here. He'd like to see you."

"Was his flight early?" I tried to act cool, as if seeing a young man murdered was all part of an evening's work.

"He's waiting."

"Oh, dear. Have I been a bad boy? Is the boss going to give me a spanking?" I moved close to Jackson, whispered in his ear. He flinched.

"Please, Greg . . ."

"It's okay. I'm not going to tell him anything."

I walked into Vaughan's office without knocking. He was all affability. "Ah, Greg. Thanks for coming by."

"How was Florida?"

"Very nice, very nice." He thought for a second. "You know. Hot."

Hot, my ass. You weren't there at all, were you? "I must get back there some time."

"Actually, it's about your travel plans that I need to talk to you."

"Okay."

"I want you to go out to the US for me."

"Did you leave something behind?"

"We've got a chance to get Craig Lukas a fight."

"I know. Next month, isn't it?"

"Something new has come up."

"Great. When and where?"

"New York City, the day after tomorrow."

"Short notice. What's the plan?"

"You will fly out with Lukas in the morning. Get him ready to fight. Keep him in check."

"And what kind of fight is this? Another invited audience, like this evening?"

Vaughan scowled; he obviously didn't like direct references to his unorthodox business activities. "A boxing match," he said. "A promoter that I know over there has a fighter he's keen to . . ."

"Promote?"

"Yes." Vaughan was used to his subordinates doing as they were told; I made him uneasy. "We're setting up an exhibition match as a way of raising his media profile before the big fight in Miami."

"Sounds like a great idea." I could smell bullshit, and Vaughan knew it. "I guess you've got lots of interviews and photoshoots set up."

"Yes, yes, of course . . ."

"Are we taking Bill Brett with us?"

"What?"

"Your in-house photographer."

"Of course not." He was getting cross with me now. This was fun.

"I suppose there are plenty of photographers in New York City who do that kind of work. Perhaps your promoter friend can hook you up."

Vaughan was losing patience, and wanted me out of the office. "Tom has all the travel details. There will be further instructions when you get to New York."

"And when are you joining us?"

"What?"

"When are you flying to New York? You're not going to miss your golden boy's first American fight, are you?"

"I'll come out if I possibly can. I have a lot of things to sort out over here . . ."

I interrupted. "Yes, you do."

"What's that supposed to mean?"

"Are we going to pretend nothing happened tonight? I assume you know."

"That's being taken care of."

"I spoke to someone who said he was a police officer."

"You . . ." He took a breath, and started again. "Yes, he mentioned how cooperative you'd been. Thank you for that, Greg. I value cooperation very highly."

"And is that what happens to people who don't cooperate?" I put two fingers to my temple, and mimed a shooting.

We looked at each other in silence for a while.

"I've been advised not to discuss this," said Vaughan.

"And what about me?"

"What about you?"

"I'm a witness. Won't I be needed for the police investigation?"

"If anyone needs you they can talk to you when you get back."

"Right." Of course there wouldn't be a police investigation. Oz would disappear, no body would be found, no missing persons report. I knew how Vaughan worked. His associates would close ranks to protect themselves. Lukas and I were being sent out of the country on the first available flight. What about Dakota and Kieran? They'd heard the shots too. Perhaps Vaughan thought that they could be more easily intimidated into silence.

"I can rely on you, can't I, Greg? I'm not going to start having problems."

"What kind of problems?"

"We hired you because we understood that you could follow orders."

"If you want that, don't hire officers."

"Ex-officers."

"And you know why I'm an ex-officer, don't you? Because I wouldn't take their bullshit."

"Yes, Greg. We know all that. And we value your independent spirit." What the fuck was this, the royal "we"? "But at this point in time, I need to know that I can trust you to run things in New York."

"Yes, you can trust me. I'll get Lukas to wherever he needs to be, doing whatever he needs to do, whether it's fighting or fucking. I just ask one thing in return."

"You'll be paid well."

"That's not what I mean."

"Then what?"

"Let's not lie to each other, Vaughan. I'm not one of these kids you recruit from foster care. If I'm going to work with you, I'd appreciate honesty."

"Would you now."

I stood with my arms folded, and said nothing.

"Very well. You've seen enough of the business to know how it works. I've been obliged to diversify."

"You can say that again."

"But this trip to New York is core business. I mean boxing."

"Thanks for making that clear."

"Are we good?"

"We're good. I shall await further instructions."

"Thank you, Greg. Have a good flight."

I had to get out of there before I started laughing. As

international criminal masterminds go, Vaughan was strictly third-rate.

I emailed MI6 on the encrypted server.

> Panoply murdered this evening. Among witnesses/
> suspects is man 40s claiming to be senior police
> officer. I am flying to NYC tomorrow morning.
> Urgent require support and instructions.

I gave them the address of the shooting, and my flight numbers. An acknowledgement came back within a minute. No orders. No advice. Once I boarded that flight in the morning, I was stepping into the unknown.

It was my first night in Manchester without one of Vaughan's employees spinning around on the end of my cock: Kieran on the first night, Joshua and Dakota on the second, Jackson on the third. After what had happened this evening, not to mention all the other fucking I'd been doing, you might think I'd sink into an exhausted sleep, but nothing doing. I lay awake, going over and over in my mind what could have happened to Oz—and what was waiting for me on the other side of the Atlantic.

Oz had turned up at my house in the early hours of yesterday morning, fucked up on drugs, beaten and bruised. He'd been with a client, and taken—or been forced to take—a large amount of GHB. He'd escaped with his life, and come to me for help, but had either thought better of it and fled, or been forcibly removed by persons unknown. Somehow he'd got hold of a gun, and turned up at the house of one of Vaughan's wealthy associates where he knew he would meet the person or persons he was looking for, making threats and firing a shot. He'd then been killed. Maybe the first shot was a setup. Maybe Oz never had a gun at all, and the weapon I saw lying near his hand had been placed there for my benefit. Was I meant to be a witness? Had they been keeping Oz there until the very last moment, when they let him out, fired the gun, and then shot him in the back? An execution, pure and simple, dressed up to look like a botched attack.

I had a list of questions that kept getting longer, each leading to another. Why did they need Oz's silence? Who was threatened by him—Vaughan, or one of his clients? I'd taken Oz's place in the "wrestling match"—was I now about to take his place in a more deadly game? What had prompted this sudden trip to New York? Why not New Hampshire, where Vaughan had just been? Was that misinformation? And what of Lukas—was he a victim, or a perpetrator? I'd heard so many times that he was stepping out of line—but this, too, could be a smoke screen. The date of the suspected terror attack was close with the date of the hastily arranged fight, if it existed . . .

Around and around I went, trying to figure it out, flashing on the image of Oz, dead, his blood on the marble floor, and the cool, handsome, dark-haired police officer putting something away in a suitcase.

Finally, at four a.m., I fell asleep. The car arrived at five. A black Mercedes, with one of Vaughan's drivers. Lukas was already in the back. He mumbled a greeting, and stared out of the window. We had a long flight ahead of us, a nice little holiday in New York City, plenty of time to get to know each other. I would get my dick back into his ass before the sun set over the Hudson River, I promised myself. And with that pleasant thought in mind, I closed my eyes and let myself be carried along. Just to be on the safe side, I'd slipped a tracking device into my own ass before I left, and emailed my details to MI6. You never know when it might come in useful. I had plenty left. Perhaps I'd get one into Lukas. I was getting hard thinking about it. I lay back in my seat and closed my eyes.

Time passed. I dozed.

"Greg. Hey! Greg!"

A hand on my arm. "What?"

"We're at the airport, man."

"Shit." My dick was sticking straight up in my pants. Lukas kept glancing down at it. "Fuck. Morning wood."

He gave it a squeeze. "Better get that down before we go through security."

Perhaps Lukas and I could make a good team. Vaughan hadn't counted on that. He must have thought that Lukas would still be furious about last night's party. Perhaps he was. But his love of getting fucked was stronger. He wouldn't be the first arrogant macho dickhead I've turned into a compliant subordinate. That's the good ol' USMC training.

We checked in, got through security, and found coffee.

"Excited about the fight?"

"Excited? Fuck off."

"What?"

"He hasn't paid me for the last one yet. And this one is crap. He knows it, and I know it."

"Then why are we going?"

"When Vaughan tells you to do something, you do it."

"What's he got on you?"

"Same as he's got on everyone."

"You mean he filmed you fucking."

"Yeah. Fucking bastard."

"Who?"

Lukas shrugged. "Some guy that used to work for him when I was starting out, four or five years back. He was supposed to be a personal trainer at the gym, but you know . . ."

"That wasn't what Vaughan really employed him for."

"Yeah."

"Like me."

"I suppose so." Lukas sighed, as if his world was ending. "Oh, it's all so fucked up. Why did I ever sign with him?"

"Believe me, he's no worse than the rest of them."

"I just wanted to fight, that's all."

"And you've done well. You're famous. You go to all the right parties, and you date all the beautiful girls."

He said nothing, just stared into his coffee as if it was a deep dark well that he wanted to jump down.

"Am I supposed to feel sorry for you, Lukas? Jesus. There are boys out there who would sell their fucking souls to have what you've got."

"And that's what they do, isn't it? All those kids who think they've got a shot at the big time. Vaughan chews them up and spits them out."

"Guys like Oz, you mean?"

Lukas said nothing for a while. "That was him, wasn't it? Last night?"

"Yeah."

"Oh, shit." Lukas's voice was shaky. It took a few seconds before I realized he was crying.

"I'm sorry, Craig. Did you like him?"

"He was a sweet guy. He didn't hurt anyone."

"Do you have any idea what happened?"

"No." He put his huge hands over his face, rubbing the black stubble on his chin and cheeks. "Oh, fuck. Fuck. This is my fault. It's all my . . ." He couldn't talk any more. People at other tables were starting to glance over. This wouldn't do; Craig Lukas had a reputation to uphold. Someone would recognize him, photograph him, and it would be all over social media. Boxing star cries like a baby at airport.

"Let's go for a walk." I pulled him to his feet and marched him around the departure lounge. "Tell me exactly why you think this is your fault."

He blew his nose. "Because if it wasn't for me Oz would never have become part of Vaughan's organization."

"You mean because he admired you?"

"Yeah. He was a . . . I don't know. A fan."

"And did you . . .?"

'Christ, no. Not at first, anyway. Not until he was working for us. And then . . . yeah, I let him do stuff that he wanted to do. I told you, I liked him. Oh, Jesus . . ."

"Don't start crying again, Lukas."

"I'm sorry." He blew his nose.

"I liked Oz too. And I'll find out what happened to him."

"What makes you think you can do anything? You

know what those guys are—Vaughan's associates. Senior policemen. Lawyer. Judges. It's hopeless."

I thought it best not to mention MI6 or the CIA just yet. "When did you last speak with Oz?"

"The day before yesterday. He phoned me in the evening. He was drunk. He sounded confused. He said Vaughan had sent him on a job that he didn't want to do."

"What time was this?"

"About nine. I was out at a party."

"What did he want?"

"He wasn't making much sense. He kept asking me to go and get him."

"Why?"

"I'm not sure. He kept repeating himself. He was on his way to see a client. He didn't want to go."

"Did he say anything at all about where he was going, or why he didn't want to go?"

"He said a lot of things. It was hard to make it out. I should have listened to him."

"Had he ever made calls like this before?"

"He used to ring me up in the middle of the night. I was actually going to block his number, he was becoming a nuisance. He'd say all sorts of shit, like he wanted to be with me and stuff."

"He was a lonely, frightened boy."

"Oh, fuck, Greg, don't make it worse."

"And you don't know where he was going?"

"No."

"Who sends the boys out on jobs?"

"Bill Brett, usually. Sometimes Jackson."

"And is Vaughan blackmailing his clients as well as charging them for services?"

"He's capable of anything."

"Including murder?"

"He'd never have the courage to do it himself, but he'd put people in a situation where they had no alternative but to kill."

"Who do you think killed Oz?"

"It could be anyone."

"It's happened before, hasn't it?"

Lukas said nothing. We'd done one full circuit of the lounge by now, and started another.

"How many times?"

"I don't know. It's better not to know."

"You just concentrate on the fame and the money and the women, and you don't care if a few young guys get killed."

He stopped and turned on me. "It's not like that!" His face was red, and a vein was sticking out in his forehead.

"And then one day, out of the blue, it's you."

That took the air out of his balloon. "What's that supposed to mean?"

"Think you're too important? Think again."

"He wouldn't touch me."

"You keep bitching about the money, and threatening to walk out on him, and see what happens. Vaughan is afraid of you. You know too much, and people will listen to you. Wouldn't it be in his interests to arrange an accident for you? Perhaps on foreign soil, where it's easier to make you disappear."

"Oh, come on, Greg . . ."

"Maybe he's sending you out there with the assassin he's paid to kill you."

Now the blood was rushing away from his face. "That's not funny."

"It's not true either. But did it not occur to you that Vaughan wants both of us out of the way?"

"It's not like that. It's a chance to generate some publicity . . ."

"Before the big fight in December. I know all that. It's not true."

"Why?"

"Who organizes a fight like this with two days' notice? No time to get anything organized. He just wants us out of the way. And I bet you, when we get there, plans have changed. We'll be sent on some wild goose chase." I was thinking New Hampshire. "The fight won't happen."

"Then I'll be really pissed off. I'll talk to the first cop I can find. I'll tell them everything."

"Don't be so fucking stupid. And don't get any ideas about talking to the media either. Or tweeting anything. Let's find out what's happening, and then you have to let me make the plans."

"Why should I trust you?"

"If you do as you're told, I'll fuck you again."

I walked ahead; he had to jog to keep up. "Okay, Greg. Okay. I'll do as you say, right? Just . . . you know, it takes me a while to . . . to get my head around it . . . I didn't realize what was going on . . . I swear."

I let him ramble on for a while, confident in the knowledge that his ass was now taking control of his brain. When the gate number was announced, I interrupted him. "I need the bathroom. Come on."

I got him into a cubicle, locked the door behind us,

and pulled my dick out. I really did need to piss. Lukas watched for a while, then joined me, crossing streams, getting as close to me as possible, splashing over the edge of the bowl. When we'd both finished, our cocks seemed reluctant to be put away.

I snapped my fingers and pointed to the floor. "On your knees."

He didn't argue. He dropped down like a good soldier and took hold of my balls. His mouth opened, his tongue slid out like a welcome mat, and I was in.

For a straight celebrity, Lukas was a pretty good bathroom cocksucker. We'd have to watch that. Don't want any entrapments. His hand was down his pants, working away.

"Get up," I said, when I was close. There was no room to fuck him in there, and I couldn't be bothered with condoms and all that jazz, but I turned him around, pulled down his pants, bent him over so I had a good view of his hairy ass, and stuck one wet finger inside him. Lukas sighed, and started shooting his load all over the bathroom floor. What he didn't notice was that I'd managed to insert a tracking device. With luck, that would last all the way to New York and beyond. Once he'd finished, I span him around again, pushed his head down and managed to get into his mouth just as I started ejaculating. He took the lot, and swallowed. I pulled him up, kissed him long and deep, then cleaned myself up with a wad of toilet tissue.

There were other guys using the bathroom when we came out of the cubicle, our faces flushed and (in Lukas's case) sticky, but nobody dared say anything.

We boarded the plane, and Lukas had a smile and

a friendly, flirtatious word for all the cabin crew. I was ignored. I guess they thought I was his bodyguard. It was as good a cover as any.

We slept for most of the flight. Only our tracking devices remained awake, and working.

13

It took me a second to recognize the man in the chauffeur's uniform holding the COOPER sign. Uniforms, as I know very well, obliterate identity. The cap was pulled low over the eyes, and even they were covered with dark glasses, so it was the mouth I recognized first, and with good reason, if you cast your mind back.

Luiz, who'd done a great job of sucking me back to health in the Navy Med.

"Captain Cooper. I'm your driver for today. My name's Aurelio."

"Yeah, of course it is."

He picked up Lukas's suitcase. Everything I owned was in a backpack.

"The car is this way, gentlemen."

"We'll follow." I watched his ass, rounder than ever in his tight chauffeur's pants. The efficiency of the CIA, or the FBI, or whoever was giving Luiz his orders these days, was impressive, right down to the details.

If there had been a flicker of recognition on my face, Lukas didn't notice it.

There were envelopes on the back seat of the car with our names on them. "Mr. Vaughan asked me to give these to you," said Luiz/Aurelio, glancing in the rearview mirror. "Welcome to New York."

"How thoughtful," I said. There was a guide book, some refreshing wipes, an energy bar, and $200 cash in each package. And a shiny new smartphone. "Mr. Vaughan thinks of everything. Doesn't he, Craig?"

Lukas was already playing with his phone, swiping through the apps, checking his contacts. "This is brilliant! I can text my Mum. Look, I've taken a photo, you can see skyscrapers and everything. I'm sending that to her."

I checked my email app. The encrypted stuff was all there, including an email telling me that Lukas and I—or, rather, the tracking devices in our asses—had successfully crossed the ocean.

I improvised some small talk with Aurelio, trusting his training to make the right inferences.

"How's the weather?"

"Warm for the time of year."

"Looks like there might be a storm coming."

"There's one forecast in a couple of days."

"Oh, yeah? Here in the city?"

"The reports say it's coming down from the north-east."

"Then coming here?"

I glanced at Lukas to make sure he hadn't picked up on the subtext of our weather talk. He was happily oblivious.

"Not sure about that yet."

"We'd better get some winter clothes then, just in case."

"You'll find everything you need at the apartment, sir."

"Mr. Vaughan again?"

"Just as before."

"It's good to know we're in such safe hands, Aurelio."

"We didn't want to think you'd been forgotten."

What I really wanted to know was what Vaughan had sent us over here for. Was the fight real, or were we being used for something more sinister?

"So, Aurelio, where are you taking us?"

"You're staying at an apartment in midtown."

"One of Mr. Vaughan's?"

"It belongs to a client of his."

"He has some pretty fancy clients."

Luiz said nothing.

"And who do you work for, Aurelio?"

"I'm just a driver for the limo company."

"I see. Did Mr. Vaughan book you, or his client?"

"I came through the agency."

That was as clear as he could make it without screaming "I work for the CIA." Lukas probably wouldn't have understood or cared, but Luiz was trained to be careful.

"That must be useful if another driver has to cancel unexpectedly."

"Funny you should mention that, sir. Your original driver was taken ill very suddenly. Had to go to the hospital."

So the CIA had hacked into Vaughan's emails, found out who was supposed to be collecting us from the airport, abducted him or otherwise put him out of action, and sent Luiz in his place. Vaughan would never know. The CIA had ways of ensuring that limo services keep quiet—like, for instance, threatening a visit from the US Immigration and Customs Enforcement to check up on their drivers' paperwork. The CIA was running me now. The Brits had plenty to deal with—keeping an eye on Vaughan, investigating the death of Oz Rafiq, protecting the rest of Vaughan's boys, and, in the fullness of time, handing over a big fat file of evidence to the police. That was something to look forward to. I'd given them what they needed. Now we were in unknown territory.

Luiz dropped us on Third Avenue, near Grand Central Station. One of those anonymous apartment blocks that used to look shabby and full of transients, but now have fancy security systems and rents that only crooks can afford. It said a lot about Vaughan's American associates that they had an empty flat in east midtown empty and waiting for us. The place stank of organized crime.

We showered, fucked, showered again, ate, and slept. There were two bedrooms, but we only needed one. By the time we woke it was early evening, New York time. I'm used to crazy time zone shifts. I can get by on coffee. Lukas, on the other hand, was groggy and disorientated, possibly because he wasn't used to getting so much dick up his ass. In boxing terms, he was punch-drunk. Fuck-drunk, I guess. He was only calm when he had my cock. The rest of the time he was nervous and bitchy, complaining about Vaughan, endlessly telling me he wanted to find new management, worrying about tomorrow's fight but also dismissing it as a waste of time.

Details were sketchy. An "exhibition match," Vaughan had said, but that could mean anything from two men in satin shorts pretending to box for a roomful of dirty old men all the way to a hired venue with press and promoters and champagne for the front rows. I needed, at the very least, a time and a location. The longer I waited, the more I believed we had been sent here simply to be out of the way.

I kept Lukas busy. I can put the toughest athlete through his paces in a tent, in a patch of desert, in the back of a transport lorry if necessary, so the Third Avenue apartment made a pretty good makeshift gym. I had him skipping without a rope, doing tuck jumps, push-ups, planks, the whole repertoire. In between training sessions I kept Lukas's hole well stretched with my fingers and my dick, and I gave him every opportunity to improve his oral technique. I don't subscribe to the theory of sexual abstinence before a fight. I was determined to get as many orgasms out of Lukas as possible, each and every one of them with my cock in one hole or another, until he couldn't come without it. Basic operant conditioning.

We watched TV on the couch, making out like a new couple. We went to bed.

The intercom buzzed at 8:00 a.m. Lukas was in the shower, washing off the jizz.

"Delivery for Cooper."

I put on a bathrobe and waited at the apartment door. The courier was wearing a motorcycle helmet and a leather jacket. Could be a hit man. I could overpower him, unless he had a gun.

He did have a gun, as it turned out. It was in a large

padded envelope which he handed to me. Then he left.

A 9mm semiautomatic Walther Creed, two magazines and enough rounds to stage a major incident. It was good to be home.

There was a letter in the package as well. A compliments slip from a company called HomeWay Investments Limited, that said simply "See you there!", no name, no number. Stapled to that was an itinerary.

G. COOPER
C. LUKAS

Arrive Hammond Hotel, W 43rd/8th Ave, 1700
Identify yourselves at reception and ask for Peter Logan, HomeWay Investments.
Event is taking place in 3rd floor meeting venue space, look for the sign reading Investors in Sport Annual Conference.
Please note you are responsible for your own security.

There was no information about the "event," what was expected of us, what kind of equipment we should bring, but from what Vaughan had told me about "core business" I assumed that Lukas would need his boxing kit. I would obviously need the gun, and the note about "security" told me that there was some concern that there might be another attack. This time, I guess, it was me who was supposed to be doing the shooting. Another young guy like Oz, with me in the role of the executioner.

It was not a role I relished, but if they believed me

capable of that then my penetration of Vaughan's inner circle was complete.

Lukas came into the kitchen, naked, drying his hair. He saw the gun.

"What the fuck is that for?"

"A gift from our clients in New York. It feels good to have firearms again."

"I suppose you know how to use that thing."

I didn't bother to reply, just grabbed him by the dick and pulled him in for a kiss. Once I'd got him good and hard, I said, "Now, we've got nine hours. We're going to spend that time getting you in peak physical condition. How do you feel, champ?"

In reply he dropped to his knees, undid the belt of my towelling robe, and started sucking my cock. I began to think more seriously about that cabin in the woods. Perhaps we could keep the outside world away. Yes, I've thought about this before, with other men, and it's always gone the same way—I fuck it up, they fuck it up, the world fucks it up for us. But wouldn't it be funny, I thought, as Craig looked up at me with tears streaming down his face, as my cock entered his throat and he controlled his gag reflex, if he was the person I came out of this with. Not any of the obvious ones—not Oz, not Kieran, not Jackson, none of the boys that I would usually go for—but Craig Lukas, the straight celebrity boxer with the bad attitude. When it was all over, when Vaughan was behind bars and I was free of my obligation to the CIA, I'd tell him the truth about Greg Cooper, I'd lay it on the line and we'd build a future together . . .

I saw it so clearly, both of us with beards, up in the woods, chopping wood, fucking like animals . . .

And then I came.

I was so focused on Lukas's training that I almost forgot to check the phone that Luiz had given me. I guess this happens to everyone who goes deep undercover—you start to forget who you really are, and who you're working for. When I noticed that there was a new email waiting for me, I resented the intrusion. There were only a few hours until we were due at the Hammond Hotel, and I had planned to spend at least two of those fucking. They could be my last.

Once I'd gone through the necessary sign-ins, this is what I read.

URGENT meet with Agent Oliver 1430 today at Finnegan's Bar E40th Street. Come alone.

Who the fuck did they think they were? I didn't have time to go out and meet some uptight spook in a phony Irish pub. And then, fortunately, I remembered Ethan Oliver's tight little ass and preppy haircut, and I gave him the benefit of the doubt.

"Hey, lover boy, I'm going out for a walk. Need some fresh air."

I thought he might take some persuading—Lukas was following me around the apartment like a puppy dog, and I expected him to sulk if I left him alone. But in fact I'd fucked him into submission.

"That's okay, I need more sleep. You're wearing me out, man."

"When this is over, I'm going to show you a few new tricks."

"What's left?"

"Oh, we've just begun." I kissed him on the mouth. He was turning into a good kisser.

"Don't be long, man," he said, his voice croaky with sleep. "I'm just gonna . . ." He padded off to the bedroom. Okay, I might have overdone it. Maybe Lukas wouldn't be on top form for this sham boxing match this evening. I didn't care much. The sooner he gave it all up, the sooner we could get clear of Vaughan and find that cabin in the woods. And, of course, it didn't matter how well he fought in terms of my operational objectives. I reminded myself of that as I walked down the stairs. Don't lose sight of the mission. Don't let it become a second thought.

Sitting at the bar, Agent Oliver looked like any other daytime drinker, down on his luck, drowning his sorrows, in between jobs or hiding from his wife.

I took a stool near him. There were only three other people in the bar, and they looked like they were on serious meds, but even so, I played the game of discretion. The barman got me a beer, which I sipped once and ignored.

"Hey," said Oliver.

"Hey." I played my part, scowling, avoiding eye contact. We sat in silence for a while, then, once Oliver was satisfied that I hadn't been followed, we moved to a table in the back corner, as far from the window as possible.

"You're still alive, then."

"As you see."

"And are you still Dan Stagg?"

"He's in here somewhere."

"I'm pleased to hear it."

"So, what am I here for?"

"You've done well, Dan. London is satisfied."

"You mean they're going to bust Vaughan?"

"Maybe."

"How much have they told you?"

"Enough."

"About the murder?"

"They're not calling it murder."

"What are they calling it? A young man accidentally walked into the path of an oncoming bullet?"

"The case will be handed over to the relevant authorities at the appropriate time."

"I see."

Oliver was pissing me off. Perhaps if I hadn't spent the last couple of days fucking and falling in love with Craig Lukas I might have given him a fair hearing; as it was, his disregard for Oz's death, and his tunnel vision about Vaughan, just annoyed me. He couldn't see the bigger picture, and he certainly didn't give a shit about the human cost. Why had he summoned me here? To check that I was still following orders? To reprogram me?

"Luiz tells me that you and Lukas are being well looked after."

"He told you that, did he?"

"Have you received further instructions from Vaughan?"

"Why ask me? You know everything."

"Is there anything on your mind, Dan?"

"Just waiting for my orders."

"Hmmm."

We sat in silence for a while. I wanted to get back to

Lukas, to get the match done. I wasn't in the mood for CIA bullshit, the hints and evasions.

"So," he said, "he hasn't contacted you."

I showed him the itinerary.

"Anything else?"

"It came with a free gift." I tapped my coat pocket. "Nine mill Walther Creed."

"Why would you need that?"

I shrugged. "The boxing world in New York is still run by the Mob."

"Really?" Oliver raised his eyebrows. "I hope you won't be using it."

"Only if necessary."

"Please remember who you're working for, Dan." He looked so fucking prissy when he said that, like a junior schoolteacher losing control of his class.

"You mean if I start shooting people it might be inconvenient for you?"

Oliver moved his glass around the tabletop in a neat geometrical pattern. I watched his hands—very nice hands, with hairy wrists and neat nails—and wondered what was coming.

"We believe that you and Lukas, or possibly just one of you, will be moved up to Concord, New Hampshire, later tonight."

"What's happening?"

"The extreme right-wing group that Vaughan has been funding is planning an attack on an army base."

"Why? That's insane."

"They're not expecting the attacker to survive."

"A suicide mission."

"Exactly. And that's where Osman Rafiq fitted in.

Send a Muslim in to attack the US Army. Increase terror and paranoia. Legitimize the aims of the extreme right."

"Not so extreme anymore."

"And this is how they're planning to secure their position in the mainstream: attacks by the enemy within. Oz was perfect. A British Muslim. Synonymous with terrorism."

"And now that he's dead?"

"You're the replacement. Or possibly Lukas."

"In other words, if you can't get a Muslim, send in a queer."

"You've got it, Dan. Maximum headlines. Set back the equalities agenda by decades. Give every redneck an excuse for gay-bashing."

"But we're not going to do it, are we?"

"You'll have to go along with the plan up to a point."

"You mean one of us might get killed."

"We hope not. As soon as we have credible evidence of the plot . . ."

"Yeah, I know, you send the cavalry in, we get rescued in the nick of time, screen kiss, roll credits."

"That's the plan."

"I guess I have to trust you, then."

We sat in silence for a while, staring at our drinks.

Oliver broke the silence. "What happened to Oz, Dan?"

"I'm not sure. I think one of Vaughan's clients treated him too roughly. He was beaten up, covered in bruises and cuts, they gave him an overdose . . . poor little bastard."

"Are Vaughan's clients into S&M?"

"What do you know about that kind of thing, pretty boy?"

"Enough to realize that some clients will pay a good deal for a prostitute that they can torture without fear of prosecution."

I felt something cold and hard in my throat, and for a moment I thought I was going to be sick. I needed that beer now, and took a swig to wash down the disgust.

"Oz wanted to get out of the whole thing. I should have listened to him, shouldn't I?"

"It's too late for him, Dan. But we can still stop this."

"Why don't the state troopers just go in and bust these assholes? Why do you need me?"

"Because they won't show their hand until they believe the attack is going to succeed. And for that, they need the hit man that Vaughan promised them. An outsider, someone who has nothing to do with the organization. A foreigner. Oz would have been perfect, but you or Lukas will do just as well."

"Lukas has a lot more to hide than me."

"People like that are easy to manipulate. Vaughan's been blackmailing him for years."

"Says who?"

"The information you supplied to London about Vaughan's business activities encouraged them to look closely at the bank transactions of a few key individuals. Some of them were the businessmen whose addresses were being visited by Vaughan's sex workers. Among the others was Craig Lukas."

"You mean he's been paying Vaughan to keep quiet about him?"

"Apparently."

"Jesus." Was Lukas lying to me? He'd mentioned prize money that hadn't been handed over—but if

Oliver was right, it went a lot further than that. Now, perhaps, Vaughan was offering to let him go if he'd do one last job for him . . . Delivering a package to a synagogue in New Hampshire . . . Lukas would be desperate enough to ask no questions.

"Will I go with him?"

"We don't know for sure. Vaughan may have sent you here just to get you out of the way after Oz's death. But he may also want you to go in with Lukas. We expect you to receive instructions after the fight."

"If it is a fight."

Oliver looked puzzled. "What else would it be?"

"The last exhibition fight I did for Alan Vaughan involved more fucking than fighting."

He flushed a little, and swallowed before he spoke. "What do you mean?"

I gave him a brief, brutal resume of the four-man event that preceded Oz's death. Whose cock went where, who came in which hole, and so on. Oliver licked his lips and said, "Do you think Vaughan's flown you all the way to New York to do that?"

"Why not? We're very good at it. Want to come along and see?"

"No thanks. I'm not into public sex."

"Perhaps I can give you a private demonstration."

He drank, holding my gaze. "Perhaps you can."

"But not now, I guess."

Oliver laughed. "Definitely not now."

"But if we had more time?"

"The mission will be over, one way or another, very soon."

"So if I survive, I get to fuck you."

Oliver smiled, leaned back in his chair, and crossed his arms. "I thought I made that clear the first time we met."

"I guess you did."

"I've thought of little else." From the bulge in his pants, it looked like he was thinking about it right now. "Fortunately for the Firm, and for homeland security, I'm good at switching that side of my brain off."

"I'm not." I pressed my knee against his leg.

"You better learn to be, Dan, if you're going to be useful to us in the future."

"Who says I want to be useful? Fuck usefulness. I've given Uncle Sam the best years of my life. Can't you just put me out to pasture now? All I need is food and shelter and plenty of young tight ass to fuck."

"Maybe I could do with a change of direction myself."

Now, how would Ethan Oliver look without the sharp haircuts and the close shaves? How would he look in that log cabin in the mountains? If he grew a beard he'd probably just look like a hipster, but what the hell? I'll fuck hipsters.

We looked at each other for a while, trying to imagine what kind of couple we'd make. The preppy young agent and the battle-scarred veteran. One with a career and a public reputation, the other dead to the world, past caring, with a head full of bad memories. Was there a future for us? Was I the only one imagining this? Had I lost my mind? Only a few minutes ago I was dreaming up a future with Lukas. Christ, I needed a vacation. PTSD must be kicking in.

"So what are my orders?"

"We know it will be difficult for you to communicate with us. You'll be observed all the time. The phone you have been given contains a tracking device, of course, but it will probably be taken away from you. Do you still have the tracking devices you were issued in London?"

"There's a couple left."

"Use them."

"On myself?"

"On yourself."

"Sure you don't want to help me put one in?"

"You can manage."

"Shame."

"Hopefully they'll last long enough for us to pinpoint your whereabouts. Think you can get one into Lukas?"

"Of course I can."

He sighed. "Yeah. Of course you can."

"It's a bit late for jealousy, Oliver. You recruited me because I have the morals of an alley cat, remember?"

"I remember. Now, just try to keep out of immediate danger, Dan. But if necessary . . ."

"I can look after myself. And I have my friend here." I patted my pocket, where the gun weighed reassuringly heavy. "I've faced worse enemies than Vaughan and his pals."

"I know." He stood up; he was still erect. "See you on the other side, Dan."

We hugged like two old buddies, and Oliver walked out of the bar.

14

The Hammond Hotel was an ugly, anonymous building, the kind of place where I've attended military briefings, second-rate from the crappy carpet in the lobby to the frayed furniture in the events room. It hadn't been decorated since the 90s, and it must have looked like shit even then, with tacky mirror panels and acid green wallpaper. I'm no decorator—my idea of perfect décor is a double bed with a naked man on it—but this gave me a headache before I'd even got to the reception desk.

We were given name badges and welcome packs with the HomeWay Investments logo on them. When we stepped out of the elevator at the third floor we were met by a fat, sweaty man in a cheap suit.

"Peter Logan. Greg, Craig, nice to meet you." He had a damp, flabby handshake. "Welcome to the conference."

"Okay. Where do we get changed?"

"We'll get to that later."

"Is the other guy here yet?"

"So, if you just want to come through for some refreshments, we're having a break at the moment . . ."

"I need a timetable, and I need to see the venue."

"That's all in your welcome pack, Greg. Now, why don't you come through? Everyone's looking forward to meeting you, Craig."

Lukas looked like a rabbit in headlights, and followed Logan down the dingy corridor towards the function room. What the hell was this? A boxing match? A sex party? Nothing made sense. The room was big enough for a fight, but the chairs were set out in rows, and on the platform at the front—a raised dais, about twelve feet by six—there were three chairs, a lectern with a microphone, a low coffee table with carafes and glasses, and, behind it all, a screen for presentations.

Not an ideal boxing venue.

"What the fuck," I muttered to Lukas, as we were led towards a table at the back, where coffee and tea were laid out. "This is weird."

"Maybe it'll happen in another room or something." He stepped towards a crowd of eager, smiling faces and outstretched hands. "Time to do the meet-and-greet."

I guess Lukas was more used to this than I was; he'd been on the boxing circuit for a few years, he'd tasted success, and you don't get that without smiling at idiots, talking crap, and kissing ass. Maybe this really was the Investors in Sport Annual Conference. Perhaps all that was required of Lukas was a bit of sparring as window dressing for the fat cats in suits who were putting up the money for his December fight. Vaughan could have arranged this little junket precisely for the reasons he claimed—to raise his boy's profile with US investors and media before the main event.

Lukas certainly seemed relaxed, chatting with strangers, talking the talk. I was the one on the edge of the group, scowling and ill at ease—but no one was looking at me. It was Lukas they were interested in, the fresh meat from across the ocean.

So why was I armed? And why had there been no security? We'd walked straight into the conference without so much as a patdown. If it was such an innocent event, why had Vaughan felt it necessary to provide me with a weapon and give those instructions about being "responsible for your own security"? What kind of trouble was he expecting?

There must be some clue, if only I could see it. Some false note that would betray the real purpose of this event. But it all looked right: a group of thirty-five, maybe forty middle-aged white men, most of them overweight and badly dressed, speaking in loud voices about money and sport and media access. And they were straight. They weren't even checking out Lukas's ass, which was looking particularly round and fuckable in a pair of tight black pants.

Okay, if they're not queer, they must be members of this extreme right-wing organization that I've been hearing so much about. That was more plausible; I always think that being fat, ugly, and straight predisposes you to being a right-wing asshole. Idiots on the left tend to be grungy dickheads with beards, but at least you could fuck 'em if necessary. This lot wouldn't provoke a hard-on in a roomful of teenagers. I studied their lapels for badges and insignia; Nazis can't help flaunting it, even if it's just some crappy button with a lightning bolt or a cross that looks a tiny bit like a swastika. But there was nothing. It was only their blandness and lack of diversity that made me suspicious.

There was nothing on my phone, nobody approached me, and every time I tried to catch Lukas's eye he was deep in conversation with another shiny-faced jerk, nodding and smiling like a true pro. He seemed to be basking in the attention. I guess it made a pleasant change to be treated as a talented boxer rather than a piece of meat. I was expecting another phony weigh-in, a forest of sweaty hands groping the front of his shorts, but for once things were exactly as they appeared to be.

I looked around for Peter Logan, our designated contact at the conference, but he was nowhere to be seen. I opened up the welcome pack, assuming that there would at the very least be a timetable of events in there, some clue to what was expected of us, but all it contained was glossy brochures about HomeWay Investments, some flyers for future events, and a pocket-sized guide to sports fixtures in the New York area, fall/winter edition, already half out of date.

No mention of Craig Lukas, Alan Vaughan, or today's event.

I glanced through the boxing section of the guide, looking for Lukas's name in December. Nothing. The whole affair took on an air of unreality. Did everyone know something that I didn't? What was I doing here? It was like one of those stupid dreams when you're meant to be going on stage and you haven't learned your lines. I've gone into combat situations with inadequate briefing, but at least there I could rely on firearms and my own two deadly hands. Here I was lost. I had a gun in my pocket, sure, but there was nothing to shoot at. No target, no enemy.

"Okay, gents." An amplified voice made me jump. Peter Logan was up on the platform, speaking into the microphone. "If we could take our seats, I think we're ready to resume."

There was a general rush for seats. Lukas was led straight up to the platform. He seemed to know what was going on. I just had to hang around and make sure no one tried to murder him, I guess. I took a seat at the back. It would have been nice to know what the threat was, if indeed there was one. I might be bored to death by Peter Logan's endless, drivelling welcome speech. That was the only danger I was in.

Perhaps armed men would swing down from the ceiling and pluck us out of the room into a secret network of tunnels. . .

Perhaps there was a bomb somewhere in the building, and we would be among the victims pulled from the debris. . .

Fuck this, I was falling asleep. The beer I had with Oliver was catching up with me. It didn't matter. Even if Lukas and I were abducted by aliens, we had tracking devices in our assholes. I thought about how smoothly my finger slid inside him, the hot, wet walls of his pussy . . .

I woke with a start, jolting my head backwards. Logan was still talking. Jesus, it was stuffy in the room. I could hardly breathe. If I slipped out for some air, nobody would notice, would they? Lukas was in no danger.

I slipped out of the room and strolled along the corridor for a while; there was no one around except a chambermaid, not even a cute bellboy that I could push into a broom cupboard for ten minutes.

Better get back to the main event: for all I knew, one of the fat men in suits could have whipped an automatic weapon out of his briefcase and be threatening Alan Vaughan's Great White Hope. I went back in. No: they were still enjoying the sound of their own voices. We seemed to be on some kind of question and answer session, with most of the questions being directed to Craig. What was the boxing world like in the UK? How did he feel his style of fighting would go down in the US? What were his ambitions, and how far did he think he could go? He gave the usual boxer-type answers, bragging enough to sound confident, talking crap about technique and the psychology of boxing. As far as I'm concerned, the only psychology that matters is terrorizing your opponent with the sheer force of your fists. Everything else is show business.

I remembered some of the guys I'd trained over the years—the marines and other forces who came to learn the art of unarmed combat. I remembered young bodies, nineteen, twenty, twenty-one, pinned to the mat with my elbow on their throat, I remembered the smell of sweat, the slippery, smooth skin, the look on their face when they realized that Dan Stagg, the killer, the tough guy, wanted to stick his cock up their tight little asses . . .

I was drifting off again, staring at the ceiling, when I heard something. A noise that instantly set all my senses on high alert. Quite close, perhaps not in this room but nearby. The click of a safety catch being removed.

I stood up quickly, pushing my chair back. People in the seats in front of me looked around in surprise, whispering to each other, frowning at me as if I was crazy. Someone actually shushed me—as if I was talking at a movie theatre. But I wasn't imagining this. I knew what I'd heard.

"Is there a problem, sir?" asked Logan from the stage.

I said nothing, just walked quickly up the aisle to be close to Lukas. From the raised platform I scanned the room. Nothing. The sound must have come from beyond the doors. Could I have been mistaken? Could it have been one of the housemaid's trolleys, or the sound of a distant door clicking shut?

No. You don't spend twenty years in and out of combat zones without developing a sixth sense about these things. Someone had a gun.

"Greg, what the . . ."

"We're leaving."

"Sir, I would ask you to sit down."

"Shut the fuck up, Logan." He gaped like a goldfish, and gripped the sides of the lectern. "Lukas. Now."

I took him by the upper arm and started leading him away, but just as I stepped down there was a weird, strangled scream from behind me. I turned to see Logan, his face red and distorted, grabbing Lukas from behind, his forearm around his throat. Lukas was caught off guard, and staggered back, knocking Logan over. Three or four guys in the front row jumped up on to the stage, pushing me, kicking Lukas, even stamping on his hands. Madness had broken loose. What was this? A sabotage mission by a rival promoter? Lure Lukas in and then render him unable to fight?

"Stand back," I shouted, and drew my gun. They froze. And as I pulled Lukas to his feet, the doors at the back of the room burst open. Three police officers in bulletproof vests, with weapons pointed towards me. I let go of Lukas's hand. He ran to the side of the room with Logan and a couple of others—they were not attacking him now, they just stood and watched.

"Drop your weapon," said one of the officers.

There were three of them, and only one of me, and I had no desire to spend the rest of my life in prison for shooting a cop, and so I lowered my gun. I was about to throw it on to the floor when I heard a hiss behind me, and was just in the act of turning when something hit me very hard on the back of the head.

I remember falling to my knees, and that was all.

I woke up in a prison cell. A small, square room, about eight feet by eight feet, with a single bed, a basin, and a bucket. White walls and ceiling, gray floor, one fluorescent tube overhead. A metal door with a small barred opening.

I was dressed in the clothes I was wearing before, but my pockets were empty. No wallet, no ID, no cell phone.

I felt the back of my head. There was an egg-sized lump there, and a thick clump of dried blood. I've been knocked cold plenty of times. I know what it feels like. This was something different. The pain was there, the nausea, but there was something else, a sense of detachment, numbness, floating.

I'd felt it before. Most recently, when I came around from surgery at the Navy Med.

I'd been under anesthetic.

Shit! What have they done to me? I stuck my hands down my pants and checked. Yes, it was all still there, thank God. Nothing had been removed. I felt my limbs, my stomach, my face. All normal. My asshole didn't hurt. Nothing had been stuck up there.

I remembered, with relief, that I'd inserted a tracking device inside myself just before setting off for the Hammond Hotel. Whatever happened since then, no matter how long I'd been unconscious, someone would have followed my movements, at least in the hours directly after the attack. For all I knew, my rectum was still sending out signals.

I yelled "hey!" It sounded loud in my tiny cell. Nobody responded.

I had no idea if it was day or night, or how much time had elapsed. I had no idea where I was. Jesus, I could be in Thailand or Russia or Manchester for all I knew. In those first moments of waking, I was able to believe five different things at once. I never left the UK. I'm in barracks in Afghanistan. I'm in my bedroom at my parents' house. I'm in the hospital. I'm dead.

As my head cleared it became obvious that I was in prison. The faucets on the basin said "hot" and "cold": an English-speaking country, at least. And somewhere in the distance I heard a siren—a good old American police siren.

"Hey! Anyone there?"

I needed to shit and piss, and while I have no problems about doing it in a bucket, I thought this was a good excuse to get some attention.

"I need the fucking bathroom. Come on! Somebody? Hey! Hey!"

I picked up the empty bucket and started banging it against the bars; the clang would travel down empty corridors far more effectively than my voice.

It took a while, but eventually someone got pissed off enough to shut me up. I heard the clang of keys and doors.

"What the fuck is all the noise about?"

"I need the bathroom."

"Use the bucket."

"Where am I?"

"I said, use the fucking bucket and shut the fuck up."

Yeah, sounded like I was still in New York, or at least on the eastern seaboard; you don't get those vowels anywhere else.

"I want to see my lawyer."

"Yeah, yeah."

"What's that supposed to mean?"

"Pipe down, pal. Everything's under control. Use your bucket. Food's coming soon."

"I can't eat in here with a bucket full of shit."

"Aww, little baby." He was going to die. "Better get used to it."

"Tell me where I am."

"Well you ain't in the Holiday Inn, I'll tell you that much."

I heard his laughter receding down the hall.

Fuck: I really did need the bathroom. The bucket served its purpose. I washed myself in the sink. There was no toilet tissue, nothing to dry myself on. No matter: I stank anyway. My armpits were ripe, like I hadn't washed for three, four days. Is that how long I'd been out? My belly felt empty too, but I wasn't hungry. Maybe that would come. I remembered to drink from the faucet, cupping the water in my hands; dehydration would make me weak and crazy.

The smell from the bucket was foul. I pulled off my T-shirt, and covered it. And then, with nothing else to do, I lay down on the bed, put an arm across my eyes to block out the light, and tried to sleep off the anesthetic.

I was woken by a key in the lock. The door opened, and a hand pushed a tray across the floor. Before I could even stand, the door was closed again.

"Bon appetit, motherfucker."

I was hungry now. I've had worse food, I guess. I can't quite remember where, or when, but I must have. Stale bread, an apple, a lump of cheap sausage, possibly from a pet food store, and, weirdly, some Ritz crackers. They tasted good. I needed the salt. I ate slowly, knowing from experience that if you eat too fast after a period of starvation you can easily throw it straight up. So I took my time, chewing each mouthful, feeling the sugar reaching my bloodstream. It was only when I started eating that I realized how hungry I'd been. How had they fed me—if at all?

How many human rights laws had been breached in the last few days?

Where was the legal representation to which I was entitled?

Where, for that matter, was the fucking CIA, or the FBI, or Major General Wallace Hamilton? Had it been operationally necessary to throw me to the wolves? Was I going to die in here, the mad bastard in solitary confinement who keeps yelling about how he was forced to change his identity and had a tracking device implanted in his anus?

It was all a bit too Twilight Zone for my liking.

I am Dan Stagg, I said to myself. I will survive this. I don't know who my friends are, I don't know where the fuck I am, but I will get out. The metal door seemed to argue against that, but I've never really listened to reason.

For the next few hours I slept, paced the cell, did some push-ups, shit and pissed in the bucket, ate another plate of food that was pushed across the floor, and tried to get a glimpse of the person on the other end of the arm when I was fed and slopped out. All I could see was a blue polyester shirtsleeve, a hairy hand with a wristwatch, the gleam of a black leather boot. My attempts at conversation ("I want to see my fucking lawyer!" and so on) were met with silence, or snorts of laughter.

Wherever I was, it was not a regular correctional facility—or, if it was, someone was doing some very private freelance work. You read about these things: detention facilities in the New York area have come under intense media scrutiny in recent years for just this. You hear about illegal immigrants or suspected terrorists being thrown in these places and forgotten.

How convenient if that happened to me.

As the haze of anesthetic wore off, one fact was becoming crystal clear.

I had been set up.

The trip to New York, the conference at the Hammond Hotel, Peter Logan and all those other fat cats in suits, the armed police—possibly Craig Lukas himself—were part of a conspiracy in which I was the pawn, the patsy, the punch line.

Alan Vaughan must be behind it—Alan Vaughan

and his American confederates. Something had gone catastrophically wrong with the CIA's intelligence. We were never destined for New Hampshire. Whatever we'd been sent to New York for had happened in that dreary conference venue in a hotel near Times Square. I was the fall guy in an intelligence operation that had gone badly wrong. Maybe it was in the CIA's interests to leave me where I was, to remove a witness to something they should never have been doing in the first place. Maybe it was the CIA that had put me here in the first place. Agent Ethan Oliver would always put the Agency first.

All I could do now was conserve my energy, look after myself, and wait. For how long? Days? Months? Years?

I didn't even jack off. That shows you how bad things were.

Time passed. Two days? Three? It's hard to tell with no variation of light, no variation of meals, just the exact same ingredients shoved through the door every few hours. My body clock was fucked, I was sleeping and waking in no discernible pattern. The only chronometer I had was beard growth. I'd shaved on the morning of the conference; this felt like a four-day growth. Four days since I was in the bathroom on Third Avenue, showering and shaving after fucking Lukas up his hairy ass for the thousandth time.

I had no contact with the outside world. For all I knew, Vaughan's neo-Nazi pals could have blown up the White House, dismantled the federal government, and be handing out firearms in school classrooms. Armageddon could have come and gone, and I'd be none the wiser. No phone, no access to the media. That microchip in my asshole was my last link to the world, and that had been shit into a bucket. Right now it was probably working its way through a sewage treatment plant on its way to pollute a river somewhere.

In retrospect, the idea of turning into Greg Cooper didn't seem quite so smart. It's all very well cutting your ties with the past—we'd all do it if we could, leave everyone and everything behind and start again—but then you find that your new life comes without a safety net, you keep on falling and nobody is looking for you because you're already dead. No concerned relative or friend was going to start asking questions, because anyone who cared—if there was anyone—had been to my funeral. You only die once.

And here, or in some other detention facility, was where I would die. Whoever I was. The rations were getting smaller: they were starving me, I got no exercise, and I saw nobody. Even for someone who basically hates ninety-nine percent of the human race, that's tough. What I wouldn't give for half an hour with a college football team. . . I started hallucinating, or at least dreaming so vividly that it was hard to distinguish between dream and reality. It felt like they were drugging me. The fluorescent light was always on, day and night had no meaning, and after a while I became snow-blind, unable to see clearly, everything in my cell the same flat bright white, the images in my head so much clearer. Perhaps I'd been there for longer than I thought. Perhaps there were drugs in my food. Why didn't they just kill me, and get it over with? What was the point of keeping me alive? Was I useful to someone—a hostage to be bargained over?

Time passed. Nothing happened. I got weaker, or the drugs got stronger, and although there was a little jarhead in there somewhere who wasn't quite ready to give up, the rest of me was failing fast. My legs were wasting away. My hands were shaking. I couldn't wash or shave or clean my teeth. I stank, but in that enclosed space it was impossible to distinguish smells. I felt like I had flu, shivering, exhausted, bruised.

I was dying.

15

A line of light. Greenish white, then gone.

The sound of dishes being washed, chink chink chink, or is it bells, distant bells?

Silence, a roaring silence like a never-ending explosion, and a sudden pounding in the chest, hard, like someone's hitting me with their fists, thumping into me, breaking my ribs. Panic, flight, a jerk in the spine and the legs, prepare to run. Fear.

Awake.

Everything is white and blurred. I think there's a TV on somewhere, a screen of some kind. Too much light. Movement, vague circles white out of white, puffy clouds coming closer and receding. Is this death?

A face at the end of a long tunnel, like looking down the wrong end of a pair of binoculars, ridiculously far away and tiny, so tiny it makes me laugh, the breath coming out through my nose.

The face getting closer, a brown sun in a blue sky, white clouds, coming towards me like a dolly shot in a movie, taking up more and more of the sky until all

I can see is brown skin and white teeth and eyes that look into mine and a mouth that smiles and speaks, *hey, you're awake, hey Dan, how are you doing, buddy? Welcome back.*

And then the clouds cover the sun and the picture goes down to a line like on the old TV at home, a line and then a dot and closedown.

Don't worry. This isn't an episode of *Dynasty*. The last couple of hundred pages weren't just a dream. But it took me a while to figure out what was going on—was I still in that prison cell? Everything was familiar, the bed, the room, the face at the end of the tunnel, the sound of the voice, the words, the pain in my body, and for a second of panic I thought that I was doomed to repeat this forever, like some soul in hell.

Jesus, they must have messed with my brain. I haven't thought about souls or hell or eternal damnation since some horny priest tried to interest me in religion thirty years ago.

"Dan?"

That name. The old name. Dan. Me, I think. "Hmmm?"

"Hey, welcome back. It's me, Dan. It's Luiz."

No, this was too much. It's a dream, Dan, Greg, whoever you are. Don't trust it. We've been here before. It's never real. Soon you'll wake up, with the pain in your guts from starvation, the pounding hammer behind your eyes. . .

"Can you hear me?"

A hand grasped mine.

"Dan? Can you hear me? Squeeze my hand."

I was frozen. I couldn't move. This was fear, pure

and simple. Fear that what seemed so good would all disappear, and I'd be back in my own filth, dying. . .

"Doctor, he seems to be in some kind of . . . I don't know. He's awake, but he's unresponsive."

The hand never let go of mine. Someone touched my face, my eye, a light shone into me, I winced.

"It's okay, Luiz. He's alive. Just give him time. Stay with him. I'll be back in half an hour. Call me if there's . . ." The voice faded. I think I might have slept.

The hand was still there when I checked again.

"Luiz." This time I managed a word. The fear was receding, and with it the paralysis. "Hey." My voice was cracked, old, distant.

"There's my man. Good to see you, Dan." Cool fingers on my forehead. "You're safe now. Everything's okay."

My breathing felt weird, like I'd just run a mile. My guts were cramping. I guess this was relief.

"Okay, buddy. Calm down. You're going to be fine. The doctors are looking after you. Jesus, you're a tough old bastard."

"What . . . where . . ."

"We'll tell you everything later. Try to relax. Listen to my voice. It's a beautiful day out there. Blue skies, sunshine, really cold. It's nearly Christmas. Think about that, Dan. You'll be okay for Christmas. We'll have a party, yeah? Food and presents and all that jazz. I don't want a lot for Christmas. . ."

He sang softly, slowly, stroking my forehead, holding my hand, and I drifted off again, this time into something that felt like sleep rather than prolonged incarceration.

* * *

Two days later I was sitting in a chair. The tubes that had been feeding and rehydrating me, and pumping me full of antibiotics, were out, leaving purple bruises where the cannulas had been. I was clean, my hair and nails had been cut, but I'd kept the beard. It covered up the sores and rough patches on my sunken cheeks.

Luiz had just taken me through the morning's physical therapy session, and now I was eating my second breakfast, or first lunch, whatever it was. I was on a regimen of five small meals a day.

And where was I? You guessed it. The dear old Walter Reed National Military Medical Center in Bethesda, Maryland. The Navy Med. Back where we started, completely fucked up again, being nursed by Luiz again, waiting for some cunt from the top brass or the Agency to tell me what a great job I'd done and please, pretty please Dan, would you mind dying again and turning into someone else so we can fuck you up just one more time . . . the last time . . . until the next time.

This time the answer would be no. Not because I had anything better to do, but because, as I advance into middle age, I've begun to think that there might be more to life than risking it for some abstract idea of duty.

I'd been thinking about that cabin in the woods, and even if every potential companion had let me down, I could still go it alone. I'd be happy. I'd get a dog. Become the crazy guy who turns up at the grocery store once a month, fills up his truck and drives back into the wilderness. Just me and my dog.

Luiz's phone rang.

"Hello. Okay, right. Yeah, he's ready. Give me two minutes. Thanks."

I finished my meal in three mouthfuls. Luiz took away the plate, gave me a cloth to wipe my mouth, brushed the crumbs off my lap. He was not authorized to tell me what had happened. That was the job of whoever was coming up in the lift right now. I vaguely wondered who had drawn the short straw. "You see, Dan, the mission didn't quite work out as we expected . . ."

Luiz held the door open, admitted my visitor, and left.

What do you know? Agent Oliver in the flesh, just as cute as the last time I saw him, before he sent me into an ambush that landed me in prison and nearly cost me my life. Well, he had guts, I'd give him that. Not everyone would have the courage to walk in and face a man they'd nearly killed by their own fuckups. Central Intelligence Agency, my ass. What intelligence? Central Ignorance Agency would be more like it. I was framing a remark along those lines, but I couldn't be bothered. Let him say his piece and scuttle back to Langley. They'd be pleased with him: Dan Stagg was not going to cause any trouble. It was Oliver, not me, who'd get the promotion.

He'd dressed for the occasion in informal clothes. Gone were the sharp suits and Brooks Brothers shirts; today he was in the national dress of sports casual, which could have come from Target but, I suspected, came from some designer store in the city. The informal, friendly meeting. The soft goodbye. Hey Dan, I'm just a regular guy like you, look, I wear sneakers, some days I don't even shave, okay? Let's try and forget my vastly superior status. We're just people.

Oh, sure thing, Agent Oliver. What's that? Call you Ethan? How nice. Of course I'll keep my mouth shut. Two thousand bucks? That's too generous. Goodbye, and thanks.

"Good to see you, Dan."

He pulled up a chair. His face registered no shock. They train them well in the CIA, because I knew I looked like shit.

"Yeah. Right."

"You're probably wondering what . . ."

"You didn't come and visit me in prison."

He didn't like being interrupted, and for a second he scowled. Then the bland, smooth expression returned. "That was not possible."

"So I understand."

"You don't understand." He raised his voice by a decibel or two—but for Ethan Oliver, that was the equivalent of yelling. He took a breath. "We didn't know where you were."

"You didn't know."

I let the words fall into silence. Oliver fidgeted.

"So with all the tech and all the informers and all the surveillance, you couldn't find me in whatever prison I was in."

"A detention facility in Queens."

"You are fucking kidding me."

"No."

"Queens? Fucking Queens? I mean, all that time I was in Queens and you couldn't even fucking find me? In fucking Queens?"

Oliver was pale. Perhaps he'd never come across a traumatized veteran before. Well, he had one right here.

He was alone in a room with him. I was angry, and even on heavy medication I could kill him before he had time to call for help. Even if he was armed.

Armed. 9mm Walther Creed. I could feel the weight of it against my torso. A phantom weapon.

"Okay, Oliver. Tell me what happened. I guess that's what you're here for."

"Yes." He wiped his upper lip with the back of his hand; I was making him sweat. Good. When I'd finished with him, he'd be as wet as if he'd just stepped out of the shower. "That's what I'm here for."

"Let's pick things up in the Hammond Hotel, shall we?"

"If I'm going to make sense of this, I have to go back a couple of weeks." He bit the corner of his thumbnail.

"Take your time. I'm not going anywhere."

"When you were in Manchester, you met a young man named Osman Rafiq."

"Yes. Oz. Who is now dead."

"Correct. How would you describe his role within the Vaughan organization?"

I shrugged. "He was a minor player. A wannabe. He hung around in the hope of getting a break as a fighter, and while he was waiting he was pimped out to dirty old men."

"That's one side of the story," said Oliver. "But there's more to it. Rafiq was also involved in the drug trade."

"I never saw evidence of that."

"Nonetheless, he was dealing to Vaughan's associates. And others, it appears. His network was extensive."

"And Vaughan supplied him with the stuff?"

"Oh, no. Vaughan is prudish when it comes to drugs. He's no fool. He knows that the police would soon find him if he was involved in that business."

"You mean Oz was dealing independently?"

"That surprises you?"

"I was surprised that he could tie his own shoelaces. He was such a . . . I don't know. A follower."

"That's the side you saw. But behind the façade, there was an efficient businessman who used his connections with Alan Vaughan to work his way up in the drug trade."

"Where is this going?"

"Rafiq made the mistake that all dealers make. He started sampling his own supply."

"How do you know all this?"

"Your friend Andrew Reeve in MI6 has excellent relations with the greater Manchester police. They had been aware of Osman Rafiq for some time."

"And they didn't bust him?"

"The case was blocked at a high level."

"By senior police officers."

"Exactly. Who, we believe, were in Alan Vaughan's circle."

"I can ID at least one of them for you." I remembered the cocky, brown-haired bastard at the fatal party, putting something away in his briefcase. "I'm pretty sure he fired the shots that killed Oz."

"In return for taking the heat off Rafiq, Vaughan demanded services."

"You mean sex?"

"For once, no. Vaughan was planning to bring Rafiq

to America and lend him to his associates. He was going to be framed for a terrorist attack on some high-profile members of an extreme right-wing political organization."

"Not, by any chance, the right-wing political organization that sometimes calls itself HomeWay Investments?"

"You've got it."

"And what went wrong? How did Oz end up dead?"

"We're still not sure. It seems he was trying to muscle in on Vaughan's operation—trying a bit of blackmail of his own. That didn't go down well. Vaughan knew how to keep his clients happy, and they paid well for his discretion. Oz, it appears, started making threats."

"But the night before he died, he turned up at my place, covered in blood, off his head on GHB. He said he'd been beaten up and drugged."

"It's possible. It's equally possible that he got into a fight with another dealer after using too much of his own stuff. Maybe the police will figure it out. Whatever happened, it left Vaughan, and HomeWay, without a hit man."

"So I went in his place. What the fuck was it supposed to achieve?"

"That's what we didn't figure out until it was too late. We were distracted by what we thought was the main event: the attack on the army base in New Hampshire."

"Yeah, what about that?"

"Oh, it happened." Oliver smiled. "After a fashion. They found some crazy bastard to drive a truck into the perimeter fence. There were explosives in the back, but they didn't do too much damage. Blew the doors off the truck, gave the driver a few nasty burns, but he'll survive."

"And what minority did he represent? Muslim? Gay? Democrat?"

"As far as we can make out, he was your average small-town meth head. Lots of Nazi material in his trailer home. But there was some attempt to dress it up." Oliver coughed; he was trying not to laugh. "They packed the cab with gay magazines and Lady Gaga CDs."

"Wow. That's a pretty cunning plot."

"Unfortunately, the driver didn't die as planned. Once we got him into custody, he sang like a canary, especially when his drugs started wearing off. Not much of it made sense. We couldn't establish a credible link to HomeWay."

"So the mission was a failure."

"On the contrary. The attack on the army base was a sideshow. The real deal was what happened at the Hammond Hotel, two days earlier."

"For real? At some shitty sports conference?"

"HomeWay has its fingers in many pies. They put resources into things like boxing; it looks legit, but it's basically money laundering. The core business is political. They're also known as the American Way and Home of the Brave. You'll find them online if you know where to look, recruiting lunatics like our poor Lady Gaga fan."

"And I was set up to attack them."

"The whole thing was a performance. They staged it to look like you had pulled a gun on them for political reasons. Maximum publicity for HomeWay, maximum sympathy, makes it look like they're not the terrorists, it's people like you. Loners, outsiders. They got the photos and the video footage, which went straight on to social media. The cops who arrested you were fake."

"Jesus."

"HomeWay has its own security. They apprehended you, and they made you disappear. The news stories that they put out named you as Greg Cooper, and gave all the details that you had supplied to Alan Vaughan. They said you were in police custody, which was officially denied, but that doesn't matter—HomeWay just said it was a federal cover-up. Their followers swallow any conspiracy theory they're fed. HomeWay had the photos and the perpetrator. They could present themselves as victims of an attack by the left. It might have been more effective for them if Oz Rafiq had been the guy with the gun, as originally planned, but you were an acceptable substitute."

"And what about Craig Lukas? Was he part of this?"

"Craig Lukas was acting under orders."

"From Vaughan?"

"From Vaughan."

"I see." I thought about this for a minute. "You mean, everything?"

"I'm afraid so, Dan."

"I thought he was too good to be true."

"If it's any consolation, he was one of Vaughan's biggest victims. MI6 obtained details of payments he's been making to Vaughan over the last five years. Huge sums."

"The prize money."

"And more. Every penny he earned from his media work."

"And where is he now?"

"In prison, while it's decided whether to put him on trial here or extradite him to the UK."

"He'll get plenty of cock in prison. He'll be happy."

Oliver said nothing.

"And what about Alan Vaughan?"

"He was apprehended at Manchester Airport, trying to fly to Colombia."

"Jesus."

"He's remanded without bail while the list of charges against him grows. Blackmail, terrorism, rape, conspiracy to murder, you name it. The press has had a great time. His wife is telling everyone it's a pack of lies."

"Poor woman."

"Don't feel too sorry for her, Dan. There's a proceeds of crime investigation hovering over her head."

"And all this happened because I pulled a gun in a room full of fat men in suits?"

"You provided the one piece of evidence that we needed: a link between HomeWay and Alan Vaughan. As soon as they mentioned your name, and the details we'd planted, we knew there was only one possible source. If Vaughan was providing HomeWay with that kind of information, it was safe to assume he was providing them with money. The attack on the army base confirmed what we already knew: HomeWay was involved in homeland terrorism."

"But it's all theory. No proof."

"We got our proof. You remember Peter Logan?"

"The sweaty guy at the hotel?"

"He talked."

"About Vaughan?"

"About everything. Eventually. After a little persuasion."

"I still don't understand what was in it for Vaughan. Why jeopardize everything to fund some bunch of crazy bastards in the US? Surely he didn't believe their crap. He isn't stupid."

"Alan Vaughan is exactly what he appears to be: a boxing promoter. Everything else was in the service of that. He wanted to get out of the UK—it was getting too hot for him there, people were starting to find out about his other activities, people like Oz were starting to break ranks—and move to the US. That's where the money is. HomeWay would have made that possible for him. They have all the connections in the sporting world, they could get him an entrée. And in return, he gave them the people they needed for one of their plots. Foreigners. Outsiders."

"And they ended up with me."

"In the absence of a Muslim, a mad gay ex-marine would do nicely. That plays well with their anti-federal agenda."

"So that's the end of Vaughan."

"And thanks to the information you provided to MI6, a senior police officer has been charged with the murder of Oz Rafiq."

"I knew it."

"Several other prominent individuals are under investigation."

"I bet they are."

"And City Fitness has closed down."

"What about the boys?"

"They're being looked after."

"Tom Jackson? Is he in prison?"

"There are no charges against him," said Oliver, with a smile. "In fact, your friend Reeve from MI6 is very interested in young Mr. Jackson."

"I just bet he is." I could see Jackson riding Reeve's thick cock—and I could also see him making a very good career for himself in the intelligence services. Perhaps, one day, he'd be briefing me.

"You will be interviewed by the British police at some point. They are trying to piece together exactly what happened to Oz."

I remembered his mysterious disappearance from my Manchester apartment, the tidy bed, the clean bathroom. Perhaps I would never know the truth of his final hours. "Does that mean I have to go back?"

"I think, under the circumstances, we could ask them to come to you. You've done enough."

"Yeah. I nearly died in prison."

Oliver pressed his hands between his knees, and looked at the floor. "I know."

"Are you going to tell me about it?"

"Yes, I am." He took a deep breath, relaxed his shoulders, and began. "As soon as we heard what happened, we were looking for you. NYPD, FBI, all our agents. We tracked you as far as a warehouse on Long Island, and then the trail went cold."

"I must have taken a shit."

"What do you remember?"

"Nothing. I woke up in that cell."

"They must have sedated you. By the time the police got to the warehouse, it was empty. We lost you. They led us on a wild goose chase, planting false information to keep us busy. As far as we now, you were moved straight to a detention facility in Queens."

"Was it a federal prison?"

"Run by a private company. The corruption goes further and deeper than we suspected. You were admitted under a false name. It took a while to prove that you were the person we said you were."

"How did you manage that?"

"MI6 were very thorough. They had your DNA on file."

Of course: my audition with Reeve and Radek.

"How long was I in there?"

"A month, more or less." Oliver's voice cracked. "We nearly lost you, Dan."

"And how did you find me?"

"Logan again. It took a while."

"Is he still in one piece?"

"He'll live."

And that seemed to be the end of that. They got the bad guys. Vaughan, Logan, and the rest of them were in prison. The boys were safe. Dakota, Kieran, Jackson: I'd never see them again, but I'd saved them. As for Craig Lukas—his career was over, his reputation destroyed, maybe he'd serve some time and then follow the usual path of disgraced boxers, into private security. Or he'd kill himself. I didn't much care.

Everyone was pleased with me. Major General Hamilton, Andrew Reeve, Ethan Oliver, all the politicians who controlled them, would be content with a job well done. I'd been promised a pension. That would be enough for me. It doesn't cost much to live a simple life. I've got twenty, thirty years left, hopefully not too much more. I don't want to be old. If I buy myself a place to live, I can afford food, a car, the essentials of life, and I'll probably have enough left over to pay for trade.

Not much of a life after decades of service, but it could be worse. I could be dead again.

I became conscious of Oliver staring at me. His face was pale and tense.

"What?"

"We so nearly lost you. When we found you . . ."

"It's okay." I reached out and took his hand. "I've been in worse shape before." This wasn't true, but I wanted him to feel better. "They keep trying to kill me, but I'm still here."

"Thank God." He squeezed my hand. That felt nice. We didn't speak for a while.

"So, Agent Oliver," I said, as much to break that silence as anything, "do you consider the operation to have been a success?"

"Actually, it's not Agent Oliver."

"Oh, you got a promotion? Congratulations. What is it now, then? Special Agent Oliver?"

He shook his head.

"Chief Special Agent Oliver? Deputy Director Oliver? Give me some help here."

"It's just Ethan Oliver."

"That either means you're so senior that you no longer have a rank, or . . ."

"I quit."

"You did what?"

"This is my last job. I am officially leaving in March, but you know what the CIA is like. As soon as you say you want to go, they make sure you are out in the cold. I insisted on debriefing you, but I had to put up a fight. I think I should be allowed to clear up my own messes."

"Why the hell did you throw away a career like that?"

"Because I can longer work within a system that treats human beings as expendable resources."

"Don't join the army, then."

"I wasn't planning to."

"Surely you guys are trained to understand the concept of casualties of war."

"I understand the concept just fine. I've seen agents and other operatives die in the course of duty. I'm okay with that, in general."

"So?"

"Just not in this particular instance."

"Why? Because some asshole in the prison service conspired with some asshole in the NYPD to kill someone in police custody? Come on, man, this shit happens every day."

"We should have found you earlier. You were nearly dead. You were . . ." He choked, and had to stop.

"The mission was a success. The bad guys were caught, the attack in New Hampshire was a failure, and here I am, still alive."

"I don't care about the fucking mission." His voice was rough, his eyes wet. "Don't you get it?"

I was beginning to think I did, but he was going to have to spell it out. "Explain."

"I didn't want to lose you."

The words could not go back. I waited.

"It was your death I couldn't accept. Your suffering. I realized that I . . . I just can't . . ." Poor bastard was struggling for words, almost for breath.

"It's okay, Ethan. I know what you're trying to say."

"You don't know, Dan."

"Then tell me."

He wiped his eyes, blew his nose, cleared his throat.

"I love you, you fucking idiot. I love you."

16

As declarations go, that was badly timed, inappropriate, and unexpected. Much as I'd wanted to fuck Ethan Oliver ever since I first met him, my motives were more to do with punishment and revenge than that other thing he'd mentioned—that thing I always struggle with—love. He was a jerk in a suit. A spook. A representative of everything I hate—order, control, dishonesty, secrecy. I like breaking those guys down with my dick, turning them into drooling sex addicts and then moving on. And let's not forget that he was directly responsible for what I'd endured in that prison cell. I might pretend that it was all in a day's work, but I suffered in body and mind more than I've ever suffered before. I'm not going into details. I can't talk about that stuff. I file it away and I forget it. One day it'll all come out, and I'll be that lunatic who walks into a shopping mall with an AK-47, but that's what you get when you train men to suppress their emotions. It's very effective and useful in the armed forces. It's shit in civilian life— but I had no plans to reenter civilian life. I tried it. It doesn't suit me. I wanted a new mission. I wanted Major General Wallace Hamilton or Andrew Reeve from MI6 to give me a job. I needed an objective in my life. A reason to move on.

What I did not need was some guilt-ridden spook telling me that he was in love with me. Okay, he was an attractive guilt-ridden spook, I got stiff when he started spilling his guts, and I did admittedly kiss him and hold him, but that didn't mean that I was planning a future with him. It did not mean that I loved him back. I didn't fucking know him, for Christ's sake. He didn't know me. We were strangers. Hot strangers, yeah, but that's all. You don't base these decisions on some stupid moment of attraction. You don't fall in love with someone just because he cares about you and is willing to sacrifice his career for you. You don't. You just don't. You don't fucking fall in love at all. Every time you fall in love with a man, he dies. So stay out of trouble, get a new job, put yourself in the firing line again, and hope this time that a bullet or a bomb gives you a nice clean end.

But things never seem to go the way I want.

Here was former agent Ethan Oliver in my arms, awkwardly clambering on top of the hospital chair to sprawl in my lap, his mouth glued to mine, his hands all over me, and for some reason, obviously to do with medication and recent trauma, I seemed to be reciprocating.

It couldn't go on for long. My leg muscles were weak and wasted, and his weight was hurting me. I was in pain.

Our idyll was interrupted by a soft cough.

"You'd better let Colonel Stagg breathe a little, sir."

Luiz, of course, standing in the doorway in his dazzling white nurse's uniform, arms folded across his chest, a smile on his face. Oliver jumped to his feet, and tried to rearrange himself.

"Hey, Luiz. Care to join us?"

"Three's a crowd, Dan. Besides, I have other patients to attend to."

"I just bet you have." Who was receiving Luiz's special therapeutic attention now, I wondered? Some new patient who was about to be issued with a new identity and sent out into the field, sucked back to health?

"I'm going to have to ask you to leave, Mr. Oliver. The doctors will be here in a couple of minutes. There's the round of meds, and physical therapy, and then he has to rest."

"Okay." Oliver was flushed, ill at ease. "I'll go. Thank you for . . . thanks for your understanding, Dan."

Come on, Stagg. Wave him off. Dismiss him with a gruff remark. Get rid of this thing. This need. This emotion.

He backed off a couple of steps.

I said, "See you," and his face resumed its habitual bland expression.

He turned, and walked towards the door.

And then I thought of that cabin in the woods, and the empty bunk beside mine, and the boredom and loneliness of life without companionship. And I hastily rearranged the picture to see if another face would fit.

"Wait."

Luiz was making himself busy with a piece of paper.

"Hey, Oliver! Wait."

He turned. "What?"

"Just . . . just hold it. Luiz—can't he stick around?"

"Not really. The doctors are . . ."

"I mean, if I tell them that I want him to."

"It's not usual."

I pushed myself up in the chair. "And how about if I give orders?"

Luiz scratched the back of his head. "Well, Dan, you're the senior officer here."

"You bet your fucking life I am. And it's about time people remembered that."

Ethan Oliver seemed frozen to the spot, his mouth hanging open. I caught his eye, and we looked at each other. Five seconds, ten seconds, twenty.

"I'll leave you alone, then," said Luiz. "If that's what you want. Sir."

"Dismissed," I said, and the door closed softly behind him.

About the Author

As **JAMES LEAR**, he is the author of the Dan Stagg Mystery series and The Mitch Mitchell series, which includes *The Back Passage*, *The Secret Tunnel*, *Hot Valley*, *The Low Road*, and *The Palace of Varieties*. He lives in London.